"For all who believe that reaching age sixty-five marks the end of adventure, *Road Trip Trio* is a must read. Triple-header suspense, liberally injected humor, and a delightful sprinkling of romance make *Road Trip Trio* a Hallmark movie just waiting to happen; but don't wait, enjoy the fun right now."

—Dannie Hawley, author of
Dealing With Our Fears When Letting Go Seems Impossible

"I have thoroughly enjoyed [Smith's] jam-packed thriller, *Road Trip Trio*. [It is] filled with all types of twists and turns, ups and downs, and sandwiched in-between the adventures, managed to impart Christian ethics. This story is a must for readers who like romance, comedy, and fast-paced action scenes. Overall, a most fascinating adventure!"

—Jeanne Webster, published writer of
Christian articles, poetry, and blogs

"Doris has woven a delightful tapestry for her readers. Baby boomers will easily identify with these three girlfriends whose travels hold adventure, mystery, humor, and an abiding faith in God. The *Road Trip Trio* characters quickly become your intimate friends, and each chapter keeps you hungering for more!"

—Pam Ford Davis, freelance writer and
on-air radio and television personality

ROAD TRIP TRIO

ROAD TRIP TRIO

Doris Aldrich Smith

DORIS ALDRICH SMITH

TATE PUBLISHING
AND ENTERPRISES, LLC

Published by Tate Publishing & Enterprises, LLC
127 E. Trade Center Terrace | Mustang, Oklahoma 73064 USA
1.888.361.9473 | www.tatepublishing.com

Tate Publishing is committed to excellence in the publishing industry. The company reflects the philosophy established by the founders, based on Psalm 68:11,
"The Lord gave the word and great was the company of those who published it."

Book design copyright © 2013 by Tate Publishing, LLC. All rights reserved.
Cover design by Rodrigo Adolfo
Interior design by Mary Jean Archival

Published in the United States of America

ISBN: 978-1-62563-786-4
1. Fiction / Contemporary Women
2. Fiction / Christian / General
13.04.03

Acknowledgments

I am very grateful to the Tate Publishing Co. and their staff who have been immensely supportive in the preparation of *Road Trip Trio*. Their suggestions and direction have been most helpful.

I am grateful to three special women in my life who have encouraged me throughout my new adventure of writing Christian fiction. My best friend and retired English teacher, Annette May, sat with me for many long hours as we honed the final editing for this book. Our own road trips over the years inspired the adventures of Kathleen, Lucille, and Bernice. Kelly Sellers, my only child and my great encourager, gave me the support I needed to pursue publishing my books. Kristin Harp, a young friend who is like a daughter, has also been a great cheerleader and is working with me in marketing. Thanks to my photographer, Shannon Thayer.

To the numerous family members and friends who have kept up with the progress of my work, I thank you for your interest, prayers, and encouragement. Thanks to my husband Roy who gave me the space I needed to create *Road Trip Trio* and didn't question my sanity when I laughed aloud at the adventures of the trio.

Chapter 1

The silver Lexus backed out of the condominium parking space with three old friends. Lucille Shuman, the owner of the car, laughed as she put the car into drive. "The three musketeers ride again. Road trip," she shouted out her open window. Kathleen Keller rode in the front seat, juggling a coffee mug and a bag of doughnuts. She felt the perspiration beading on her forehead.

She had just lifted her two suitcases into the stuffed trunk, and she then rushed back into her condominium to pick up the coffee mugs and the bag of doughnuts. Kathleen had double-checked the lights, the range, and the computer to make sure they were off. Bernice Meyers waited for her at the door and took two of the insulated coffee mugs. Kathleen locked her door. Lucille was waiting in the car, yelling for them to hurry. Finally the three friends took off on their annual two-week vacation together.

"Please, Lucille, I do have nosy neighbors, you know," said Kathleen. She opened the bag and handed Lucille a glazed doughnut with a napkin and then passed the bag back to Bernice who took a jelly doughnut. When the bag came back to her, she selected a chocolate cake doughnut with chocolate frosting. Chocolate had always been her friend. Their vacations always started with a bag of doughnuts and mugs of coffee.

Lucille laughed and said, "Girlfriends, we are going to the Florida beach and we are eating doughnuts. Forty years ago, we would eat ice cubes and celery sticks to keep our girlish figures for our bikinis. Guess that ship has sailed," she said, looking down at her ample belly. Lucille had thin legs and arms, but she had a little Humpty Dumpty body going for her.

Bernice finished her doughnut and asked for another. Kathleen passed the bag to the backseat and said, "Bernice, you are the only one of us who can afford to eat the first doughnut. You are such a skinny thing. You have always been a little thing. Eat up. No matter how many calories you inhale, you still stay so thin. It isn't fair, is it, Lucille?" Kathleen had fought the spreading behind for twenty years. She appeared chubby now, chubbier than she liked. The muffin top made her uncomfortable. Since retiring from the ministry, she changed her wardrobe to polyester slacks with elastic waistbands, bright floral or striped blouses covered with a variety of jackets and sweaters. Years ago, she had been much thinner. When she wore high heels, she felt more fashionable, but now, she did not care as much. Now, she felt content to wear her black socks covered in a variety of flats and walking shoes. She was no longer concerned about keeping up her image. She just wanted to be comfortable. She kept her salt-and-pepper hair short in a variety of styles from haircut to haircut.

Bernice said, "Girls, if I could take a few of your inches for my, uh, you know…and my hips, I would. I do not enjoy being this skinny. I don't have much to hold up a bikini, if I were ever crazy enough to try to wear one." She laughed and the two women in the front seat joined in. Her two friends often accused Bernice of buying her clothes in the girls' department. She always laughed, but never denied it.

Lucille had always been the most flamboyant of the three old friends. She and Kathleen had taught high school together when they were just out of college. Lucille had always been a bleached blonde, which she still maintained even though she thought her hair might be grey. She had blue eyes and a pretty face for her age. Her wardrobe consisted of bright colors, gauzy full skirts, and many scarves. She never went out of the house without her makeup. At age seventy-one, she still wore high heels everywhere she went. She oozed happiness, always smiling and laughing so people just gravitated toward her. Most of her students had liked and respected Ms. Shuman. It seemed strange when she started to have students who were the grandchildren of her first students. None of them ever forgot her. They all had a funny story to tell about Ms. Shuman's class. She reveled in the fact that so many students remembered her fondly. If she could not have children of her own, she would claim her students as her kids.

These three friends had known each other for many years. Kathleen and Lucille had been bridesmaids in Bernice's wedding to her now deceased husband Zackary. They had been present for her children's baptisms and their weddings. In fact, Kathleen had officiated at the baptisms and weddings of Bernice's two sons and her daughter. The children and grandchildren called Bernice's friends Aunt Kathleen and Aunt Lucille.

By lunchtime, the friends were discussing the menus at some of their favorite restaurants. Lucille said, "I need to fill up the gas tank before lunch," as she pulled into a gas station. She grumbled about the price of gasoline while she pumped the gas. Kathleen and Bernice got out and stretched their legs. They both stood beside the car with their hands at their waists, bending one way and then the other.

Lucille said, "What are you doing, girls? You think if you stretch out now that when we get to the restaurant you can get out of the car and walk like normal people? I told you we would stop along the road before we got there so we could all stretch. That way we would not look like three arthritic old ladies getting out of the car at the restaurant." She giggled. "However, no, you could not wait. Now those old men having coffee at the window table have seen that you are two old arthritic women, with a younger blonde friend who is pumping the gas." She laughed aloud and told them to get back in the car.

After looking at the gaggle of men sitting in the window of the coffee shop, Bernice waved and they grinned and waved as the girl friends got back in the car.

After lunch, Lucille drove again. There was not much traffic, so they were all relaxed. Suddenly, she began to slow down. The other two friends sat up straight to see what the problem might be. Ahead on their side of the road sat an old blue Buick with five teenage boys standing beside it. They waved their arms, trying to get Lucille's attention to have her stop. She continued to slow down.

"What are you doing?" Bernice questioned. "You aren't really going to stop, are you? We are outnumbered."

"It is broad daylight, and they may need some help."

"What they need is your Lexus instead of the old junker they have. Tell her not to stop, Kathleen."

"It is a definite no-no for three old ladies to stop because someone flags them down, but it is very hot today. The doors are locked, so don't unlock them and don't get out of the car."

Lucille pulled up next to them and Bernice rolled down her window halfway. Three of the boys came over to the open window and one said, "Our car overheated. Do you by any chance have any water we can buy?" They looked like seniors in high school and presented a variety of teenage looks. They did not appear threatening at all.

Kathleen pulled out several bottles of water attached to a plastic ring and handed it to Bernice in the front seat. "Give them this water. We can wait to be sure they get on their way. They look harmless to me. The boy over there looks like he could be one of your kids."

Bernice nodded and handed one of the boys the water bottles. "How much do we owe you, ma'am?"

All three women said, "Nothing."

Kathleen rolled down her window and said, "Guys, you just pay it forward. Next time you see someone in distress, give him a hand. However, use good judgment and do not put yourselves in jeopardy. Stand back because we need to get off the road behind you." Lucille put the car in reverse and pulled off the road behind the Buick. They waited while two of the guys poured water into the radiator. They had one bottle left, which they passed around, and each took a long drink from it. The guys put the empty bottles on the floor of their car, thanked the women as they piled back into the old junker, and waited for the driver to start the car. After a couple of tries, the motor started. The guys were giving high fives to one another and waving at the Good Samaritans in the car behind them. Some of the boys stuck their upper torsos out of the windows and yelled words of thanks and waved. Both cars pulled back onto the road, and after a few miles, Lucille passed them and left them behind.

They stopped to fuel up later and to take a restroom break. When Bernice and Lucille came back to the car, Kathleen had decided to drive so she sat behind the wheel. She waved at the old Buick as it pulled out onto the highway. The other women waved as well, and then Kathleen said, "Look on the floor of the backseat." They did so and saw a six-pack of water bottles. "The boys replaced our water. Now what do you think about those boys? They are good people from Kentucky who are traveling for a month before they head off for college. Two of them are going to Indiana University. The one who looks like your Nick is going to Ohio State. They are such nice young men and very appreciative of us old women who were not afraid to stop and help some stranded strangers. However, it may not always go this smoothly, Lucille. Do not stop for just anyone along the way. You hear me?"

"I hear you. Nevertheless, it is hard to pass up high school students in need. Who knows, one of them could have been a former student of mine."

"Give me a break," Bernice sarcastically said. "What makes you think you could run into one of your former students all the way down here? That is hardly possible. However, you did teach long enough that there could be hundreds of thousands of your little scholars down this way this summer. We'll watch for them, dear." She felt ashamed of herself for being so sarcastic. "Sorry, Lucille, I didn't intend to be so mean. You could absolutely run into a former student. Stranger things have happened."

"No offense taken, dear. Just wait and see. I could very well spot one of the hundreds of thousands of students I have taught over the years. They would recognize me before I could recognize them. I have not changed all that much in forty years, but teens becoming adults sometimes become unrecognizable. By the way, there were not hundreds of thousands of students, just thousands."

"No, dear, none of us has changed in the past forty years," Kathleen said with a grin.

By the end of the conversation, each one buckled her seatbelt, and Kathleen drove south, continuing their road trip. Lucille put in a CD and they listened to oldies from the 1960s as they sat in silence.

Lucille heard an old Elvis song, "You're the Devil in Disguise," and remembered her first year of teaching when she chaperoned the senior prom. The science department head had asked her to be his date as he also was a chaperone. She tried to remember his name. It was Robert something. That had been their first and last date. He was not particularly handsome, but he had a lean body and dressed like a male model. He had made it clear that he had no strings attached to any woman. At the prom, they danced a few times, and the seniors applauded for them and encircled the two teachers who danced to "You're the Devil in Disguise." After the prom, he had taken her to a nearby town for a midnight dinner. During dinner, he had asked her some impertinent questions and then told her, he actually did have a girl back home. He would probably marry her if no one better came along. He said he needed to have a pretty girl on his arm. His fiancée Merry, four years his junior, was finishing her graduate work. After she graduated, they would plan a wedding, if no one better came along.

He asked the small band playing in the restaurant to play "Georgia on My Mind" twice, and finally when they finished the meal, he asked her to dance. She declined and said, "Does Merry know you have a date for the prom?" Before he could answer, she said, "Robert, I think my stomach is getting upset. The meal was great, but the unveiling of your true character has made me nauseous. I do not want to be in the role of 'no one better coming along.' Take me home."

She remembered standing up and going to the ladies' room while he paid the bill and left a tip.

He had waited for her by the exit and shrugged his shoulders when she opened the door for herself. He had asked if she had lost the corsage he had given her. She admitted she had. Lucille snickered aloud remembering she had lost it when she dropped it in the wastebasket in the rest room.

"What's so funny?" Kathleen asked.

"Oh, just remembering my last prom date at the old age of twenty-four."

"Robert Jones, the science department head. I remember what a slime ball he was. I wonder if he ever married his girlfriend back home. For her sake, I hope not." They returned to silence and Lucille slammed the CD player off when "Georgia on My Mind" started playing. Talk about coincidence and not a good one.

The following day, they crossed the state line into Florida. Bernice drove the Lexus and had the seat pulled up close and elevated so she could see over the steering wheel.

"Tell me again which exit I take to get to Sarasota. I do not want to be responsible for getting us lost. Last year, I got us lost before we got to Phoenix. You remember. I don't need to be set up for all your ribbing again this year."

"Okay, dearie, I'll give you some warning. Sorry, it is your turn to drive. It always seems you are behind the wheel when we get close to our destination. Do you want to pull over and I will drive?" Lucille offered.

"No, just watch for signs for me."

"There. See that sign. Turn right at the next exit," Kathleen said, who had been watching for the road sign, as the two women in front discussed not getting lost. She wiggled her index finger at the sign. Bernice turned off at the right exit and drove a while until they arrived in Sarasota. Lucille had been to the hotel where they had their reservations a few years earlier, so she gave the directions and they arrived in short order.

They checked into their suite and then had no help getting all their suitcases out of the trunk and onto the luggage cart provided. They dragged the carrier rack out of the elevator and found their suite on the sixth floor. They had two twin beds and a loveseat, which opened up into another twin bed in the living room area. Bernice said she would take the loveseat. The other two were grateful because it looked like it would fit her small body better than theirs. In addition, Bernice was the loudest snorer of the three of them. She could have her own room. They opened the curtains and the sliding door that led out to a small balcony. The sky was a clear blue, the blue water in the Gulf of Mexico glittered, and the waves lapped on the sandy shore. The heat at the middle of the day hit them as they stepped outside.

"I think maybe we should have waited until November to come down here."

Lucille grinned and said, "Don't be so pessimistic, Bernice. We are going to have a great time on the beach and at the pool, and we will check out the museums, which will be air-conditioned. We are going to have fun. If we are lucky, we might find three rich old guys who think we are hotties." She laughed.

Bernice and Kathleen both moaned, "Oh, no, here we go again."

"Lucille, you look all you want, I do not want to replace my Zackary. What about you, Kathleen? You want Lucille to bag a man for you?"

"I doubt she could find one to meet my specifications. He must be handsome, youthful, tall, with hair on his head, and be riding a white horse. Actually, I prefer to search for my own," Kathleen said as she turned to go back into their room. She thought, *Actually, I have given up the search. No one will ever compare to Tyler. I am content with my memories.* She had a sad feeling come over her.

They unpacked and hung up their clothes and loaded the drawers. Bernice placed their suitcases under the clothes racks. They heard a knock on the door, and a member of the staff stood there to take the luggage dolly. "Sorry, ladies, that I couldn't be available to bring your luggage up for you," he said with hesitation. "I helped an elderly couple, and they were very slow."

"No problem," Bernice said. "Thanks." She shut the door and whispered, "I think he wanted a tip. For what? For being sorry he was not available. No way. He wants a second tip for helping an elderly couple? No. We are an elderly trio. Well, at least you two are elderly." They all laughed.

"Get your bathing suits on and let's hit the beach, girls. Slather on the lotion, grab your beach towel, and put on your thongs. I mean your flip-flops. We used to call those sandals 'thongs' when they had the strap between your big toe and the next one. You know. Now you cannot call those things thongs. Have you ever thought you would wear a thong? I cannot imagine anything more uncomfortable, can you? It reminds me of dental floss. Maybe we ought to try on a thong in the store just for fun when we go shopping tomorrow," Lucille said and then giggled.

"Ew. No, Lucille, we are not trying on thongs. Surely, nobody tries those on in the store before they buy them, do they? Oh, I may gag. I am ready. Let's go. Who has the room keycard? Do not lose it. I am not taking mine. What time is it? We cannot stay out too long on our first trip out in the Florida sun. We don't want to get sunburnt," Kathleen said.

"I am most susceptible to sunburns. What with my fair skin and blonde hair, I have to be extra careful," Lucille said. She took one last look at herself in the mirror. With her little finger, she wiped some lipstick that bled outside her lip line. *Funny,* she thought, *I do not feel as old as I look. Where have the years gone?*

"Honey, your skin may be fair, but your face is not going to get sunburnt because you have it coated with so much makeup. And your blonde hair, well, never mind," Bernice said. "Let's hit the beach, beauties. Moreover, do not mention thongs again. I am with Kathleen. Ew."

The three friends headed for the beach, each wearing a beach cover-up and a hat with a big brim. They found three wooden lounge chairs together and unloaded their arms. They spread out their towels and put their beach bags next to the chairs. Then they took off their flip-flops and walked quickly toward the water. The sand felt like a hot skillet and their feet were the fried eggs. They lifted each foot gingerly as they scurried down the beach to the water.

"Dearies, I didn't know we could trot this fast, did you?" Lucille said with a giggle. As they got to the water, they stopped and let the warm water soothe the bottoms of their feet. Lucille slipped out of her beach cover-up and threw it on the dry sand. She held her hat on with one hand and started to wade out into the water. A bald-headed man stood up out of a small wave right in front of her, wiped the water off his face, and grinned.

"Well, hello, dolly. Where have you been all my life?"

Kathleen and Bernice looked at each other and rolled their eyes. "Does he really think that line still works?" Kathleen whispered out of the side of her mouth. Bernice laughed aloud. Lucille's two friends pulled up their cover-ups above their hips and waded out to their knees to the left of Lucille and her friend. They watched as Lucille conversed with the bald-headed man. Lucille flirted as they talked. As she came back up to the edge of the water, she introduced him to her friends.

"Girls, this is Shorty Alexander. Shorty, meet my two best friends in the entire world. This is Kathleen Keller and Bernice Meyers. Shorty is from Texas and he is down here on an oil deal.

He wants to take us all out to dinner tonight at a famous seafood restaurant. What do you say?"

"Let's talk about it, and Shorty can call you after we get back to our room. Okay?" Kathleen said.

"Sounds great to me, little ladies. Room 614, you said, Lucy? Well, I need to dry off. I have been in the water too long. I will call you shortly. You call me Shorty, and I'll call you shortly." He guffawed and slogged out of the water.

Again, Kathleen and Bernice rolled their eyes and looked at their friend who waved as her new friend walked to his beach chair. "Call me, Shorty. 614."

"What in heaven's name is wrong with you, Lucille? You just met the man in the ocean and you have a date already. When they say there are more fish in the sea, I guess they are right. She snagged another one," Kathleen said with her hand on her hip. "I'm going back to the beach chairs. Lucille, you just beat all. And I can't believe you are shouting our room number all over the beach."

Bernice joined her as they disgustedly marched quickly back to the chairs, covered with their towels. Lucille stopped to pick up her cover-up, shook the sand out of it, put it on, and followed her friends.

Lucille approached the beach chairs. "Well, he invited all of us. I would not go alone with him, but there is safety in numbers. He offered to buy us a fantastic seafood dinner on our first night in Sarasota. Why would it hurt for him to show us an extraordinary seafood place? What is wrong with being wined and dined?" She pouted.

"Nothing is wrong with that I guess, *Lucy*," Kathleen said. "He got awfully familiar with you in a short visit there. You be careful. Moreover, I thought you did not want us to call you Lucy. You won't let us call you Lucy."

"When he says Lucy, it is kind of cute with his Texas drawl, don't you think?"

"Okay, Kathleen, are we going with Shorty and *Lucy* to dinner tonight?" Bernice purred with a grin.

"Oh, I guess so. I do not want *Lucy* traipsing off with some stranger. We don't want her kidnapped on our first night here."

"Oh, goody. We'll look for a couple of nice oil men for you two also."

"No, we won't," Kathleen and Bernice, proclaimed in unison.

"I remember the man you tried to find for me before I met Zack. Kathleen, tell her. She is not to try to find me a man because her first try bombed and I don't want another one now."

Kathleen reminded Lucille, "Remember that guy you introduced to Bernice? I cannot remember his name. Barney. Barney and Bernice. You thought the names fit so well. Barney was short and skinny. He looked like Barney Fife. In addition, he was so bashful that he did not say more than three words the entire evening. Lucille had a nice date, I had Tyler, and Bernice had bashful Barney. Barney and Bernie. You served shrimp, and he did not tell you he had allergies to shellfish, so after dinner, we had to take him to the emergency room. I felt so sorry for the guy. He confided in Tyler that you were his first date, Bernice. Poor guy. He still lived with his mother. Lucille, you are not a good matchmaker. Just find your own boyfriends, dear."

"I had forgotten about Barney. He had been the librarian's assistant in town. After his mother passed away, he went to Indianapolis and got a library job. The last time I heard about him, he was dating another librarian. Bernice, you must have helped him get over his fear of dating."

"No, I would guess you helped him, Lucille. You talked and asked him so many questions while we sat with him at the hospital, that he finally started communicating. You have a gift, you know," Bernice said with a grin.

Chapter 2

At the appointed time, Shorty knocked on their hotel room door. He had on white slacks and a multicolored Hawaiian shirt. His face and balding head looked beet red from too much sun. They smelled his aftershave from inside their room. Lucille invited him in.

"If you are ready, we can go. I made a reservation for seven o'clock. After my big swim this afternoon, I could eat a whale or a horse, a seahorse." Then he laughed at his own joke. Lucille laughed with him, and her two friends looked at one another and rolled their eyes yet again.

Kathleen had put on white slacks and had on a colorful blouse. She had added earrings and a little lipstick. Bernice wore her pink pants and hot pink T-shirt that said "Sarasota" on it. She had put her grey hair in a neat bun on the top of her head. Lucille, on the other hand, had on bright-blue stretch pants with a long, knit, fitted top displaying rhinestone designs all over the front. Her freshly applied makeup and her blonde up-do announced this fun lady was ready to go. She wore orange high-heeled sandals with a touch of the bright blue in the flowers positioned on the toes of the sandals. Shorty directed them to the elevator, put his hand on the back of Lucille's waist, and claimed his real date for the evening. In her heels, he barely came up to her earlobe. Nevertheless, he appeared ecstatic to be with her. To Shorty, Lucille was a real looker, and he proudly escorted her to the elevator. He had called down to the desk and had his rental

Cadillac brought around to the front entrance. He made sure to put Lucille in the front seat with him, and the other two gladly got in the backseat.

As they sat in the unique, tastefully decorated seafood restaurant, they perused their menus. Shorty suggested the lobster and Lucille decided she would have lobster. Kathleen looked for something less expensive on the menu. Bernice considered something from the kids' menu, but changed her mind. She would just ask for a doggie bag and take it back to their room. On the other hand, she might eat the entire thing right now. After they placed their orders and they all had drinks in front of them, Lucille told Shorty that the three women at his table had known each other for years. She and Kathleen had taught high school English together for a couple of years. Then Kathleen answered God's call to ministry and went to seminary. They remained best friends. Bernice and Kathleen had been best friends and roommates in college. Kathleen introduced Lucille and Bernice to one another and they became the three musketeers. For years, they had been there for one another in the good times and the bad.

"Shorty, Bernice is a retired photographer. She had a spread in the *National Geographic* a few years ago. She and her husband traveled together after their children were on their own and photographed some fantastic places around the world. Our Kathleen, besides being a teacher and a preacher, is also quite a detective. Katie, tell Shorty how you solved a murder in seminary," Lucille said.

Shorty leaned toward Kathleen, "You don't look like a detective or a cop, honey. I like a good story. Tell me." He took a long drink of his beer.

Kathleen gave Lucille a disgusted look that meant, "I can't believe you got me to repeat this story again." She turned her head toward Bernice, crossed her eyes, and pursed her lips, which said it all. She took a deep breath and began the story.

"When Lucille and I were teaching, I became engaged to the love of my life, Tyler Hart. What a handsome man, a godly man, and just a great guy. He could make me laugh, yet he could be serious. He was the kindest, most helpful man I have ever known. He had already proven he would be an outstanding pastor."

Bernice added, "Tyler put movie stars to shame with his handsome face and gentlemanly ways. You were a cute couple, honey."

Kathleen smiled at her friend. "He was in seminary at the time getting ready to graduate. He had his first church appointment that should have begun a month after graduation. God had been dealing with me also. I felt called to the ministry, but fought it. I enjoyed teaching and felt it was my ministry. Tyler gently encouraged me to apply to his seminary. I should have been on campus with him, but I am stubborn."

Lucille added, "Shorty, she is a fantastic pastor. At least Bernice and I think so, don't we?"

Bernice nodded in agreement.

"Tyler was on his daily jog when a hit-and-run driver slammed into him. He was dead on arrival at the hospital. I was eighty miles away and didn't get to say good-bye." Kathleen stopped and looked at her left hand on her lap. She still wore the engagement ring Tyler had given her. She twisted the ring on her finger and still felt the loss.

"Two years later, God still nagged at me, and I gave in and applied to the same seminary. Anyway, once I got there, I checked weekly with the police to see if they had any leads. The police had not apprehended the hit-and-run driver. It made me angry that the police had not found the driver who killed my Tyler. Therefore, I started my own investigation. I interviewed everyone who was on campus when the accident happened. The only students on campus who had been there then were the seniors preparing for graduation. I questioned every professor, staff member, and senior. Most of them had nothing to add to what I already knew."

Lucille interrupted, "Shorty, she is a persistent woman. Go on, honey."

Kathleen stirred her iced tea with the straw and continued, "The business manager found out from one of my friends that I had a heart for missionary projects. Being in charge of setting up the missions fair that spring, he asked me to help him. We met to talk and he asked me out to dinner that evening to continue our planning. I really did not want to go to dinner with him, but he convinced me it was a business dinner or a planning meeting. He said two other students would be with us. However, when he picked me up, he told me the other students had tests the next day and had backed out. I thought he lied to me.

"Bruce Bailey, the business manager, must have been in his late fifties and was single. He tried to date the older students and tried wooing the female dean. She wanted nothing to do with him, but he did not give up easily. Some of the other girls called him a slime ball. His short stature with grey stringy hair on a balding head tended to be a turn-off for the young girls he chased. He wore horn-rimmed glasses over his dull blue eyes and sported a moustache. I am sorry to say that the students made sport of him behind his back. He had an array of plaid jackets that he wore with bow ties, white socks, and loafers with tassels. The word around campus, okay the gossip, portrayed him as a drunk who had been showing up late for work and sometimes appeared to have a hangover. One of the students who had a wild streak and stayed out late most nights had seen him leaving a bar several times weaving out to his car. Yes, we gossiped about him."

"No one ever said that seminary students were perfect, they just try harder," Bernice said. Kathleen raised her eyebrows at her that caused Bernice to shrug her shoulders and grin.

"Anyway, I went out to dinner with him and took my notebook. He started drinking before we had ordered our meals. Instead of talking about the missions fair, he started digging around to find out what information I had uncovered about Tyler's death. I told him I knew the driver of the blue van to be a short man. Some of the things I told him were from the police report. I wondered why he wanted to know so much. He really irritated me, and I decided no more dinner meetings. He didn't like that decision."

Their dinner arrived and Kathleen hoped she could drop the story right there. The women made yummy noises over their food. Shorty began eating and very quickly consumed half his dinner. "Go on, Katie, finish your story," he said while pointing at her with his fork.

She put down her fork and picked up the story where she had left off. "As I helped to set up the missions fair booths, one of the custodians overheard Bruce pressing me to go out to dinner with him again. After Bruce left, Frank, the custodian, suggested I be careful. He had seen Bruce get physical with another student the year before when she turned him down. Obviously, she had not reported the incident. We saw Bruce walk out of the building and jump in his dilapidated old white Buick. I asked Frank why he drove such an old car. He said he used to drive a rather new dark blue van. Frank thought this car was his mother's car. I asked Frank why he had not reported the blue van to the police and he said they had not asked him. He needed his job and did not want Bruce to get him fired. Then I decided I needed to snoop around Mr. Bailey's garage and see if he still had the blue van.

"So around midnight, I dressed in black and drove down the alley behind his house. I parked a few houses down and walked quickly to the back of his garage. I looked in the side window and the white Buick sat there. Defeated, I went back to the dorm. I could not sleep. As I went through the facts I had so far, I remembered Bruce telling me he owned the house next door to his wonderful elderly mama. So the next night, I got into my black garb again and went back to the same spot and parked my car. The moon shone brightly so I did not need a flashlight.

"As I sneaked around Mama Bailey's garage, a dog started barking. I quickly got to the side of the building, but I could not see in the window. I jumped up and down a few times and there appeared to be a dark van inside.

"When I heard the barking dog getting closer to me, I turned around. A flashlight blinded me. I took off running down the alley, jumped in my car, and backed out to the street. I assumed Bruce's mama had caught me. The next night, I persuaded a friend across the hall to drive me to the neighborhood and to wait while I took a picture through the window. I went prepared with a cleaning bucket from Frank's closet to stand on. Carolyn, my friend, let me out at the end of the alley, and I carried my bucket and camera to the back of the garage. I listened and did not hear a dog or any other noise. I stepped on the upside-down bucket and took a few flash pictures of the van and verified that the front right fender had a huge dent. I grabbed my bucket and camera and ran back to the car. We went to an all-night pharmacy and printed out the pictures."

"You were a brave one, weren't you Katie?" Shorty said with a grin. "Then what happened? Oh, do you girls want some dessert? The strawberry cheesecake here is really good." The three women all declined.

"Bernie, you little thing, you need to eat some dessert to fill out those curves," Shorty said.

"My name is Bernice, not Bernie. Furthermore, no thank you to the dessert." She turned to Kathleen and whispered, "And my lack of curves is none of his darn business." Kathleen patted her arm, commiserating with her.

The meal had been very filling and tasty, but Kathleen had eaten less than half of hers. She had been too busy telling her story. She took another bite of the shrimp scampi and decided she could no longer eat the cold buttery dish. Kathleen felt disappointed because the garlic butter had made it so tasty, and she felt bad about wasting so much. However, she knew she would appreciate it when she stepped into her bathing suit in the morning.

"I took the pictures to the police station. A detective supposedly in charge of the case met with me. He said he would investigate the car and let me know. He told me to stay away from the Bailey property. Caleb was a handsome guy with red hair. The problem for me was that he knew he was handsome and was too cocky. He wanted to take me out to dinner to discuss the case further. I had already had enough dinner date meetings for a while. I never did date him because I wasn't over Tyler."

Bernice said, "It is *still* too soon after Tyler. You still aren't over him, Kathleen."

"Maybe not. How about if I finish this story another time?" said Kathleen as she pushed her chair back from the table. She excused herself and went to the ladies' room. This was not how she wanted to spend her vacation…retelling the story as it always made her sad. She wiped a tear from her eye before pushing open the ladies' room door.

"Well, did they arrest this Bailey guy?" Shorty asked.

Lucille said, "You'll just have to meet us on the beach tomorrow to hear the rest of the story. Do you have plans in the morning, Shorty? We'll be at the beach around ten."

"I have no plans yet. Girls, I would like to take you all out for breakfast in the morning. I know a classy little café you girls will enjoy. What do you say?"

Bernice tried to make eye contact with Lucille, but it did not work. Lucille said, "I think we'd like to go very much. Thank you. Here comes Kathleen. Are we ready to go?"

Kathleen and Bernice were not too happy that Lucille had made another date with Shorty for all of them. "Lucille, we will go out to breakfast with him, then lunch and dinner will be on our own. Please," Kathleen begged.

Bernice agreed wholeheartedly. "But Shorty is decreasing our expenses for us." She giggled. "But I'm with Kathleen. We planned this trip for three girls, three old friends. The three musketeers—and now we have four mouseketeers—three mice and a rat." Lucille took offense at that for her new friend and told her so.

Bernice apologized. "You are right. I'm not nice. I am sorry."

The girls sat around the small table in their room for a game of rummy before going to bed. They decided that after breakfast, they would spend some time on the beach and after lunch would shop around the quaint little shops. When all three girls were ready for bed and Lucille had all her makeup off, Kathleen and Lucille crawled into their beds, while Bernice perched on the end of Kathleen's bed. Kathleen read a scripture and prayed, Bernice went back to her bed, and they turned out the lights.

The next morning following breakfast with Shorty, the girls prepared for the beach. Lucille asked the other two if they did not find Shorty entertaining. They agreed that Shorty had many funny stories to tell. The café radiated quaintness, and the food tasted delicious. It deserved another visit next week perhaps, with just the three of them. Kathleen came out of the bathroom with her black bathing suit on and complained about the fit. "I ate too much breakfast. Maybe when I am buying my own meals, I will cut back a little. I tend to be a little frugal when I am paying for my own." She chuckled as she put on her cover-up and flip-flops. She packed her beach bag as Lucille changed into her bathing suit, including a paperback book that she wanted to finish. She knew, however, that with Lucille chattering, she likely would not open the book. Bernice did not tell Kathleen that their friend had invited Shorty to the beach to hear the rest of her story. Bernice closed her cell phone and reported that all was well with her daughter Bethany.

"Bethany told me to be very careful about talking to strange men. In addition, she said to keep a tight rein on Aunt Lucille because she does not know a stranger. She knows her well. I didn't tell her about the boys we helped on the way down."

Lucille walked out of the bathroom in her bright purple suit with a flounced skirt. "She knows who well?" she asked as she had only heard the last part of the conversation.

"Bethany said to keep a tight rein on you around strange men. I didn't tell her you had already found a strange one."

Lucille stuck out her tongue at Bernice, grabbed her purple and white striped beach robe and her white hat off her bed, slipped into her flip-flops, and said, "Let's hit it, girls."

The three friends had not been on the beach more than fifteen minutes when Kathleen groaned, "Here he comes." She put her head down on her arm, wishing she could fall asleep.

Lucille sat up quickly and called, "Shorty. Over here, hon. I saved you a lounge chair. Are you going to hit the waves or lie in the sun first?"

"I want to hear some more of Katydid's story. She has me hooked. If I am ever in trouble, I want her on my side." Shorty laid out his large beach towel, sat down, and began applying lotion on his face and arms. Kathleen mouthed "Katydid" to Bernice and made a face.

Kathleen rolled over, sat up, and sighed loudly. "Okay." She looked at Shorty who now had Lucille smearing suntan oil on his hairy, chubby back. "I waited for the police to go check out the blue van in the Bailey garage. Apparently, Caleb had a couple of days off, so he waited until his return. In the meantime, life went on at seminary. We had a choir recital on Thursday night. As I stood in the front row of the choir and sang, I noticed Bruce Bailey and his little old mama sitting in the third pew. She pointed her little skinny, crooked finger at me and whispered to Bruce. I knew she recognized me as the girl sneaking around her garage. Oh, how I wished I could have been in the back row hiding behind the tall girls. No such luck."

"You can't do much about your height, dear," Shorty said. "I know from experience."

"The next day, Bruce had Molly, the registration clerk, phone me to come to the business office to clear up a financial situation. When I got there, she shrugged her shoulders when I asked what he wanted. She whispered, 'Bruce has a burr under his saddle over something. He is getting more mean-tempered as the months go by.' She buzzed his phone and told him I had arrived. She pointed for me to go on in. 'Good luck,' she whispered, lifting her eyebrows.

"Bruce told me to sit down in the chair beside his desk. He shuffled some papers as if he were looking for something. Then he looked at me and said gruffly, 'Ms. Keller, we don't seem to have a record of your tuition payment this semester. It may be an oversight on your part, but it needs to be paid today or you will be dismissed.' He looked at me sternly over his horn-rims.

"I said, 'Mr. Bailey, I paid my tuition and I have a receipt in my room. I can bring it over to Molly later.'"

"'You leave Molly out of this. I'll come to your room to see the receipt later this afternoon.'"

"I told him, 'No, I said I'd bring it to the office later. In addition, sir, I do not think you have the authority to threaten to dismiss me from seminary. Shall I check with President Bondi on the issue? I saw him in his office as I came down the hall.'"

"'Well, see that you do bring it in,' he stood up to dismiss me. 'By the way, how are you coming along at finding your boyfriend's killer?'

"I answered that I had not given up on helping the police find the person. I left his office and shut the door behind me. I stopped at Molly's desk and told her what he said."

"'Why, Kathleen honey, I remember you bringing in your check. I don't know what he is talking about,' she said. 'Well, bring in the receipt and I'll make a copy of it for him. I'm leaving early today, so try to get back by three-thirty.'"

Chapter 3

"At three o'clock, I heard a knock on my door. I did not keep it locked during the day, so I said, 'Come in.' Bruce came in with a bouquet of roses. To make a long story short, he gave me a shifty smile and pulled back his jacket so I could see a gun in his belt. He said, 'We are going out to dinner, Ms. Keller. We are going to walk out this door, and you will carry these flowers and act delighted to be with me.'"

"I said, 'I am not a good actress, Mr. Bailey.'"

"He said, 'If we see anyone, say hello and keep walking. I will shoot you and whoever you try to tip off, you nosy witch. Could you not just let well enough alone? Let's go.'"

"I started to pick up my purse and he told me to drop it. I did drop it and spilled the contents out on the floor. 'Mr. Bailey, I don't think you are supposed to carry a gun on campus,' I said. I acted braver than I felt. He told me to button my lip. He scared me. When I am scared, I tend to get giggly. I started to giggle when I thought about how buttoning my lip would look. What kind of button should I use? When I tell that now, it seems ridiculous, but at the time, I felt giddy as a little girl and could not stop the image in my head or the giggling. It made him angrier.

"He told me to shut my mouth. He had his arm around me as we walked to his old white Buick, which was a piece of junk. He helped me in, waved at Frank the custodian who stood next to the trashcans. Frank did not wave, but just looked at us with his hands on his hips as if he did not believe I would get in a car with weird Bailey. I could not believe it either. I thought about giving Frank some kind of signal, but did not know what. Then the moment for help had passed.

"He headed south and drove for nearly an hour until we went up a single-lane rutted road through a bunch of trees and underbrush. We came out at a ramshackle log cabin. His mama came out on the front stoop in her cotton dress and rubber boots and waved at her baby boy. He came around and jerked me out of the car. When he got me inside, they tied me to an old kitchen chair.

"I asked him why he wanted to do this. I tried to play along as if I did not know his secret. He was guilty of Tyler's death. 'Mr. Bailey, I don't understand. I had my tuition receipt ready to bring to your office. Really I did. I paid my tuition. Take me back to my room and I'll show you.'

"Mama Bailey laughed with a hoarse voice and told her son I must think they were awful stupid. 'Didn't you think I could recognize you after catching you snooping around my garage? You know too much. You are a nosy parker.' I watched as they had their dinner of tuna on crackers and warm cola. They gave me a metal cup of water, which I would not drink. It looked like water from the muddy creek behind the cabin. At night, they laid me on the floor with a blanket, still tied up."

"Kathleen, dear, are you sure you want to talk about this again?" Bernice asked.

"I'm sorry, Kathleen. I shouldn't have asked you to retell this story," Lucille said.

"That's okay, Lucille. I really did not think it would upset me, but it has. Let's change the subject." She remembered the shivering and fear she felt as she laid on the rough-hewn floorboards of the dirty cabin. She stood up, took off her sunglasses and hat, and headed for the waves. She did not want to think about those days any longer. She would wade in the water and wash away those bad feelings and thoughts. She felt the warmth of the waving water lapping up around her feet. She walked out until the waves washed over her knees and then went further until she felt the waves moving her body while her feet were sinking into the sand. She took a few more steps out, then lay down in the water, and started swimming. Bernice had come to the edge of the water and watched. When Kathleen had swum out too far for Bernice's comfort, she started yelling for her to come back. Just then, Kathleen turned over and headed back in. Bernice exhaled the pent-up air in her lungs. As Kathleen got closer, Bernice waded out to meet her.

"Girlfriend, you scared me."

"I did? I am sorry. It just felt so good to glide through the water so freely, but I promise to be more careful." The two of them walked back to the sandy shore and saw Lucille and Shorty had their heads close together chatting and were oblivious of anything around them.

When the girls started packing up their beach bags, Shorty said, "Well, little ladies, I wish I could take you all out for lunch."

Bernice interrupted him and said, "Oh, no, we really couldn't let you do that."

"I *wish* I could take you to lunch, but I have a business lunch today. But there will be another chance," he said as he stood up to accompany them back to the hotel lobby. They told him good-bye when they stepped out of the elevator on the sixth floor, and then he continued up to the ninth floor.

While Lucille touched up her makeup in the bathroom, Bernice said in a whisper, "I am glad he had a business lunch. It is high time the three of us have some fun together. Where shall we go for lunch? I do want to see the Ringling mansion. It looks cloudy now, so this would be a good time to be inside."

"Any place is fine for lunch and a mansion tour sounds good to me. Hopefully, Lucille will agree," Kathleen said as Lucille came out of the bathroom all dolled up again and proceeded to put on another pair of high-heeled sandals. "We were thinking about taking the Ringling mansion tour, so you may want to wear more comfortable walking shoes, dear. There will be too much walking for those high heels to be comfortable."

"Sounds like fun. Okay, I will go with my walking shoes. I want to be able to keep up with you two. Anyway, Shorty won't be there to see how scruffy I look without my heels."

All three of them enjoyed a delightful afternoon. They had not seen such opulence since they were at the mansions at Newport, Rhode Island, two years before.

Kathleen read from the information she had picked up at the door of the mansion, "The mansion is named Ca'd 'Zan, meaning the house of John. In 1927, John Ringling bought land and moved his circus to Sarasota for their winter headquarters. John and his wife had been wintering in Sarasota for about sixteen years and over time helped to make Sarasota the city it now is. The thirty-room mansion was inspired by the Venetian Gothic palaces."

Bernice said, "Thirty rooms. Wow. How comfortable could it be to live in a mansion? Mr. and Mrs. Ringling did not even have any children to help fill it up. I guess they had to have many guests. Actually, they could have housed their star circus performers, but I bet they didn't. It is too bad they did not have children. Can you imagine children living there, sliding down the banisters? What fun it would have been."

Lucille added, "That room at the top with the circus motif painted on the ceiling and walls would be a child's delight."

"Well, they didn't hang out there in their cut-off jeans and T-shirts," Kathleen said with a chuckle. "I think it would have been an adventure to just be part of the housekeeping staff and enjoy the surroundings. I doubt that any of us will have to worry about the angst of owning a mansion. Imagine the taxes on such a place or cleaning the place or washing the windows."

"If you owned a place like that, you wouldn't have to worry about the taxes or doing any of the work, washing windows, cleaning, or cooking. Your staff would take care of it. I wonder how many people were on their staff."

Lucille said, "I have no idea. But if it were a bed-and-breakfast, I'd stay for a couple of nights or a month." "Well, that might be fun," they chimed in.

They drove back to their hotel and decided that after walking miles through the mansion and up and down hundreds of steps, they wanted to put their feet up. They did not want to go out for dinner, so they decided to eat in the hotel dining room.

"We can see who else is staying at our hotel. There could be some interesting guests besides Shorty," Lucille said. "I hope he had a good meeting today."

Kathleen suggested they get their bathing suits on, go to the pool, and soak their feet. It sounded like a good idea to the other two. As they sat at the shallow end of the pool with their feet dangling in the warm water, they began reminiscing about when Kathleen introduced Lucille and Bernice. After college, Kathleen had gotten a teaching job at Columbus, and Bernice became a writer and photographer for the local newspaper. Kathleen and Bernice had plans to go to dinner one Friday night and she invited Lucille to go along.

Lucille's classroom sat across the hall from her own. Lucille's classes occasionally laughed at her antics and descriptions of characters in literature. She made her lessons memorable by using different voices as she read segments of the stories they were studying. At first, Kathleen became irritated and aggravated by the disruptions, but actually, she felt jealous because the class across the hall seemed to be having more fun than her own class. She withheld judgment of the teacher and got acquainted. It did not take long because Ms. Shuman was very outgoing and eager to make friends with other teachers. One Friday during lunch, Lucille mentioned that her date had cancelled on her for that evening, so she guessed she would have to clean her apartment and do her laundry. Kathleen suggested she go to dinner and the movies with Bernice and her. She readily agreed and offered to drive. Kathleen's two friends hit it off, and they became a threesome. Bernice worried that Kathleen might be jealous when she and Lucille planned to go to dinner one Saturday night when she had a date with Tyler, but that did not happen. Kathleen did not have a jealous bone in her body, except the time that the art teacher tried to drag Tyler on the dance floor at the faculty dinner.

"Lucille, help me here with the name of the flirty art teacher who tried to drag Tyler out on the dance floor. You remember the one who dressed like a belly dancer and surprised the principal for his birthday at the faculty dinner."

"Oh, you have asked me that before and we can never remember. Rowena, Roseanna, Rolonda, something like that. What made you think about that bimbo?"

"Lucille, be nice. I do remember that first faculty dinner we attended way back when."

"Can we wrap up this trip down memory lane and go get ready for dinner? I am hungry, how you about?" Bernice stood up, waited to get her hips loosened up, and headed for the handrail to get out of the pool.

Later in the evening as the friends were chatting and reading the dinner menu, Lucille squealed as someone put his hands over her eyes and said, "Guess who? Do you mind if I join you?" Shorty Alexander leaned down to kiss her on the cheek.

"Oh, Shorty, you surprised me, hon. Sit down. I saved a spot for you right beside me." Lucille winked at her girlfriends.

"You don't mind if I join you ladies, do you?"

Bernice and Kathleen said half-heartedly in unison, "Of course not." Bernice crossed her eyes at Kathleen, who whispered to her, "Stop it. Our crossed eyes are going to freeze like that."

"Speaking of eyes, Shorty, how did you get your shiner?" Bernice asked.

"Oh, my, Shorty, whatever happened to your eye? You do have a shiner. Honey, does it hurt?" Lucille asked as she put her thumb and index finger on his chin and turned his head so she could see better. All three women looked at his face and noted that indeed he had a black eye that he tried to cover with a little cover-up cream.

"I ran into a sign outside the restaurant where I had my lunch meeting today. It is nothing. I looked the other direction and walked right into the sign. Boom. It jumped out and hit me. I will be all right in a few days. Don't worry about me, Lucy," he said as he patted her hand. He smiled at her as if he really appreciated her concern.

They placed their orders and then relaxed a moment, looking around at the tastefully decorated room with forest green and cranberry accents. The china and crystal shone and the round mirrors the vases sat upon reflected the flowers. Guests were talking, but it seemed so quiet. They smiled and leaned back in their chairs with satisfaction. Even with Shorty joining them, they were happy with the ambience of the dining room.

"Shorty, tell us about your business meeting. Did it go well?"

"Fine, fine. I do not want to bore you with business. What I want to hear is more of Katie's kidnapping story by the revolting little man and his mean mama. Would it upset you too much to tell me the rest of the story?"

Kathleen thought that she might as well finish it and get it over and done. "Okay, here's the rest of the story." She put her napkin in her lap, took a deep breath, and continued. "The Baileys kept me tied up for three days except to go to the outhouse. Bruce went out a couple of times to get groceries. Mama Bailey harassed me before he returned telling me what a catch her Brucie was, and I must be stupid not to want to date him. I agreed with her. I told her that every young woman wanted a man her father's age with white socks, tasseled loafers, plaid jackets, and a myriad of bow ties with a bad attitude who liked to tie up women with the help of his mother. Once, she slapped me and told me to shut my mouth. I always have been a little mouthy when angry or scared."

"You can say that again," Bernice interrupted. Kathleen gave her a frown and then chuckled.

"For three days, I wondered if anyone had reported me missing. My dorm room door stood ajar and my purse's contents were on the floor, so if anyone looked, they might guess I did not leave by choice. My wallet and car keys lay on the floor and my car remained in the parking lot. It was the weekend so there were no classes going on, so classmates or professors would not miss me. However, someone had to be missing me."

"I tried to call her several times, but she never answered," Lucille said. "I got worried when I called Bernice and Kathleen's mom, and neither of them had heard from her in a few days either. Remember that, dear?"

"Yes, I know you tried to find me. However, I had not told you yet about my speculation about Bailey being guilty of manslaughter. My friend who had taken me to spy on the Bailey's garage lived across the hall from me. I knew that surely Carolyn had missed me and would have an idea of what had happened when she saw my purse dumped on the floor and could not find me. I began to think that no one would find me and my body would never be found because those two crazy people would kill me and bury me under the cabin. I spent much of the time praying and quoting scripture. I sang quietly so many praise songs and old hymns that my throat got raspy. Bruce finally told me to quit singing because I did not sound like Doris Day. I had to agree with him on that. They kept asking me if I had told anyone about the blue van in Mama's garage. I lied repeatedly and said, 'What van?' It was frustrating them badly, and it gave me strength to hang in there. On the third day, they put the rag around my mouth because they were tired of hearing me sing and talk. I refused to cry. I was sure God would send someone to rescue me. Well, I told myself that someone would come eventually."

"Now that wasn't right," Bernice said. "Kathleen, you have a fine voice. Talk about meanness on his part." Kathleen grinned at her friend who was supporting her against criticism.

"On the third night, Bruce and Mama shared a bottle of cheap wine sitting at the dilapidated table. He got maudlin and told her he would like to marry me, and then I could not be a witness against him. She called him stupid because I could not be trusted.

Time had run out, and they needed to dispose of the rubbish and go back home."

"Can you believe that? They called our Kathleen rubbish. They were just evil," Lucille said.

"Mama Bailey said he could drive the van down to the Ohio River and push it over the banks and get rid of the evidence. He could put me in the van, and they'd get rid of two problems at once.

"Then the front and back doors got kicked in simultaneously. Bruce started to cry and Mama told him to shut up. She slapped him and told him to be a man. I could not see who had come into the cabin, but I felt someone untying my hands and taking the rag out of my mouth. I gagged and breathed deeply through my mouth. What a relief, especially when he came around and untied my feet. The redheaded detective, Caleb, pulled me to my feet and gave me a hug. I was so happy to see him, that I hugged him back. He said, 'You were not easy to find, Ms. Keller.'"

"I wish you had dated Caleb a time or two. It might have helped you," Lucille said.

Kathleen shook her head no and said, "Two police officers came in with him and put the Baileys in handcuffs. The police escorted them out. Bruce actually said to the cops, 'She is going to marry me, so you can't ask her any questions.' Can you believe the audacity of that worm?"

"Caleb sounded like a nice man though, Kathleen. But I know you weren't ready to think about dating anyone else," Bernice said. "Go on, honey, I didn't mean to interrupt."

"Caleb proceeded to tell me that my friend Carolyn had reported me missing on Saturday afternoon when he went back to work. He checked out the blue van I had photographed for him. He found no one home at Bruce's house or his mama's house. He got a search warrant and went back to the garage. They identified the van because of the dent, and they found old blood on the underneath side of the fender.

"When Carolyn reported me missing, Caleb almost panicked. He went to campus and questioned folks on my floor of the dorm and some of the staff. Bruce had called in sick to the seminary on Friday. No one seemed to think much about it. Caleb talked to Frank, the custodian, and he got the clue he needed. Frank told him it surprised him to see me get in Mr. Bailey's old white Buick with a bouquet of roses and I did not wave at him. He said I did not look happy. He did not understand why I would go out with Bailey, but there is no accounting for taste. However, he thought I had better taste. And I did.

"The police were watching the Bailey's neighborhood. They searched both houses, but did not find me. A detective found after much digging in the courthouse records that the Baileys owned some property down by the river. The property belonged to Magnolia Maelene Morrison, Mama's maiden name. There are not too many women named Magnolia Maelene Bailey. A smart detective found that information. So they searched the area and found the tire tracks, which led them to the cabin."

Lucille said, "Kathleen became the big heroine at the seminary. She had helped solve the mystery of the death of her fiancé. She risked her own life in the process. Nevertheless, she did it. She had her picture in the paper and newspaper and television reporters interviewed her. We were so proud of her."

"We still are," Bernice said with a big smile. "And I think the female students were glad that she managed to get the campus letch taken away."

"Perfect timing," Kathleen said. "Our meal is here. Can we talk about something less stressful? Umm, this chicken smells delicious." They all agreed that the meals were great. Kathleen breathed a sigh of relief that she had finished her story. It had been more difficult than she thought to retell the details again. She ate part of her meal and her stomach started to rebel. She just moved the food around on her plate. No one seemed to notice.

Chapter 4

On the fifth day of their vacation, Lucille had plans to go to the dog track with Shorty. Kathleen and Bernice were beginning to see him as harmless, so they did not feel they had to tag along with them. Bernice wanted to do some shopping for the grandkids, and Kathleen wanted to go anywhere but to the dog track. Lucille got all dolled-up in her stretch purple pants and a purple top trimmed with red stones. She put on her red high-heeled sandals and a pair of big sunglasses that had red frames. When Shorty knocked on the door, he wore yet another Hawaiian shirt with purple flowers on it. "Well, look at us, Lucy. We are a matched set. Let's go, doll."

"See you later, girls. I promise I will go to the circus museum with you tomorrow. Shorty has some business to take care of, so it will just be the three of us," Lucille said as she grabbed her oversized red and purple striped bag and headed for the door. She turned at the door and waved her hand at her friends. "Bye for now, girlfriends."

They waved good-bye to one another. Bernice said, "That man seems harmless, but there is something about him that makes me suspicious. I hope it just isn't that I am jealous of him breaking up our fun threesome."

"There is something about him that I can't read. He seems well mannered, kind, and generous. However, he seems to have some kind of a secret. The story about walking into a metal sign does not ring true with the black eye. If he walked into a metal sign, the entire side of his face ought to be black and blue," Kathleen said.

"Maybe that is it. He is hiding something." The two friends had told Lucille they would take a taxi to go shopping. Shorty had asked her to drive her car because the rental agent had come to pick up the Cadillac to fix a window that would not close completely. The agency would have it back to him by tomorrow.

Bernice and Kathleen went out to lunch at a little outdoor café and enjoyed browsing through several stores. Bernice found several gifts for the kids and items for her children and their spouses. Her shopping bags got heavier and heavier as the afternoon wore on. Kathleen had found a necklace she really liked for her sister. She would save it for her birthday in November. She found a book she wanted to read and bought it, knowing it would be a winter read.

After a few hours of walking and shopping, they stopped for a piece of cheesecake and iced tea. They agreed that they were both tired of shopping, so they took a taxi back to their hotel. Bernice thankfully put down her bags. She stuck them in the corner with the suitcases.

"How about if we rest for a while and either go down to the dining room or order room service for dinner," Kathleen said.

"Lucille should be back by then. I wonder if she will be as tired as we are." She slipped out of her sandals and lay down on her bed. Bernice pulled back the bedspread on Lucille's bed and did the same. Between the shopping and the heat, they were ready for a rest.

"I can't imagine that she will feel any better than we do after spending the day walking around in those high-heeled sandals. I don't know how she does it," Bernice said. They quit conversing and lay still until they were both breathing evenly. Kathleen could hear Bernice snoring and grinned before closing her eyes again and going to sleep.

When Bernice awoke, there was no light coming in the window. She checked the alarm clock and jumped off the bed.

"Kathleen, wake up. It is eleven p.m. and Lucille is not back yet. Where can she be? I think I'll call the main desk and see if she and Shorty have returned."

Kathleen sat up too fast and felt dizzy for a moment. "I'm sure there is a good explanation for her not being here. Maybe they are in the dining room."

Bernice said incredulously, "Kathleen, it is going on midnight. The dining room is closed." She quickly pushed the button for the desk. She asked a couple of questions and hung up. "The guy on the desk says he's been there since seven and hasn't seen the blonde lady and short man. What are we going to do? Call her cell phone, Kathleen. Please."

"Well, let's not get overly excited. You know Lucille. They are probably out dancing somewhere or walking on the beach." Nonetheless, Kathleen dialed the number. The message on the phone said she is unavailable. "Let's go down to the parking lot and see if her car is back." They put on their sandals, took their purses and key card, and headed to the elevator. When they got to the front desk, Kathleen stopped and asked the clerk if he had not seen their friend come in the last few minutes. He said he would have noticed the tall blonde lady. Sorry, but he had not seen her or the man. The nervous friends walked out the front door and the humid heat hit their faces. They looked down both sides of the outside parking area and did not see a silver Lexus. Then, they took the elevator to the lower level parking and did not see Lucille's car there. Kathleen grabbed Bernice's arm and started to pray.

"I am sure she has had a nice dinner with Shorty and we are hungry. The dining room is closed for the night, we have no transportation, and my stomach is rebelling," Bernice said.

Her friend answered, "I know. I cannot believe we slept so long. We must be getting old. If she is going to keep gallivanting around like this, I think we ought to rent our own car. This is ridiculous. Do you suppose it is too late for room service? What about the bar? Could we get a sandwich there? I wonder what is in the vending machine." They had arrived back up in the lobby and walked out the front door again.

"Vending machine? Bar? You have to be kidding. See that big sign down there? It is only a couple of blocks away. It is an all-night pancake house. Can you walk that far?" Bernice challenged. Kathleen linked her arm through her friend's arm, and they strolled down the long walkway to the sidewalk.

An hour later, they were walking back into the lobby, feeling much better. They had looked around the parking lot and had not seen Lucille's Lexus. Kathleen walked over to the desk clerk and he shook his head, "Sorry, ma'am. They haven't come in while you were gone." He busied himself with paperwork.

"Maybe she came in a side door. Maybe they had car trouble. Maybe she has returned and is already worried about us," Bernice said. She knew she was mistaken, but thought it better to be positive. *Let us not borrow trouble.*

When they got to the room, it looked the same. Kathleen picked up the phone and called Shorty's room. No one answered. Bernice turned on the television, hoping that there would be no news of an auto accident or kidnapping or anything like that. They sat in the chairs and watched television. A few times, there were sounds in the hallway as other guests were returning to their rooms, but Lucille did not walk through the door. Eventually, they both fell asleep. When they awoke, Lucille was still not back. Nevertheless, they both had stiff necks and backs from sleeping in the chairs.

Bernice quickly took a shower while Kathleen called to have a rental car delivered to the hotel. When it was her turn, Kathleen stood under the shower briefly, let the hot water loosen the sore muscles, and she got dressed. Neither woman dried her hair. Bernice put hers into a ponytail fastened at the nape of her neck. Kathleen combed through hers and planned to let it air-dry. The front desk called them because their rental car arrived. Kathleen signed the papers. The delivery driver gave the key to Bernice, and the women asked how to find the police station.

They received a hatchback car with a stick shift. "It is cute, it is red, and it will be easy to find in a parking lot," Bernice said. "I can't drive a stick shift, can you?"

Kathleen grabbed the key out of Bernice's hand and said, "It's been a while, but I can. Let's go." As she pulled away from the curb, the car jerked a little, then the motor died. She tried again and gave it more gas than needed; the motor raced as they drove away. "I hope I don't give us both whiplash before I get the hang of this again."

They rushed into the police station, where the police officer at the desk listened to their story but did not seem too concerned. "Ladies, it isn't that unusual for a woman or gent to stay over with someone else for the night. Probably, she will be back in your room when you get there," he said condescendingly. "She probably had a good old time last night and forgot to call you."

"No, sir. She is not the type to go home or do whatever you are suggesting with someone she hardly knows. She is a fine lady, a little flamboyant and flirtatious I'll grant you, but she would not do that," Bernice said. Kathleen nodded in agreement. When the officer said they had to wait forty-eight hours to give a report of a missing person, they huffed out of the station.

"If that don't beat all," Bernice said rather loudly. "I am going to call Nick and ask him what we should do." Nick, Bernice's oldest son, had been her support since her husband Zackary had passed away. He lived in Indiana and could not come down, but he might have some advice.

As Bernice talked to her son, Kathleen noticed a small church on a corner and slowed down to read the sign. They had twenty minutes to wait until the Sunday service would begin. She pulled into the parking lot and parked. Bernice looked around, saw where they were, and nodded. The two friends went into the church sanctuary and prayed before the service started.

The pastor preached his sermon on trusting God in difficult times. He had read Mark 5:21–24 and 35–43, the story of Jairus, a leader of the synagogue, who came to Jesus asking that he go home with him because his daughter was near death. He wanted Jesus to lay hands on her and heal her. Before they got there, friends came and said they had waited too long and now his daughter had died. Jesus said, "Do not fear, only believe." The pastor suggested that just as Jairus's crisis made him perplexed, fearful, and without hope, there were folks sitting out there who were listening to him also who are or have been in similar crises where they feel fear and hopelessness. Look to Jesus; see the situation from the eyes of Jesus. Do not fear. Jesus brought the little girl back alive. "Do not fear, only believe."

At that moment, Kathleen's mind wandered and she feared for Lucille's safety, but knew that they would trust in God's protection.

After the service, they got back to the car, and Bernice noticed that her door had not locked. She did not mention it because she did not want to hear a lecture about the safety issues involved in not locking one's car. They talked briefly about being glad they had gone to church. Now what could they do? Kathleen pulled out of the parking lot and turned left.

The two friends were at their wit's end to know what to do next. "I say we go out to the dog track and ask around to see if anyone remembers seeing them yesterday. I have her picture in my wallet. How do we get there? I remember seeing a sign somewhere. I am going to pull over and you ask that old man waiting for the bus. He ought to know where the track is," Kathleen said as she pulled over into the bus stop area. Bernice rolled down her window and shouted to the man who appeared to be sleeping, "Hey, how do we get to the dog track from here?" He did not look at her. "Hey, how do we get to the dog track from here?"

He looked up and said, "Eh?" He had been snoozing and looked very much like a resident retired senior citizen in his oversized plaid Bermuda shorts, striped shirt, white socks, and brown sandals. He leaned forward and pushed up his hat off his forehead so he could see them better.

"I said how do we get to the dog track from here? Can you give us directions? We are in a hurry. We have to find a lost friend," Bernice shouted.

"Oh, he doesn't need to know that, Bernice," Kathleen said.

He stood up slowly and said, "The dog track you say? Yeah, I know where it is. That is where I am headed."

Without a second thought, both women said, "Get in the car. Show us the way." He shuffled over to their car and tried to climb into the backseat. Bernice got out and pulled the seat forward for him. He tried to find something to hold on to before stepping in. She pointed out a handle over the window. He got his right foot in. She encouraged him to step back out and begin with the left foot. He carefully maneuvered himself back out. He got his left leg in the backseat by lifting his leg with his hand. By then, the bus behind them tried to get into the parking spot for buses only, but their car had it blocked. The impatient bus driver honked the horn repeatedly while he waited for the old man to get in the car. Bernice so much wanted to push his behind in and down into the seat, but felt maybe she did not know him that well. The bus driver shouted something at them as he waited for Kathleen to restart the car and move. She waved at the bus driver out her window. Finally, Bernice put her seat back into place and got in the car. She shut her door, Kathleen let up on the clutch, and the engine died. She started the car again and gave it too much gas, but the car moved on. The bus driver laid on the horn one last time. Bernice waved as if to thank the bus driver for his patience and quickly rolled up her window.

"Patience is not that man's strength." They all chuckled.

"My name is Rusty, and I appreciate the ride because taking the bus every day is a pain in my backside. My wife has the driver's license in the family, and she refuses to take me to the track five days a week."

"This is Kathleen and I am Bernice. We are looking for our friend who is missing." Kathleen held up the picture of Lucille for him to see.

He took it, looked, and thought. "Was she wearing some tight purple pants? Is she a real looker with a short guy? Yeah, I saw her yesterday. She seemed to be having a good time."

They pulled into the parking lot. Rusty thanked them for the ride and told them he hoped they found their friend. Rusty slowly shuffled, so the women left him in the dust as they scurried up to the entrance. They spent a couple of hours asking people if they had been there the day before and if so had they seen this blonde older woman. After a hundred or more people looked at the picture, only one person remembered seeing Lucille. The guard at the gate remembered Lucille and the short guy hurrying out the front gate about four o'clock. The guard said he remembered her because she had on a colorful blouse, purple tight pants, and she was having trouble running in her high heels. He remembered that the short man with her ran as if he had a bear on his tail and dragged the lady faster than she could run on her own.

At dinnertime, Kathleen and Bernice gave up. Even with the information they had, they had not come close to finding her. They headed back out toward their little red car and the guard waved at them as they went by.

"Well, we didn't accomplish much there. Another couple of hours and we can go back to the police station and fill out the paperwork. Maybe we should call our hotel room again," Kathleen dialed and let it ring about twenty times and no one answered. Bernice called Lucille's cell phone and she did not answer. At the car, Kathleen touched the button on the key fob to unlock the doors. Both women tried to open their car doors, but they had no luck. Kathleen pushed the button to unlock the doors repeatedly, but nothing happened.

Bernice went to the hatchback, and when the door opened, she squealed with joy. She climbed in, carefully crawled to the front seat, and unlocked the doors. Kathleen got in and grabbed the paperwork she had tucked under the visor. She called the rental office.

"This is Kathleen Keller, the renter of this stupid red hatchback. We are at the dog track and cannot get the car doors unlocked. Luckily, the hatchback unlocked. My friend had to crawl through to the front seat. We are both almost seventy years old, and we surely cannot keep doing this. She is skinny and spry, but I am not skinny or spry, so we need you to bring us another key for this car, or better yet, bring us another car. Why did I get this little kiddie car when I had asked for a midsized rental? What do you mean you do not have any more cars? Give me a break. You want us just to leave it unlocked. No, we are not leaving belongings in the car, but you want us to leave your car unlocked in the parking lot of the hotel all night. Okay. As soon as you get another car, preferably not a stick shift, I want it delivered to our hotel. We are not getting any younger here. Someone has to be turning in a better car by tomorrow. You have my name and phone number. Right? Okay." She punched the off button and stuck out her tongue at her phone.

Bernice had been listening to the conversation and she laughed aloud. "We are not getting any younger here? How right you are, Katie." Bernice's phone rang, and she flipped up the lid and saw her son's name. His advice fell in line with what his mom and Aunt Kathleen had already done.

"Mom, you be careful. This does not sound good. Keep in touch, and don't leave the hotel after dark," Nick said. Bernice thought it best not to tell him that the two of them had walked down the street the night before to go to the pancake place.

After a quick meal, the two distraught friends decided to go by the hotel and check again to see if Lucille had returned. No luck. When they got to the police station, a different officer sat behind the front desk. He did not hassle them, listened to their story, and commiserated with them. They let the kind police officer make a copy of Lucille's picture.

He said, "Ladies, go back to your hotel, and if we find her, we'll call you right away."

They thanked him and headed back to the temperamental car. Kathleen got them back to the hotel and they drove around looking for a silver Lexus. They slumped in their seats with disappointment. Kathleen parked under a light and said, "Remember, don't lock your door. You cannot keep crawling through the car. If we are lucky, maybe someone will steal the stupid thing."

They waited up half the night. Kathleen again led them in prayer for their friend Lucille. Kathleen read the Gideon's Bible from the nightstand and Bernice played solitaire, drank iced water, and ran to and from the bathroom. They prayed again about three o'clock and tried to sleep, but neither of them had much luck.

When they awoke, they brushed their hair and their teeth, put on comfortable clothes and sandals, and headed out the door. They would go to the police station before stopping somewhere for breakfast. They walked over to the little red car that they both were beginning to dislike and opened the doors. Her driver's seat lay back like a bed. They saw empty pop cans, a bag of empty sandwich boxes from the Golden Arches, and a big wad of wet bubble gum stuck to the carpet on the floor on the passenger side.

"What is this? I cannot believe someone has been in our car. I cannot believe they had a picnic and left their trash. Who knows what else happened in here. That is bubble gum. I suppose they will charge us for that mess stuck into the carpet. Let us clean up this mess so we can get on our way. Here, Bernice. Take this clean napkin and see if you can pull up that bubble gum." Both women worked at cleaning up the mess.

When they had thrown the trash in the trashcan, they got in the car. Kathleen adjusted her seat, put on the seat belt, and inserted the key. It would not turn. She took it out and inserted it again. It would not turn. She took it out, turned it upside down, and tried again with no results.

"What is this? Yesterday, we could not get the door unlocked. Today, the key will not start the car. I am getting livid over here," Kathleen said as she looked up to the clouds and prayed for patience and help. The interior of the car was too hot. Bernice got out and stood by the open door.

"Are you going to call the rental place? Our papers are not in the visor now. These car invaders stole our paperwork. Here, the business phone number is on the sticker on the back window," Bernice said.

Kathleen angrily punched in the phone number and began to walk around waiting for someone to answer. "Hello? Yes, this is Kathleen Keller. This lemon of a car you rented us has another problem now." As she talked, she walked down past three cars and paced as she talked. She turned and noticed a red car with a hatchback and a sticker on the back window for the rental company right behind her. "Let me call you back," she said and closed her phone. "Bernice, shut that car door and get over here. Hurry up." Kathleen opened the driver's door and looked inside. They found the rental papers tucked behind the visor. She got in and inserted the key. She turned it and the car started running. Bernice jumped in the passenger seat. They looked at each other and started to giggle, to chortle, and then shrieked with laughter.

"What just happened here?" Bernice asked.

"Well, girlfriend, it seems that we cleaned out someone's rental car for them. Can you imagine what they will think when they get in their car and realize the trash and bubble gum are gone and the car seat is in the upright position? And what are the chances that two identical rental cars would park a few cars down from each other at the same hotel?" They both laughed some more.

Bernice said, "I hope they weren't saving that bubble gum for today. Wait. Wait. I have to go back in to the ladies' room. I've laughed too hard and too long." She jumped out and walked swiftly to the entrance, keeping her knees close together. Kathleen waited in the car with the air conditioner running.

Before Bernice returned, a young couple came out and jumped into the other red car. The girl jumped back out and said, "Chuck, someone has been in our car. We did not leave it this clean. Did you come out earlier and clean out the car?" She got back in the car and they drove off.

Kathleen really laughed when she picked up Bernice at the entrance. "Bernice, a young couple just got in their clean hatchback over there and didn't even thank me for cleaning it out." They laughed.

"We have to quit laughing. Lucille is missing and it is serious. I am feeling guilty." Bernice agreed.

Chapter 5

Kathleen drove to the police station. They walked in and stopped at the main desk. The first police officer who had not been very helpful sat behind the desk. "What can I do for you, ladies?"

"We are reporting our friend Lucille Shuman and a Mr. Shorty Alexander missing. We do not know his real first name. We tried to report Lucille missing yesterday, but they told us we had to wait, sir. Have you heard anything about her yet? Or her Lexus? We came down here in a silver Lexus. We are worried about her. She is seventy, very bright, and really with it. Therefore, it is not dementia or anything like that. She went to the dog track with Mr. Alexander, and a couple of people reported to us that they saw them scurrying out to the parking lot."

"Let me get someone who can help you here, ma'am," he said slowly as he picked up the phone. "Sergeant Miller, come to the front desk please."

Kathleen said under her breath, "I can't believe he let me tell the whole story again and we have to talk to someone else."

He told them to go sit on a bench under a huge bulletin board filled with pictures of criminals. Kathleen sat down, but Bernice started browsing through the pictures of wanted characters. Finally, an officer in uniform came out and listened as Kathleen told her story again. The officer said they were keeping an eye out for her car, but there are many silver Lexus vehicles in Sarasota. They would keep in touch with the women. Defeated again,

Kathleen and Bernice went back to the hotel. Kathleen decided to go sit on the beach and watch people to see if maybe Lucille and Shorty would come walking down the beach. Bernice said she had to lie down because of a splitting headache. "Don't be gone too long, Kathleen. I do not want to find that you disappeared too, and I am left all alone. Too much like *The Twilight Zone*. Don't be gone long, you hear me?"

"Yes, Bernice. I promise," Kathleen said, as she left the room with her beach paraphernalia. She moved to a different beach chaise lounge off by itself and took off her cover-up. She took time to slather suntan lotion all over herself. She pulled out her paperback book and tried to read, but could not concentrate. The sun lulled her to sleep. A couple of hours went by and her own snoring woke her up. She felt the open book on her tummy slide off and wiped the drool that was running out of her open mouth. "How gross. How embarrassing." Between the sounds of the waves slamming the sandy shore, she could hear two men's voices. Without sitting up, she opened her eyes and saw them down the beach. The mothers had taken their children in for lunch, so the beach looked deserted and rather quiet.

Her ears perked up when she heard, "Kill him, Slim. The boss said to get it done now."

"But he is with that old blonde broad."

"Don't matter. If she sees you, take her out too," the gruff voice said. "Do it before they move again and you can't find them." She noticed that the two men were looking around and she pretended to be asleep. She snored again. She peeked out of one eye and saw the heavy-set man look at her and shake his head. She knew he thought she was just some old goofy lady who was probably deaf too. They walked off in different directions.

When Kathleen saw they were no longer looking back at her, she grabbed her bag and other belongings. She put her feet into her flip-flops and marched off quickly to the hotel lobby. Her heart pounded in her chest. She turned around to be sure no one followed her and she scurried to the elevator. When she opened the door to their room, Bernice looked up from putting on her sandals.

"Where have you been? I told you not to be gone too long." Bernice stood up and put her hands on her hips.

"I'm sorry. I fell asleep on a chaise lounge. When I woke up, I had been snoring and drooling. How embarrassing. However, it gets worse. I heard two men in suits and black dress shoes talking from a short distance away. The beach was almost empty so their voices carried. The heavy-set man said, 'Kill him, Slim. The boss said to get it done now.' The other one said, 'But he is with that old blonde broad.' Then the big man said, 'Don't matter. If she sees you, take her out too. Do it before they move again and you can't find them.'"

"Oh, dear, I wonder who they are going to kill."

"Think about it. Shorty had a business meeting and came out with a black eye. Someone is not happy with him. They are going to kill someone, and he has an old blonde woman with him. That could be Lucille. Our Lucille. Although I do not appreciate him calling her a broad. We have to go to the police station again. Let me put on some clothes and we are out the door." Kathleen grabbed the pants and bright blouse she had worn that morning and dashed into the bathroom.

She dashed out still buttoning her blouse and said, "Come on, Bernice, don't just stand there. Let's go."

The two friends headed back for the little red car with the stick shift. "I hate this car," she mumbled. When they got to the police station, again the police officer at the desk acted as if he had not seen them before. They asked to see the officer they had talked to that morning and again they were told to wait on the bench. Bernice got up and started looking at the wanted posters again.

"The photographer who took these photos is sure lousy. I could do a better job," she said.

"Well, I would hope so. You had pictures in the *National Geographic* magazine, for goodness sake. And these are wanted posters, dear." She stood up and looked at a few of the pictures. "You are right. Poor photography. But they serve the purpose." She started to turn around and sit down when an ugly face stared at her from the wall. She went over and looked more closely. "He looks familiar. Bernice, do you know this man?"

"Why would I know that man? I don't hang out with robbers and thieves?"

"Where have I seen that face before? Hmm. Oh, my gosh, I know. This is the heavyset guy on the beach. This is the one who said to kill," Kathleen whispered.

She jumped when the uniformed police officer came back out and said, "Hello again, ladies. Sorry to say we have not found anything that would tell us there has been any foul play with your friend. Maybe she ran off with the man and they got married," he said and laughed.

Bernice said, "That is not funny. Lucille is friendly, but not stupid."

Kathleen then told him about overhearing the conversation on the beach and pointed to the fat face on one of the posters. "That is one of them."

"Ma'am, are you sure? You said you had been sleeping. Are you sure you weren't dreaming? How far away were they? What are the chances that his picture would be on this wall? Maybe he looks similar to the man. Are you even sure you heard him say *kill*? Maybe you misunderstood," the officer said.

"I may be getting old, but I am not blind and I am not senile. I know what I heard and what I saw. They may be planning to kill Shorty and the woman he mentioned could by our friend Lucille. What are you going to do about it?" Kathleen said with some fury brewing within her.

"Okay, we'll see what we can find out about this guy," he said as he pulled down the poster with the fat-faced man. "We'll get on this right away. We will call you. You do not need to keep coming back. Ma'am, I know you are concerned, but we are looking for the Lexus. When I have a man free, I will send him around with her picture to other hotels and see if she has checked in somewhere else."

The two women thanked him and turned to leave. Kathleen turned back to look at him and saw him grin at the officer at the desk and twist his index finger around his ear to indicate a crazy person.

"Now that makes me angry." She grabbed Bernice's arm and stopped her as she turned to go back toward the officers. "Gentlemen, I may be old enough to be your mother, but I am also smart enough to know when I am being placated, appeased, and ridiculed. Is this how you treat all senior citizens? This is a serious matter. If I do not hear from you by evening, I will be calling the mayor. I do not know her personally, but we will become acquainted very quickly. She will hear how poorly you treat visitors who are in need in her fine city."

Bernice popped up and said, "And she will be the lawnmower and you will be the grass, if you get our drift." She pointed at Kathleen and stomped her foot and said, "Let's go, Kathleen." Both women huffed and puffed as they went through the glass doors. When they were out of sight, they turned to each other and did an old-peoples' victory dance because they had stood up for themselves.

On the way back to the hotel, Kathleen pulled in line for the drive-through window at an ice cream store. "We need ice cream," she announced. They each ordered an oversized item, and when they got them were surprised they were so large. Kathleen pulled over under a tree, and they got out, consuming their treats at a picnic table.

Bernice said, "What are we going to do? We have to find her before something bad happens, if it hasn't already." She had tears running down her cheeks dripping on her large hot fudge sundae.

Kathleen started eating her extra-large banana split and shook her head.

"I have to think this through. Let me eat and think." They ate in silence. Finally, Bernice said, "If I eat any more of this, I am going to be sick."

Kathleen scraped the last of the melted ice cream out of the bottom of her dish. She reached for Bernice's plastic bowl and said, "I'll finish it for you. No use wasting it."

Bernice's eyes got big as she watched her friend finish off the huge sundae and scrape the last of the melted ice cream out of her plastic bowl. She shook her head and said, "Kathleen, are you all right?"

Kathleen said, "I am fine. Why?" She looked down and realized all she had eaten. "Well, maybe I am going to be ill. Yuck. I cannot believe I ate all that. Why didn't you stop me? Let's go." Kathleen picked up the trash, tossed it in the barrel, and they got in the car.

As they entered their room, Bernice saw the red light flashing on the phone. She thought that maybe one of her kids had called. She got the message, but it was not one of her kids. "Kathleen. Listen."

The woman's voice on the phone said, "I am scared and I can't come back right now. Someone is trying to kill Shorty, and the killer has seen us in my car. I have to protect him. One does not run and leave a friend in distress. We are hiding out, but I cannot tell you where. I will call you back later tonight. Do not leave the room. I hope whoever is after Shorty has not connected me to the both of you. Be careful."

"Lucille is scared. Why didn't she call my cell phone?" Kathleen pulled it out of her pocket and saw that it was off. "Oh, fudge and peanut butter."

Kathleen called the police station and asked for Officer Miller, whom she had reprimanded earlier. She told him about the phone message left by their friend. He seemed to be a little more interested. Perhaps, he began to believe the two friends' story. He asked if she could play the message over the phone for him, which she did.

"Are you sure that was Lucille?" he asked.

"Yes, we recognize her voice and we can hear the fear. She is in trouble. Yes, we will call you if she, when she calls again," Kathleen said as she hung up the phone. "I think he is finally beginning to believe us."

The friends took turns getting their showers, ordered a light supper from room service, and waited for Lucille's call. They ate little of the meals before deciding to pray together again. Bernice suggested they while away the time playing rummy. They played in silence, slapping the cards down quickly. Bam, bam, bam. Bernice wrote down the score, and Kathleen shuffled and dealt again. Bam, bam, bam went the cards. They were slamming the cards on the table as if they were slapping Shorty's face for getting their girlfriend in such a dangerous situation.

"If he gets Lucille back here alive, I am going to kill him," seethed Bernice.

"Bernice, that is not a very Christian attitude, is it?" Kathleen said with a grin.

"No. You know what I mean," Bernice said, cringing from her own anger.

Bernice's cell phone rang and she grabbed it. "Hello, yes, hi, dear." She mouthed to Kathleen that Bethany was on the line. "No, we haven't heard a word from the police. Lucille called while we were out and left a message. The police finally believe that Lucille is in trouble. Yes, dear. We cannot tie up the telephone. Call me tomorrow. If we find her, we will call you. Good-bye, Bethany. I love you all too."

Finally, at two o'clock in the morning, they went to bed. However, they both lay awake for a long time, wondering why they had planned this road trip. Were they getting too old to travel without younger people along to be nursemaids?

After four hours of sleep, both women were awake. Realizing they would not be able to go back to sleep, they decided to get up and start the day.

Kathleen said, "I have an idea. I think we ought to go to the print store, have a bunch of posters with Lucille's picture on them, and ask if anyone has seen her to call us. What do you think? We could tape them on lamp posts and trees around town."

"That is better than doing nothing. I thought maybe we ought to start going from hotel to motel and see if desk clerks recognize her. We could also drive around and look for her car."

"That is too much time spent in that stupid stick-shift car. They never called us back with a different car. I am calling them." Kathleen called the car rental business and stated her case again. "Do you have any cars on the lot today? You do. Did I not ask you to give me a substitute to this little hatchback with the stick shift? This car with the broken locks is a lemon. Will you upgrade us? Fine. We will be there in twenty minutes. Hold it for Kathleen Keller. Thank you."

Bernice said, "I'm ready. Let's go." They both grabbed their handbags, sunglasses, and hotel keycards. When they crawled into the little car, Bernice said, "Won't it be great to be able to lock the doors and have a little more room?"

Kathleen agreed. She drove into the lot of Big Deal Rent-a-Car and saw four rentals lined up. She wondered how long they had been available. When Kathleen got out of the car, she walked over to the cars and looked in each window. None of them had a stick shift. The two tired women went into the office. Kathleen gave her name and said, "How long have those rentals been available?"

The meek young girl at the desk said that they were back in the lot yesterday morning. "Why do you ask?"

"May I see the manager?" asked Kathleen. The manager heard the request and stuck his head around the doorway at the back. Kathleen began very nicely with, "Sir, we have your little red hatchback out there and we can't lock the doors because they will not unlock. We had to crawl through the hatchback. Well, Bernice here had to crawl through and she is no spring chicken. Now we called in the same day we rented that little beauty and asked for help. I believe you were the one who told me to leave it unlocked and you would substitute another car for us as soon as you could. Now because of that locking problem, we have cleaned out someone else's car. I know that does not make sense. We are embarrassed. Just trust me that it happened."

The manager looked askance at her, turned to the meek girl standing beside him, and raised one eyebrow.

Kathleen continued, "You said you would bring us a substitute with automatic shift, did you not? Did you think because we are retired old ladies that you didn't have to give us the same regard you would give a young businessman or woman?"

"Well, no, ma'am. I guess I forgot that…"

"I am going to give you the benefit of the doubt and assume that you could not find your way to the largest hotel on the street next to the beach or that you are getting Anheisers or Alzheimer's. Therefore, I am here to make your job easier. Here are the keys to that little car. Now I want the keys to one of those cars over there please, and I assume you will not charge me for the upgrade under the circumstances." She took a deep breath.

"Look, we have a friend our age who has been missing for a couple of days and we have to go look for her. I don't think you want Ms. Keller here driving your stick shift around town tearing up the gears with all the stops and turns she will be making." Bernice hit the counter with her fist. "We don't have all day. Can we have that black car out there?" She pointed toward the front window and accidentally hit Kathleen in the arm. "Oops, sorry, Kath."

The manager looked flustered and stared at two women who were obviously on the edge and told the young woman to fill out the paperwork for the black Chevy and not to charge for the upgrade. "Sorry, ladies." He turned and quickly left the main office.

The two friends looked at one another and nodded, knowing they had succeeded. In ten minutes, they were in a roomier sedan with automatic shift and headed for a print shop. They placed their order for twenty-five posters with Lucille's picture on it and both of their cell phone numbers. It read, "Have you seen this woman? Call—" and the numbers were listed.

They heard Kathleen's stomach growl and realized they had not had breakfast. They decided to go to the little café where Shorty had taken them their first morning in Sarasota.

"I wish Lucille were with us now. I even wish Shorty were here. I am so worried," Kathleen said. Bernice agreed. When they finished brunch, they went back to pick up the posters. They spent the afternoon displaying posters all over town and going to motels that seemed out of the way where people might go to hide out. About four o'clock, they finally found a desk clerk in a run-down motel who said the woman in the picture looked familiar.

"Yeah. I think she checked in here a couple of days ago with a short guy. She drove a Lexus, so I did not know why they would stay here. He paid for one night, and they left before my shift started the next day. Guess they were here for a short—"

Kathleen interrupted him and said, "Don't go there. Our friend is not that kind of girl. They are running from someone who is trying to kill him. May I put up a poster on your bulletin board over there? Thanks." They walked out seething that someone would think Lucille was sleazy or easy.

They got back in the car and Bernice put her head back, closed her eyes, and sighed. "Can we stop and take a break? We need some ice cream." Kathleen agreed with her. As they were eating ice cream cones, Kathleen's cell phone rang. She handed her cone to Bernice and dug in her purse until she found it.

"Hello. Lucille, is that you? Where you are, dear? Can we come get you or send the police to find you?"

Lucille whispered, "I can't leave Shorty. Someone is following us and trying to kill him. We have moved once and are in an old motel north of town. He does not want me talking on the phone. He thinks the people looking for him could have my cell phone number and find us that way. He is in the bathroom. Just listen to me. Get the police to come to the Sunset Motel. I do not know the room number. We have not been out of the room. We have a bunch of junk food. Shorty is scared spit-less and so am I. Help me. He is flushing the john now. I have to hang up." The line went dead.

Immediately, Kathleen called the police station and heard that Officer Miller was off duty. "Let me talk to anyone who knows about the case of the missing older lady, Lucille Shuman." She waited a few minutes until she heard a voice on the other end. "Yes. Lucille Shuman. We just had a call from her and she says a killer is following Shorty. She said they are at the Sunset Motel north of town. Can you go rescue them? We will meet you there. No, I know you do not need our help. We are not going to help. We just need to be there to get Lucille. We won't get in the way, I tell you."

Bernice got the tourist information out of her large floral bag. She could not find the Sunset Motel listed. They went back inside the store and asked to see a telephone book. They found the motel listed and the address. Kathleen remembered seeing the road sign for the motel. They tossed the remains of the ice cream cones in the trash and walked back to the car. They were walking slower as the day progressed. When they arrived at the motel, there were no police cars around, so Kathleen parked off to the side of the parking lot. There were only four cars parked in front of rooms. They did not see a silver Lexus. Kathleen tried to drive behind the building, but there was no access. She drove up to the front of the office and parked. They went inside and showed a picture of Lucille.

"Yes. She and her boyfriend drove out of here about twenty minutes ago. They were heading north. Are they running from something? When they signed in, he sent her in with cash for a two-night stay," said the disheveled desk clerk. His television played loudly in the room behind the office. Kathleen heard a woman laughing with the canned laughter on the *I Love Lucy* show. She said to Bernice as she nodded toward the sound, "Are we starting to look like Lucy and Ethel?" She thanked the man and they went back to the car. A few minutes later, a police car pulled in next to Kathleen and Bernice. A police officer got out and headed for the office. Kathleen rolled down her window and told them the clerk said that the couple had just driven out going north.

The police officer said they would follow and see if they could catch them. However, he would not hold his breath about finding them. The police officer told the women not to follow the police car. The officer continued into the office and came back out a few minutes later, taking his time to get into his car.

"Those men are young enough to be moving faster than we do. Why are they so slow?"

"What are we going to do? How are we going to find Lucille? I suppose we should call her niece Lucinda and let her know what is happening. She thinks her Aunt Lucille is having fun in the sun for two weeks with us. How do we explain how we misplaced her?" Kathleen said.

"We didn't misplace her. She ran off with someone we really do not know and may be a hostage. Shorty seemed to like Lucy, so surely, he will not hurt her. But the ones wanting to kill Shorty could do it."

"Well, *Bernie*, what are we going to do? I guess we'd better go back to the hotel and wait for news from the police or a call from Lucille." She felt like giving up, but knew she could not. She had flashbacks of her kidnapping by the Baileys years before. She did not want Lucille to be experiencing anything like that. When they settled into the room again, Kathleen called Lucinda and explained that Aunt Lucille was on the run with some man and they had the police chasing them. "But, honey, I think she is going to be all right and will be back with us soon. However, I want you and all your friends and family to keep praying. We will keep in touch. Bye for now."

Bernice asked if Lucinda had freaked out. "She knows her Aunt Lucille. She knows she is adventurous. I hope that they will pray and not worry too much. I am ready to pray again. How about you?" They did so.

"Are you getting hungry? I do not think we both ought to be out of the room at the same time. How about since we now have an automatic shift car that I go out and get us a pizza?" Bernice said.

"Or we could just order one and have it delivered. We can get pop from the vending machine. Go ahead and order whatever you like, and I'll go get the pop and fill up the ice bucket."

When they heard a knock on their door, Bernice got up with the money they had put together including a tip for the pizza order. She opened the door and said, "Oh, you aren't the pizza delivery guy."

"No, ma'am," said the officer who had come to the motel and had chased the missing Lexus from the Sunset Motel. "I just wanted to let you know that we never caught up with or saw your friend's Lexus. We will keep our eyes open. We have called the sheriff in the next county, asking them to stop the car if it is sighted. We just wanted to let you know that since we talked to the motel clerk, it is obvious that your friend is in a precarious situation. We have not been able to get any information on Shorty Alexander. It must be an alias. It is too bad we don't have a picture of him."

Bernice said, "What an old harebrain I am. I have a picture of him. I took a few pictures when we were on the beach the morning that he joined us. Let me get my camera." She scurried back with her camera and clicked through her pictures until she found the one with Shorty and Lucille. She removed the disk and handed it to the officer. "I do want that back, please."

"Of course, Mrs. Meyers. Thanks. This may be very helpful. We'll let you know as soon as we have any news," he said and turned to go out the door. "Ladies, here comes your pizza delivery. Hope it is still warm. Good night."

Bernice paid for the pizza while Kathleen poured pop over ice in the plastic glasses. "Let's pray. Gracious God, we need your help. You know where Lucille is and we know you are protecting her. Help her find a way to escape. Keep Shorty safe also. Lord, direct us in rescuing our friend Lucille. Bless this food and use it to nourish our bodies and to give us strength to find her. In Jesus's name, Amen."

They picked at the pizza and breadsticks. Kathleen kept looking at her cell phone to be sure there had not been a call. Bernice finally said, "Let's play cards to make the time go faster." She grabbed the cards while Kathleen cleaned away the pizza box. She wrapped up the leftovers and put them in the tiny refrigerator in their room.

Kathleen decided to get more comfortable and put on her pajamas and robe. Several games and several hours later, the phones still had not rung. Kathleen stood up and stretched her back. "I have had enough. I need a hot shower on my back."

Bernice took her hair down and began brushing. When she took her turn in the bathroom, Kathleen picked up her Bible and turned to Proverbs. As she read, she came across verse 8 in the eleventh chapter, "The righteous man is rescued from trouble, and it comes on the wicked instead."

"Lucille is a righteous woman. She is adventurous, fun, and impulsive, but she is a kind woman. Lord, I know you will rescue her from this trouble," Kathleen said to herself.

Her cell phone rang and she saw Lucille's name. *Thank you, Lord.* "Lucille, where are you? How are you?"

"Katie, I am safe for now. I am where you would least suspect. I can't tell you where yet."

"Why not? Lucille, you have to escape and get back to our hotel room. Please. What is going on? You need to call the police and have them rescue you both."

"Shorty is in a lot of trouble. I have to help him hide out a little longer. He is waiting for his brother to get here with $200,000 to pay off a gambling debt. If he does not get the money before they find him, they will kill him. I have to stay with him."

"Lucille. That is not your problem. Let me call the police and they will protect both of you. There is a nice officer who is helping us look for you," Kathleen said.

"Let me talk to Shorty and I'll call you back." Lucille hung up.

Kathleen shouted in her phone as Bernice stepped out of the bathroom. "Lucille, Lucille." Bernice looked at her with alarm.

"She says she is okay. Someone is trying to kill Shorty because he owes someone $200,000. His brother is bringing the money to him and he has to stay hidden until he gets the cash. What a mess. Lucille feels sorry for him and wants to help protect him. She is going to call us back. I told her the police are looking for them and will protect them," Kathleen said.

"What did she say? Where is she?"

"I don't know where she is. She said they were where we would least suspect. Now what does that mean?"

"Let's work on that puzzle. If we can figure it out, we can rescue them." She grabbed the small notebook with the card game scores in it and turned to a clean page. She wrote a title at the top of the page. *Where We Would Least Suspect.*

Chapter 6

"Okay, think. Where we would least suspect. The Ringling mansion? No. The Sunset Motel? No longer. The Holiday Inn? A campground? No, she does not have a tent. A homeless shelter? No. Where, where, where? The dog track? No. Our room? No, they are not here."

"Shorty's room upstairs? Do you think?" Kathleen asked.

"Surely not." She grabbed the phone on the bedside stand and called the desk. "Is Mr. Shorty Alexander still checked in here?"

The desk clerk said, "Ma'am, we aren't supposed to give that information out. Has your friend come back yet? Well, he has paid for two weeks upfront, so he still has the room. However, I have not seen him in a few days. You are welcome."

Kathleen thought a minute and said, "He has the room paid for in advance. Do you really think they could be hiding in his room on the ninth floor? How could they have gotten in undetected? Maybe we should go to the garage and see if her car is back. I guess if they had come in from the garage downstairs, they could have sneaked to his room. Let's go check." She changed her clothes, picked up her phone, put on her sandals, and looked around for a weapon. Bernice seemed to understand what she needed. She went to her bag of purchases and pulled out two heavy candlesticks she had purchased for her son and daughter-in-law. She handed one to Kathleen and she held the other like a baseball bat.

Bernice hesitated and said, "Maybe we should call that nice officer."

"No. What if Lucille and Shorty aren't there? It would be another wild goose chase for them. Let's go check it out, and if we need help, I have my phone with me."

Bernice and Kathleen walked down the hall, each carrying a candlestick in her arm like Ms. America carrying her bouquet of roses. They met one couple coming out of the elevator who looked askance when they saw them with the candlesticks. The women just kept walking. They got in the elevator and went down to the garage floor. They walked around all the parking area and did not find a silver Lexus. Therefore, they got back in the elevator and went up to the ninth floor. When they walked down the hall and found room number 914, they noticed a *Do Not Disturb* sign hanging on the doorknob. They were whispering about whether to knock on the door or not. A young married couple walked toward them, stopping to kiss before going to their room. When they looked at the candlestick twins, they did a double take. The young wife started to giggle, grabbed her husband's arm, and pulled him down the hallway.

Kathleen knocked on the door and said in a disguised voice, "Housekeeping." She heard no response. Again, she knocked and said, "Housekeeping." No response. She stood in front of the peephole and thought she saw an eyeball. "Lucille, are you in there? Let us in now," she whispered. They heard the lock slide over. The chain was removed and the door opened a crack. Lucille reached out and pulled Kathleen and Bernice into the room. They hugged one another.

"Where is Shorty?" asked Bernice as she looked around the suite.

"He's hiding in the bathroom behind the shower curtain. We are waiting for his brother," Lucille said as she locked the door.

"Shorty, get out here," Kathleen hissed.

He opened the bathroom door and peeked out. "Katie. Bernie. It is good to see you. How did you find us? If you can find us, so can the hit man."

"My name is Bernice. Why did you kidnap our friend?"

"I didn't kidnap her. She came willingly because we were in her car. She is a good lady and a good friend. I am in jeopardy here, and she is helping me stay out of sight."

"By the way, Lucille, where is the Lexus? We have been watching the parking garage and the lot for it. It isn't there," Kathleen said.

"We parked it in a neighborhood and called a taxi. We had the driver let us out in the garage, and we came up the elevator late last night. Luckily, we did not run into anyone. You figured out my riddle, didn't you? I hope you did not call the police. Until Shorty's brother gets here with the money to pay his gambling debt, he has to hide. You girls need to go back to our room and remain there until the debt is paid. Do not say anything to the police. We have to wait it out," Lucille said.

"Lucille, we need to call the police and have them come protect Shorty. Be realistic here. You are both in danger. Now we are too. You come back to the room with us," Bernice said.

Lucille pulled her friends to the door and peeked through the peephole. She quickly unlocked the door and pushed them out. Then she shut the door and locked both locks. Kathleen and Bernice looked at one another with amazement. They walked back to the elevator. When the door opened, a thin man stood aside and allowed the women to get in and he stepped out. He did not make eye contact. Kathleen hurriedly hit the button for their floor. She whispered, "Oh my gosh, Bernice. That guy on the beach who is supposed to kill the man with the woman, that is him. That is Slim." She pushed the button and got off the elevator on the eighth floor. She grabbed her phone, hit the number for the police officer, and explained that she saw the killer heading down the hallway to find Shorty. Lucille was in the room with him. "Bernice, call Lucille and tell her to put something in front of their door. The killer is there," she shrieked.

Bernice had already punched in Lucille's number and told her to push the table or mattresses in front of the door and hide in the bathroom. "Help is on the way." Kathleen took Bernice's wrist and pulled her toward the stairway. "We are going back up to protect Lucille."

"How are we going to do that? Two candlesticks do not trump a gun. What are we going to do?" Bernice said with hesitation.

"We may have to do something to distract the killer. We can make noise around the corner. I don't know, Bernice, but we have to do something until the police get here."

They huffed and puffed up the flight of stairs. They opened the stairwell door and listened. They heard someone pounding on a door. Kathleen reached over and hit the elevator button. Shortly, the elevator doors opened and the bell rang to indicate the elevator had arrived. The pounding stopped. Kathleen thought that the killer must have heard the elevator and expected guests to walk toward him down the hallway. The elevator door closed. Kathleen hit the button again. The elevator door opened once again. The pounding stopped. The elevator was not visible from the hallway in front of Shorty's door. The elevator door closed, and before she could hit the button, the elevator light above the door showed it going down to the first floor.

"Oh, no, I waited too long," whispered Kathleen. She heard the pounding on the door again, some shouting, and suddenly a gunshot. Moments later, the elevator door opened and the nice police officer and a sidekick stepped out of the elevator.

"What is the room number? You ladies get in the stairwell. Actually, go back to your room," he said.

Kathleen whispered, "Room 914. Please hurry." The two women stepped into the stairwell but hesitated in going back to their room. Bernice grabbed Kathleen's arm and tried to drag her downstairs. Kathleen told her to wait. She opened the door so she could hear. One of the officers yelled, "Drop the gun. I said drop the gun. Put your hands in the air."

Kathleen peeked around the corner and saw the killer with his hands behind his back in handcuffs, with his gun on the floor. She pulled Bernice into the hall. The officer nearest the door knocked loudly on the door and shouted, "Sarasota police, open the door." There were some sounds of movement inside. Shortly, the door opened and Lucille stuck her head out.

After the police went inside the room and coaxed Shorty out of the bathroom, they sat down to get the entire story.

It turned out that Shorty really was an oilman, but he also had a gambling addiction. He had lost $200,000 in a series of poker games in Dallas. He could not pay the debt, so he ran. His brother, the rescuer, would arrive soon but apparently had taken his time. He owed money to a man and the heavy-set man on the beach worked as his strong arm. Shorty told them he worked for his brother who was president of the company.

He hung his head and said, "Buddy says I can't be trusted with money, and I guess he is right. Lucy, I don't know what I would have done without you by my side these last few days."

Lucille patted his hand. "Shorty, you are going to be all right now. The police will protect you until your brother gets here. Isn't that right?" She looked at the police officer for confirmation.

"Actually, we did catch Everett Goodings, the man you saw on the beach, Ms. Keller. We pulled his picture off the wall and concentrated on finding him since you had seen him in town. He is in jail. The man who wants his $200,000 back is under arrest in Dallas. This fellow will be with him soon. Shorty, you will be coming to the station with us to clear up some facts. I hope this has taught you a lesson."

"Oh, yes. I have learned my lesson. All of them," Shorty stammered. "Whatever they are, I've learned them."

Kathleen felt he probably had not. The officers sent the three women back to their room with their candlesticks. Lucille grabbed her purse, her phone, and three bags of snacks that lay on the dresser. "I bought these," she said. They took the elevator back to the sixth floor and went to their room.

"Lucille, you beat all," Bernice said and she hugged her friend. "You have no idea what we have been through. We had to rent a car which would not unlock, cleaned out someone else's car, put up posters with your face on them all over town, and spent too much money on gas looking for your Lexus. I could have given poor Bernice whiplash with that ridiculous car we had to drive."

"Perhaps I caused you to have to rent a car, but what do I have to do with you cleaning someone else's car?" Lucille giggled.

"Well, the rental car doors wouldn't unlock if we locked them. Therefore, we left the car unlocked the first night, and the next morning, someone had been in the car. The seat laid back, we saw empty food cartons all over, and a big wad of bubble gum stuck to the carpet. We cleaned it up, then...oh, never mind." Kathleen sighed.

"We are glad we got you back safely. By the way, call Lucinda. We thought we ought to let her know you were missing. People all over the state of Indiana are praying for you. What possessed you to run with him?"

"Honey, I've never seen a grown man so scared. It felt like taking care of one of my high school students who had flunked a test. He told me the entire story of his addiction and how deeply in debt he had gotten in one weekend. He is so sorry and hates to face his brother when he gets here. I do not know what is taking him so long. You girls saved our lives. What good friends you are. Kathleen, you have solved a mystery again. Well, I need some sleep. What are we doing tomorrow? Do you want to go to the dog track? I didn't get to bet on anything because we were being chased."

"No. We spent half a day looking for someone who might have seen you at the dog track. I think we need to go to the circus museum. We will fit right in there. Three old clowns who cannot stay out of trouble. Maybe we can get part-time jobs in their sideshow. Lucille, you could do the disappearing act. Bernice, what do you want to do?" Kathleen asked.

"I want to do as little as possible, if you don't mind. Actually, I think we ought to spend the day on the beach tomorrow. We need to rest and relax. What do you say?"

The next day, Lucille asked if the girls could take her to pick up her Lexus before breakfast. "I think I can find the neighborhood where we left it," she said.

They got in the rental car, drove around for an hour, and did not see Lucille's car. "This street looks so familiar and so does that white house. Yes, I parked my car right there."

"I think they towed your car. What do you think?" Bernice asked. "Let's go eat breakfast and we will try to find out where it would have been towed."

As they were eating breakfast at a sidewalk café, Kathleen's phone rang and she answered. Then Bernice's phone rang. Both callers were saying, "We know where the blonde-headed lady is. We are sitting at a sidewalk café, and she is with a couple of old ladies. I do not know the name of the street. Let me go check." Kathleen looked up and saw two young people from different tables stand up with a phone to their ears looking for a street sign. She started to laugh and said, "Thank you. We found her last night. How kind of you to be so observant and to try to help. Thanks."

Bernice closed her phone and said, "I think we'd better go around town and take down the posters. People are reporting they have spotted you, Lucille. And I resent that young man saying you are sitting with two old ladies."

They heard a voice squealing, "Ms. Shuman. Ms. Shuman. It is you. I saw your picture on the light post and could not believe my English teacher is missing in Sarasota. It is you, right? Are you still lost? Remember me?"

"My dear, how could I ever forget you? Freshman English, front seat on the last row to my left. Different colored hair every week. Your puppy ate your homework. Liza, uh."

"Yes, Liza Browne then. Liza Sutherland now. Can you believe that I found you all the way down here in Florida?" All three friends were amazed that Lucille really would encounter a former student while on vacation a thousand miles away.

"No, dear, I am not lost. I never get lost. I ran away from a killer. A retired teacher's life is not dull. The police arrested the killer last night at our hotel, and I came out of hiding with a friend who owed $200,000 in gambling debts. The killer came to our hotel room last night, shot his gun trying to get in. The police came in time, saved us because these two friends found us, and called the cops. I was with a man friend, had just met him really. He took me to the dog track, and the killer found him and we had to run and hide. How have you been?" Lucille grinned at her former student.

"My life has been rather dull compared to yours. Ya'll be careful now," Liza said and walked back to her husband who was window-shopping next door. She took her young husband's arm and started to tell him the story of meeting Ms. Shuman as she waved her arm and pointed at her former teacher. He looked back at the three women, waved, and smiled as he pulled her quickly away from them.

Following breakfast, they made a few phone calls and discovered Lucille's car at the impound lot. Kathleen followed the directions given to them by the waiter. When she pulled up in front of the fence, Lucille said, "There is my baby sitting between that old Jeep and that rusted-out pickup truck. She looks like she is slumming. Poor thing." All three of them got out of the car to go inside. They had to speak through a little hole in the glass to the overweight man with the overlapped belly sitting on a rickety rusty office chair. When he completed the transaction, he went out the back door and brought her car up to the wide gate. The women waited while he got out of the Lexus, unlocked and opened the gate, and drove her car around to the front of the office. He went back to close and lock the gate. Lucille looked over her pride and joy. On the passenger side, she saw a scratch down the length of the car.

"Oh, no. This will not do. You have keyed my car. I did not leave it like this. I presume you have insurance to cover such damage," Lucille said with her hands on her hips.

"Look, lady, we didn't key your car. You apparently abandoned her in a small neighborhood, and someone did not want your car sitting in front of his or her house. Although I do not know why. I would not mind that silver Lexus in my driveway. They called us. We picked it up and parked it back there. It has been safe inside our gates, and no, our insurance doesn't cover that," the bulky man said as he turned to go into the office.

Lucille's voice became louder as she said, "Don't you walk away from me, young man. Someone has to pay for the damage to my car."

Kathleen said, "Lucille, stop. He is not one of your students, for goodness sake. You abandoned your car in a strange neighborhood. You know who is responsible for the damage?"

"Who?"

"Your friend Shorty. You will not get any money out of him. I really doubt he can help. He has financial problems of his own. You will have to turn it in to your insurance or pay out of pocket. Let's go," Kathleen said.

Bernice rode back to the Big Deal Rent-a-Car with Lucille. Kathleen turned in the rental car and profusely thanked the manager for all his help. A little passive-aggressive attitude did come in handy occasionally. He did not quite know how to answer, so Kathleen felt very satisfied. The three tired friends headed back to their hotel room for a rest.

"Why don't we rest on the beach?" Bernice asked. "We have been missing a lot of sun and fun this week." They agreed to spend some time on the beach. It felt good to stretch out in the sun, close their eyes, and listen to the waves. They each had a tall bottle of cold water, a paperback book to read, and plenty of sunscreen.

"This feels good. This is what we should have been doing every day this week. If not for Mr. Shorty Pants, we could have done so," Kathleen said.

"Girlfriends, I am so sorry to have put you through all this. I promise I will never do something this ridiculous ever again. Am I forgiven?" begged Lucille.

"Shall we forgive her, Kathleen?" Bernice asked with a straight face. Kathleen looked over her sunglasses and said she would think about it. Lucille put a pout on her face.

"Okay, you are forgiven. But you promise you will not run off with the first man who comes along ever again?"

"Oh, yes. I am going to change my ways." Kathleen and Bernice looked skeptically at one another and grinned.

The three sunbathers quieted down and began to read their books in silence. An hour later, Kathleen had put her book down and fallen asleep. Bernice and Lucille had turned over to get sun on their backs.

Out of the near silence of the waves hitting the shore and the seagulls squawking, they heard a voice far way. "Lucy. Lucy."

Lucille sat up and shouted, "Shorty. Here I am. Are you okay, honey? Are you safe?" The other women groaned aloud and sat up. Shorty trotted toward them in his baggy swim trunks.

"Hey, little ladies. You all are sure looking rested. Do you have plans for dinner? Ladies, would you let me take you to dinner tonight? I could pick you up at six o'clock at your door."

All three women looked at one another and in unison said, "No. No. No."

"Shorty, thanks but no thanks. We are glad to have Lucille back with us and do not want to lose her again. We came down here for a fun vacation, and so far, it has been frightening. We are swearing off men friends for a long time. We wish you well, but no," Bernice said.

Kathleen added, "Shorty, we do wish you well. I really hope you can avoid getting yourself into another situation like this last one. You obviously have a gambling problem. Right?"

"Yeah. I need to work on that. My brother is going to make sure I get help. Our company should not have to cover my debts. Katie, I need to be stronger like you. I have sure enjoyed spending these last few days with you fine women. Lucy, you are one great woman. If I were a marrying man, I would give you a second look. If I were a few years younger, I could be a marrying man." He chuckled.

"Shorty, you certainly gave me stories to tell back home. It has been fun, at least most of the time. I need to spend this evening with my friends. I'll miss you," Lucille said.

Shorty shook hands with the three women, suddenly grabbed Lucille, and gave her a big hug. He turned and headed back for the hotel.

"That's life," Lucille said. "I enjoyed the fun while it lasted too. I am glad I met him and I am glad he has to go back to Texas. I think it is time for the three of us to relax and be tourists for the next week. Just us girls, okay?"

Kathleen and Bernice both said, "Amen," in unison. They laughed and leaned back to enjoy the rays of the sun and the sounds of the waves on the beach.

Chapter 7

That evening, they sat in the same seafood restaurant where Shorty had taken them their first night in Sarasota. Kathleen closed her eyes as she chewed the delicious shrimp scampi while it was still hot. They discussed plans for the next day. Kathleen heard a familiar voice and looked toward the entrance. "Oh, no. Don't look toward the door," she told her friends. So of course when you hear the words do not look, you look.

Bernice and Lucille both turned and saw Shorty Alexander. Bernice grabbed Lucille's wrist because she knew Lucille would wave to him. Therefore, Lucille used her other hand and he saw her. Shorty came toward them with a big grin on his face and his brother Buddy following on his heels.

"Well, look who is here," he said. "I hoped I would get to introduce you fine ladies to my brother Buddy." He introduced them all and gave a little detail about each woman. Buddy went around the table and shook each woman's hand. He looked nothing like his brother. Buddy was tall, handsome, refined, and well dressed. Shorty was still wearing his Hawaiian shirt. Buddy had on black slacks and a fitted grey silk shirt. With his graying hair and gray eyes, he had a number of women feasting on his gorgeousness. Kathleen guessed his age near her own age.

Lucille invited them to join the table. Buddy declined, saying they did not want to interrupt the women's meal. Shorty and Lucille insisted, and finally Kathleen and Bernice chimed in that it would be fine. A waiter brought a fifth chair to the round table and the women scooted closer together to make room.

Shorty sat down beside Lucille and kissed her on the cheek, while Buddy found himself between his brother and Kathleen. Buddy thanked the women for all they had done to keep Shorty from getting himself killed. He chatted with Lucille and said, "Lucille, you seem to have captured my brother's attention."

"Well, he certainly had my attention there for a few days."

"I am so grateful that you both came out of that situation alive. Shorty has a way of getting into precarious situations and coming out smelling like a rose."

Shorty agreed that he usually survived better than he deserved. Buddy turned his head and looked at Bernice.

"Bernice, I understand you are a photographer. Tell me about your article for *The National Geographic*. Maybe I have seen it. I've subscribed to that magazine for years now."

"Oh, about nine years ago, my husband and I were in Ghana, West Africa. It was the most fantastic trip I can remember."

"I remember that one. Your shots of the Castle Elmira on the coast were stunning. The white walls against the blue water and sky were amazing. Congratulations. Wonderful job. Are you still shooting?" Buddy asked.

"My husband passed away and so I retired. It wasn't nearly as exciting to travel without him," Bernice answered and took a drink of coffee.

"I would imagine not. I understand. My lovely wife Delia passed away last year with cancer, and life is just never the same, is it?" She agreed with him. They shared an understanding look with one another.

He casually turned to his left and looked at Kathleen. "You must be the detective Shorty told me about. Let's see, teacher, pastor, and detective. Sounds like an exciting life," he said to her.

"Well, it has been eventful. However, not always action-packed as my seminary days when I was kidnapped and almost died. I retired not too long ago and I do miss some of the daily routine of the caring and preaching and helping others," said Kathleen. "But since the three of us have been taking an annual vacation together, life is never dull. Certainly, it hasn't been since we met Shorty."

"Most people say that," he said with a grin. "Kathleen, there are only two couples on the dance floor, would you do me the honor of dancing with me?" She nodded yes, he helped her push her chair back, and he followed her to the dance floor with his hand lightly on her elbow. The three people sitting at the table said nothing, but sat watching with their jaws hanging open.

"What just happened?" said Lucille. "Kathleen hasn't danced with a man since Tyler died. She did not even dance at your kids' weddings, Bernice. This is amazing. Shorty, tell us about your brother quickly before they come back to the table."

"Well, you can see we are opposites. He got the height and the looks. He is suave, smart, and astute. He had a great marriage. He and Delia have three great kids and he has five grandchildren. I have never been married. No children that I know about," Shorty said and laughed. "Buddy has a great business mind and no bad habits that I have seen. I make poor decisions, gamble, and drink too much. There you have it and there they come."

Buddy pulled out Kathleen's chair for her and they grinned at one another. "Well, I enjoyed that. I have not danced in a long time, Buddy. Thank you," Kathleen said with a smile.

"No, my dear, thank you. Neither have I and I enjoyed your company. I see our meal coming, Shorty. Will you ladies join us with a dessert, my treat, while we eat our meal?" asked Buddy.

Kathleen answered for all three of them, "Thank you, we'd like that." Lucille and Bernice looked at one another and grinned. It had been years since they had seen Kathleen smitten by any man since Tyler's death. Maybe not smitten, but she was willing to dance and flirt a little with a man. What a rare and wonderful evening.

"Yes, we would," said Bernice. The three friends ordered dessert and told the men to eat their prime ribs before they got cold.

Kathleen asked, "Buddy, what is your real name?"

"My given name is Walter Adams Alexander. However, when we were kids, our dad gave us the nicknames Buddy, Shorty, and our sister Alicia got the name Sis. Cute names when we were kids. Not so much now. No one but family and old family friends call me Buddy."

"One of my grandfathers was a Walter. What a coincidence. He preferred the nickname Walt. I like the name." Kathleen smiled at him.

"My business associates call me Walt. I much prefer it to Buddy."

"Well, I shall call you Walt. How is your meal, Walt?" Kathleen said with a little giggle. The two of them whispered to one another and laughed.

Bernice looked at Lucille and Shorty and said, "Did we suddenly become invisible? I think they have forgotten we are sitting here."

Lucille and Shorty agreed and they all laughed. Walt and Kathleen looked up at them and Walt said, "I'm sorry. Did we miss something?"

Lucille laughed and said, "No. I do not think you are missing a thing, Walter. Neither is Kathleen. Tell us about your children."

"My oldest son, Nicholas, is vice president of our corporation. The middle child is our daughter Nancy and the youngest is Ned who is in charge of sales. Nancy is the treasurer. Between the two older ones, they have given me five grandchildren. Ned got married two years ago and they are expecting their first child in seven months," Walt said proudly.

"Ned is the one who is supposed to keep me out of trouble. Now that he has a wife, she is keeping him extra busy. I work in sales, but when I go on trips, I cannot stay away from the gambling. He cannot be everywhere. Buddy, I promise I will never get myself in another mess like this," Shorty said.

"I think I've heard that a few times, brother. We are getting you some long-term therapy this time. We don't want to lose you, but we can't afford you either," Walt answered in a soft voice.

"Well, I have eaten all I am going to eat. Kathleen, how about one more turn around the dance floor?"

She blushed and answered, "I'd like that, Walt." He stood up and held her chair for her. Those left at the table watched them walk toward the dancers and grinned again at one another.

"Your little Katie is the first woman I've seen Buddy even look at since Delia died. I think she has him mesmerized. What do you think?"

Bernice said, "I haven't seen her pay this much attention to a man since her Tyler died, other than her pastoral attention. It is nice to see. She looks happy in a different way. I like what I see."

"Well, let's not assume too much too soon," Lucille said wisely.

"That's right, after all he is Shorty's brother," Bernice said, patted Shorty's arm, and giggled. Their conversation turned to Shorty. They hoped he would get help with the addiction so he could live a normal life. He might even find a nice woman someday.

The dancers came back to the table and sat down. Bernice said, "Well, I think I am ready to go back to the room. I need to call my daughter as usual. Let's get the bill so I can go."

"Please allow me to buy your dinner. I have not enjoyed myself this much in a long time," Walt said. "We interrupted your meal, so I would like to do that." The women relented and thanked him.

"Shorty, why don't we go for one last stroll together down the beach," Lucille suggested. He jumped up as if he had just won the lottery. She thanked Walt again for the meal and the three of them walked out together.

"Well, I guess they are taking Lucille's car, so I'd better tag along," Kathleen said. She started to get up, but Walt put his hand gently on her arm.

"I think they are expecting me to drive you back to the hotel, which I would be privileged to do, if you don't mind?" The waiter brought back the little tray with Walt's credit card and receipt.

"I don't mind at all. Maybe we could go for a walk on the beach also," Kathleen said as she felt her face get warm. She knew she blushed and was mad at herself for doing that.

Walt pretended not to notice and stood up, and he helped her with her chair. With his hand on the back of her waist, they walked to the entrance of the restaurant and out to his car. He led her to a Cadillac with the same sticker that her rental car had sported. Big Deal Rent-a-Car. She asked him how he had managed a Cadillac and told him the story of getting the unlockable little hatchback with Bernice. She told him the funny details of cleaning out the wrong car. He laughed with her and enjoyed the story. She explained how she exchanged the car, and he told her she had spunk. He liked that.

He pulled up in the parking spot closest to the beach at the hotel and suggested that they take off their shoes and leave them in the car. They took a long walk down the beach, and when they got back on her hotel's beach, he invited her to sit down in the same lounge chairs that were very familiar to her now. They talked for a couple more hours.

At one point, he took her left hand in his and asked about the engagement ring. She explained about Tyler being the most wonderful man she had ever known and had not met anyone who could ever take his place. Walt patted her hand and said he understood. She finally said, "I think I had better go in or the girls will send out a search party for me," Kathleen said with a sigh.

He held her hand as she stood up and did not let go as they walked toward his car. When they saw his car, Shorty and Lucille were leaning against the door. Shorty said, "We aren't playing chaperone, but we didn't want to leave you out on the beach this late at night all by yourselves." Lucille nodded in agreement.

"I really think I can take care of myself and Kathleen, little brother. Go on up. We have to get our shoes out of the car. Lucille, I will deliver Kathleen to your door in a few minutes. Thanks for the concern."

Shorty and Lucille walked toward the entrance and did not look back. Kathleen said, "I haven't had a chaperone for a long time. Actually, I never had a chaperone. I did not start dating until my senior year of high school. My dad called me a late bloomer."

"Well, you have blossomed into a beauty now. Inside and outside, you are a beautiful rose. I would sure like to see you again. I know we live half a continent away, but I don't mind flying, do you?"

"It is not my favorite activity with the airport protocol what it is now, but when I need to fly, I can."

"Well, maybe I could send my private plane up to Indiana sometime and bring you and the girls down for a visit. I'd like you to meet my children."

"You would? How do they feel about meeting your women friends?"

"I don't know. I have not had any women friends since before I married Delia right out of college. You would be the first. Kathleen, you are a rare woman. I could tell the first time I looked in your eyes that you had the love of Jesus filling your heart. Delia had that look. I am not comparing you to my wife, except to say that the love of God is hard to miss when one looks in another's eyes."

"Since you thought your wife was one of a kind, I am complimented to be on the same list with her. Thank you."

They were in the elevator and he leaned down and kissed her on the cheek. Again, she felt her face get warm. She looked up at him and touched his collar. It was not out of place, but she wanted an excuse to touch him. She just wanted to touch him. She found him extra special. The elevator doors opened, and he waited for her to step out and he followed her. They slowly walked toward her room. She stopped beside her door and turned to thank him for the loveliest evening she had had in a long time. In her mind, she told herself it had been a long, long, long time.

"I really enjoy your company, Walt. You are a fine man."

"May I kiss you good night, Kathleen?" She nodded yes. Then, he bent down and chastely kissed her on the lips. They looked into each other's eyes and she got on tiptoes and kissed him again. They smiled at one another with an understanding that there might be more to pursue in this relationship than either one had thought possible eight hours earlier. "I think I may have to stay over another couple of days before going back to Dallas. Could I take you to breakfast?"

"Oh, Walt, I would love to do that," she hesitated.

"But?" he said.

"But the three of us decided we needed to spend some of our vacation time together. Maybe we could have lunch together. Let me check with Lucille and Bernice first. Is that all right?"

"Any time is all right with me. I am in the room to the north of Shorty's room," he said and handed her his business card. "My cell phone number is on the card and it is always turned on. Good night, Kathleen." He turned and headed for the elevator. She watched him walk to the corner. He looked back longingly and she still watched him. They waved and she turned to unlock the door.

She went in quietly as Bernice slept in the adjoining room and she heard Lucille singing in the shower. She sat down at the little round table and put her head in her hands. Why did she feel that she might be cheating on Tyler? *Tyler has been gone for over forty years and would want me to get on with my life.* She had gotten on with life—her career, her calling, helping others. However, her love life had been another thing.

The week before Tyler died, they had been out by the lake sitting on the dock that her grandfather and dad had built many years before. Their feet dangled down into the cold water because it was still spring. He had his arm around her and she leaned on his shoulder. She remembered distinctly that he had said, "Katie, I want to wake up every morning for the rest of my life after we are married and look at my beautiful wife. I will thank God every day for the blessings you bring me. We will have children, they will come into our bedroom on Saturday mornings, and pile on us reminding us it is time to get up and fix the pancakes. The little girl will look like you with your beautiful eyes and cute smile, and the little boys will have your curly hair and be mischievous like their father when he grew up on the farm. Our kids will grow up, get married, and give us grandchildren. We will spoil the grandchildren and then send them home. Maybe when we retire, we will even go to Florida for the winters. We have a wonderful future ahead of us. God is going to guide us, and I still believe he is calling you to the ministry and know that you will give in one of these days."

Kathleen began to cry silently and reminded herself that it was time to let go of that dream. Tyler, the children, their life together—the possibilities were gone long ago. Tyler would be very unhappy with her for holding on to him for so long. It was time to get on with her life before it was over. Her feelings for this new man, Walter Alexander, felt good. She believed that forty-some years ago, Tyler and Walt could have been good friends. Tyler would approve. Lucille had walked into the room and watched Kathleen's shoulders shaking and quietly asked, "Kathleen dear, what is wrong?"

"I just relived one of the many poignant memories in my heart. Do you think Tyler would approve of Walt as a good date for me?" Kathleen asked sniffling and wiping her eyes.

"Oh, I think Tyler would approve. He always wanted only the best for you. He was the best, but if he couldn't be here, I am sure he would have wanted a good man for you." She put her hands on Kathleen's shoulders and kissed the top of her head. Kathleen got up, took her makeup bag and pajamas to the bathroom, and stood in the shower until her self-assurance returned.

Chapter 8

A t breakfast the next morning, the girls were asking all about her date with Buddy. "His name is Walt," Kathleen said. "He is really a nice gentleman. I think he is sincere and not faking it. That would sure disappoint me. By the way, he did offer to send his plane to Indiana to bring all three of us down to Dallas to visit him." She did not mention the part about meeting his children.

Lucille and Bernice both smiled and Bernice said, "Wow. That sounds like a fun trip. What did you tell him, Katie?"

"I said you and Lucille would not be interested in a free plane ride to Dallas. I would come by myself," Kathleen said with a straight face.

"You did not," Lucille said. "When do we go? Did you set a time? I think I could probably find some free time this winter."

"You are right. I did not say that. I told him we would love to come to Dallas. He wanted to take me out for breakfast this morning, but I told him the three of us needed to get back to our little vacation, now that Lucille has returned."

Bernice said incredulously, "Get out of here. You turned him down. What is wrong with you? Do you think Lucille would have turned down Shorty to go with just the two of us?" She laughed and her friends joined in.

"I didn't want to choose a man I had just met over my best friends in the whole world. By the way, did you see the red Cadillac the Big Deal Rent-a-car rented to Walt? He laughed at our go-round with the Big Deal. He commiserated with me and agreed that sometimes, people do not treat older women with the respect that is due them. Anyway, if you both feel that way, would you mind if I had lunch with him today? He and Shorty will be here for two more days. Maybe the five of us could go to dinner together. Would you mind?"

"We would mind if you didn't go to lunch with him," Lucille said.

"Actually, I would prefer being the fifth wheel than having to drag a man along with me," Bernice said. "And I mean it, Lucille. Don't be finding someone to introduce to me and tell Shorty not to find any more brothers."

After breakfast, the friends went shopping for clothes. Kathleen found a calf-length dress that fit her well. It had dark and light reds swirled through the fabric and a little light short-sleeved red sweater over the top. She came out of the dressing room, and the other women did a double take. "Kathleen, you look super in that. Let's pick out some sandals with just a little heel to go with it. You know, something comfortable for dancing," Lucille said.

Kathleen turned back and forth in the three-way mirror and agreed that she had to buy the dress. They went to the other side of the store, and she saw sandals that were also on sale. She found a comfortable pair with a little heel, and Lucille came over with a pair of earrings and necklace that were "just made for this outfit." She bought the entire outfit, and when she headed out the door, she had a spring to her step that she thought had disappeared a few years ago.

Maybe it is time to get out of my comfort zone, she thought.

They got back to their hotel room in time for her to freshen up and put on her new outfit. Just as she stepped out of the bathroom, she heard a knock on the door. She opened the door and there stood Shorty. He looked at her and whistled. "You look hot, Ms. Katie."

"Thanks. Are you alone?" she asked. She looked around Shorty into the hall. She knew it. Walt had decided not to come take her to lunch. Maybe he had changed his mind about seeing her again and had headed back to Dallas. She took a step back into the room and he came in.

"Yes, I'm alone. I am here to pick up Lucy and Bernie because we are going to lunch together. Oh, Walt said to tell you that he would be right down. He has a business phone call, but he is itching to get down here. The 'itching' is my observation." He grinned at her and said to the other women, "Are you ready?" The three of them walked out and the girls told one another to have a good time. Kathleen shut the door, went to the dresser, and poured herself a glass of water. She sat down next to the little round table and began to pray for guidance again. "Lord, am I being silly? Did you put Walt in my path, or is this wishful thinking?" She heard a knock on the door.

When she opened the door, this time she smiled at Walt. She smiled and he looked in her eyes and slowly looked at her new outfit and told her how beautiful she looked. She blushed, and she chided herself knowing her face turned red yet again.

"I hope you don't mind that I have chosen the restaurant. I asked Shorty where he thought he'd take Lucille and Bernice, so we could go elsewhere and not bump into them," he said and lifted his eyebrows. "Not that I don't like your friends, but I want to enjoy just your company."

"That is very sweet and also very complimentary. Where have you chosen?"

"It is a little hideaway down the beach a long way, if you don't mind the ride." He opened the car door for her and closed it gently. When he drove down the highway, she enjoyed the view. She put her head back on the headrest and said, "This is the most relaxed I have felt in the last eight days. You have no idea how scared we were when Lucille and Shorty were missing."

"Shorty has always been an accident waiting to happen. You cannot imagine all the scrapes he got into as a little kid, a teenager, and I guess still as a middle-aged man. Nevertheless, he is my brother and I love him. My kids and I try to keep an eye on him."

"Must be a full-time job," she said with a giggle. "Shorty sure impressed Lucille when they first met. She still has a soft spot in her heart for him, I think. She has not been one to settle down with one guy. She has been like a mother to hundreds and hundreds of her students. Most of them love her and some still send her Christmas cards and pictures of their children and grandchildren. She just has not found a man who wanted to share her with hundreds of kids, I guess. She is a lot of fun to be with, but she has been a teacher before anything else."

"As much fun as she is to be around, I am surprised that some good man didn't snatch her up years ago and marry her. Their loss, for sure." He pulled into a parking lot for a small restaurant with a fake thatched roof and a bridge over a fishpond leading to the door. They stopped in the middle of the bridge and looked down at the huge goldfish swimming around.

"They are so pretty. I hope this place has something besides fish. I don't think I could eat one of their relatives right now," she said as she pointed at the fish. They walked into the restaurant and Walt gave his name for the reservation. The hostess showed them to a small booth by the front window with a beautiful view of the sandy beach and the gulf waves. The booth tucked into the corner so they had a maximum of privacy.

"This is a beautiful place, Walt. The view still cannot be beat." They visited as they leisurely perused their menus.

During the meal, their conversation went from childhood experiences to what happened the day before. They both enjoyed their time together. She declined the offer of dessert. Over coffee, he said, "I do have bad news for myself. I have an important business meeting tomorrow afternoon back at Dallas. I tried to change it, but could not get it done. That means I will be flying out early in the morning."

She tried to hide her disappointment. "Well, these two days have been very nice. I've enjoyed getting to know you."

"Likewise. This is not the end, as far as I am concerned. I am serious about getting you and your friends to fly down to Dallas. Are you still interested? I hope, I hope."

"We all are interested in that invitation. I look forward to meeting your children. I am sure they are wonderful people like their father and mother," she said with a smile.

"They are wonderful like their mother. This is August. Maybe, we could plan a week in November for your first trip down. I have business in New York in September and Chicago in October, so I could drop in to see you and perhaps we could go out for dinner."

He's coming to see me. And then our first trip. Kathleen thought, *Lord, this is moving awfully fast, but I don't want it to end. Is this your plan?*

"Kathleen?"

"Uh, sorry. My mind was elsewhere because God and I were talking." She looked at him, afraid he would think she was a little too different or abnormal.

"I do the same thing. I asked God last night if I should slow down and not move so fast and if this is the direction he wants me to go. Is that the kind of thing you are talking about?"

"Mmm, yes. That kind of thing." Kathleen again felt her face getting warm. "November sounds good. Where would we stay in Dallas?"

"Well, I could put you up in a hotel about twenty minutes from my home, or the three of you could stay with me. I have the guest room and two of the kids' old bedrooms, which Delia redecorated since they got married. I would love you to stay in my home. I have a housekeeper and a wonderful chef, so you would be very comfortable. Maxim and Miriam are married and have been our live-in help for twenty years. If I had to go in to the office while you are there, I would feel better leaving you at the house with a heated swimming pool, a library, and a cook."

"Wow. That sounds wonderful. Since I retired, I have been living in my two-bedroom condominium. It is large enough for me to feel comfortable yet small enough for me to keep up by myself. When I want to spread out, I go visit Bernice on her farm. Her kids are nearby, and they still have horses there. She has a pool that she lets me enjoy in the summer. Her flower gardens are beautiful. Her photos are wonderful, so she has brought the flower gardens into her home onto the walls for winter enjoyment. Her kids call me Aunt Kathleen."

"Do you ever miss that you didn't get married and have children of your own?"

"Sometimes. Tyler and I were a few months from our wedding when a drunk driver ran over him while he jogged. I could not find anyone to hold a candle to Tyler. After a few years, I thought I wanted to find someone else. However, no one came along who could fill his shoes. I got so involved in my ministry and helping abused women through an organization I helped set up, that time has flown by."

"Time does fly by quickly, doesn't it? It just seems like yesterday that my children were small," Walt said.

"Yes, it does, and before I knew it, I reached retirement age. My mother became ill three years ago, so I retired to take care of her. I will never regret that time we had. My dad has been gone for thirty years, so she and I had been close. We traveled together some. Riding the train across Canada to the west coast and coming back by plane had to be my favorite trip. She loved it and so did I. On the way, she wrote a journal with poetry and letters to me. She named it *Your Mom's Memories* and gave it to me for Christmas that year. I cherish that more than any gift I have ever received."

"I'd love to read it sometime, if you are willing to share. I think my daughter and daughters-in-law are going to like you. Are you ready to go? There is a nice shop a little further south that has a wonderful variety of imported items from Europe you might enjoy."

They shopped and the beautiful glassware and jewelry that the shop displayed fascinated Kathleen. Walt pointed out a beautiful necklace on a gold chain and she smiled.

"Here, try it on." He unhooked the clasp and put it around her neck. He turned a mirror so she could see how it looked. He took her red necklace off, and they got the full effect of the beautiful necklace.

"Yes, it is very pretty. Now take it off before I fall in love with it." He unclasped it and put her red necklace back on.

"Well, I have fallen in love with it. I'd like to get it for you to remember me by—until we see each other again, of course."

"I can't let you do that. That is too expensive. You don't know me that well, Walt."

"It is not too expensive and I want you to wear it. It will remind you of me, and I will think of you wearing something I put around your lovely neck. I insist. Please don't say no," he coaxed.

"Okay. Thank you. I do love it. And…" She caught herself before she almost said, *And I love you.* "And I'll wear it often and think of you." He had the necklace put in a box and asked them to wrap it with a pretty bow. "You don't have to have it wrapped."

"Yes, I do. It is special because it is the first gift I have given you, my dear." They browsed more while they waited for the clerk to wrap the box and put a beautiful gold bow on top. As Kathleen walked around the store, she could not believe she had almost said, "And I love you." *What is wrong with you, Kathleen?* She wondered what she might do next. She seemed to be losing self-control with this man. She had always counseled other women not to rush into relationships, to take the time to know another person before declaring one's love and devotion. What was she doing? She certainly did not seem to be taking her own advice. She had only known him for two days, and this behavior seemed ridiculous.

Since Walt had to leave early the next morning, they decided to ask the other three to go with them back to the same restaurant as the night before so they could dance again. They both knew it would be a short evening and night before they had to say good-bye for a while.

In the middle of the afternoon, Walt walked Kathleen to her hotel room door and left her, explaining he had some business calls to make. He kissed her on the forehead and hugged her. She leaned into him and felt secure with this man as she had with Tyler many years ago. After she talked to the girls, she could call and let him know their answer for dinner and suggest a time. When she stepped into the room and shut the door, the girls were not there. She spotted a note on the dresser for her. It said that she should join them on the beach. In addition, they had bought the dress on her bed for her to wear to dinner with Walt that night. She looked at the pretty dress in the same style as the one she had chosen. The new one had black, white, tan, and red swirls on it. The red sandals she had on would match beautifully. She could wear the new necklace in the box she was holding in her left hand. What sweet friends she had. In addition, what a nice guy she had met.

She put on her bathing suit and headed down to the beach. They waved when they saw her coming. "How sweet you girls are. I love the dress. Why did you do that?"

"Honey, we haven't seen you this happy in forty-five years. We have seen you joyful and happy in the Lord, content and satisfied with life, but we have not seen this silly, happy smile on your face in a long, long time. That look is love," Lucille said. "We wanted you to have something else special to wear to dinner tonight with Walt. We assume he did ask you to dinner."

"As a matter of fact, he suggested the five of us go back to the same restaurant where we went last night so we could dance again. In addition, that dress will flow so beautifully as he swings me around. Do you want to do that? I am sure Shorty will do whatever his brother asks him to do." They nodded their agreement.

"Sit down and tell us all about lunch," said Bernice as she patted the chair between them. Kathleen set her bag down on the sand, took off her beach wrap, and sat down. As she began to rub suntan lotion on herself, she told them that they both enjoyed lunch and Walter Alexander was amazing.

Later that evening, the three friends and two brothers sat at a round table near the dance floor. Bernice declared herself happy to be the fifth wheel. Before their entrees came, Walt led Kathleen to the dance floor. He noticed that she wore the beautiful necklace. As Kathleen predicted, her dress was swirling as he turned her. They danced and laughed. Bernice finally said, "You know, I haven't danced in a long time and it looks like fun. Shorty, can you dance?"

"You bet I can, little lady. Buddy and I both had to go to ballroom dance classes when we were in our early teens. It embarrassed us then, but I have sure been grateful and enjoyed it since. Let's go cut a rug, Bernie."

Bernice started to say, "My name is not Bernie." Instead, she said, "Oh, what the heck. Let's cut a rug, Shorty. We'll be back, Lucille, and you can have your turn." Lucille waved them off with her hand. She watched the dancers and silently rejoiced that all five of them were having such a good time. She thought that maybe her escapade with Shorty had not been so bad after all. If Kathleen and Walt fell in love, she would feel successful in being a matchmaker. The dancers noticed that their meals had arrived, so they headed back to their table. Kathleen beamed. They enjoyed their dinner and had what Lucille called delightful conversation. The night ended as the night before. Bernice went back to the room to talk to her daughter on the phone. The two couples walked along the beach. Again, Kathleen sneaked into the room after her friends were in bed. As she lay in bed, she prayed that God would be in the lead in this relationship because she thought she was falling in love. She thought it ridiculous that a woman her age could feel like a teenager again. Nevertheless, she had a delicious feeling. She had tears in her eyes as she slid Tyler's diamond ring off her finger and got up and put it in her jewelry bag. "Tyler, I am moving on. I guess you would have wanted me to do this a long time ago. However, I am a slow study, and you set a high standard for me. I will always love you," she whispered.

Tears slid down her face, and she smiled with joy because she felt God telling her to relax and enjoy her newfound relationship.

"Are you okay, honey lamb? It is going to be all right. I saw what you did and I know Tyler would say that it was about time." Lucille was sitting up in her bed.

"I am fine. I know he would. It just took me a while to get over him. What do you think of Walt?"

"He is a hunk for a man his age. He is kind, gentle, and generous. In addition, his eyes tell the story that he thinks you are very special. I do not think he will disappoint or hurt you. Shorty said the same thing as we walked on the beach tonight."

"He did? Is Walt being the real Walt, according to his brother? It would break my heart if he were deceiving me. However, I do not really think he is. I think he is exactly what he is letting us see."

"I think you are right. I feel God's hand upon you and Walt. But give it some time."

Bernice rolled over and the springs in the uncomfortable bed squeaked. "All is right with the world. Now can we get some sleep? Good night, ladies. And, Kathleen, I think he loves you."

"It is much too soon to think that. Good night, my best friends." She rolled over and quickly fell asleep, but Tyler and Walt filled her dreams. Tyler bowed to her and Walt as he backed into what looked like a mist. She had tears on her cheeks when she awoke.

Early the next morning, Kathleen heard a soft knocking on their door. She had been waiting and hoping that Walt would come to say good-bye before he left for Dallas. She had been up, brushed her teeth and her hair, and put on her special necklace that Walt had given her, with her nightgown and robe. She had been sitting up in bed reading her Bible. She jumped out of bed and peeked out the peephole. Walt looked back at her with a big grin on his face. She opened the door and invited him in. They quietly walked by the beds of her friends, both who pretended to be asleep. Kathleen opened the sliding glass door to the balcony and they stepped out into the warm morning air. She slid the door closed behind them. They leaned on the railing and talked about when they would see each other next, when he would call, that she should call him anytime she wanted to talk, and how much they enjoyed one another's company. He gave her a hug and finally kissed her. She kissed him back and put her cheek on his chest. "Well, you need to be on your way," she said.

She turned around to open the sliding door and it would not budge. She looked at him and he tried to open it. The door would not budge. They both grinned at one another.

"Honey, you have locked me out here so I can't get away, haven't you?" he said with a twinkle in his eye. "I had no idea how devious you are," he teased.

"I didn't do this on purpose." She knocked on the glass and no one came to let them in. She knocked again and called, "Lucille, Bernice. Unlock the door." She continued to knock and no one came to let them in. Walt began to laugh again. "Life with you is indeed interesting, Ms. Keller."

"I am telling you I didn't do this on purpose." She stomped her foot to accentuate her statement. She kept knocking on the glass with her fist. Suddenly, the curtain moved and Bernice looked at them with feigned surprise.

"What? What do you want?" She smiled as she unlocked the door. "Kathleen, I told you not to hogtie this guy or lock him up somewhere to keep him."

Kathleen sputtered and smacked her friend on the backside. "You know I didn't do that on purpose and you know you never said that to me before. What is wrong with you, Bernice?"

Walt and Bernice laughed aloud as Kathleen stood with her hands on her hips disgusted that they caught her in such an embarrassing situation with her friend and the new man who had made such an impression on her. He took Kathleen's hand and kissed her knuckles and gently pulled her to the door. He opened it and pulled her out in the hall for one last kiss, pulling the door closed. As he held her left hand, he could not feel the diamond ring on her finger.

"I will call you when I arrive home. Now get back in there and get yourself dressed for a fun day with your friends. Bye for now, sunshine."

She turned around and turned the doorknob. *Oh, no.* Locked out again. Her face turned red and she looked up at him and grinned. He knew that the door would lock when he pulled her out into the hallway and shut the door. He knocked for her and Bernice came to let her in. He walked away with a swagger and waved his index finger on his right hand without turning around. Kathleen pushed Bernice out of the way to get back into the room.

"He did that on purpose. He pulled me out into the hall and locked me out of the room. He was getting even with me. He is fun, isn't he?" and she giggled. She gave Bernice a big hug. "I am so happy."

Lucille came out of the bathroom dressed to go to breakfast. She looked at Kathleen and Bernice hugging. "What did I miss?"

Kathleen went over to her and gave her a hug. "Oh, Lucille, isn't he wonderful? I have not been this happy and giddy in forty-five years. Girls, let's go have breakfast and then play on the beach for a while. Do you want to build a sandcastle? Would you want to go waterskiing? How about parasailing?"

Bernice and Lucille looked at Kathleen with all the love that two friends can share with a third who has finally found someone to love again. Lucille said, "I vote for breakfast and that other stuff is a big no. How could we explain to Walter that we lost his new girlfriend as she parasailed off into the clouds? I would vote for another visit to the beach with our books and sunscreen." Therefore, Kathleen gave in to activities that sounded more sensible.

Lucille's cell phone rang, and when she answered it, she said, "Oh, Shorty. I will miss you too. You take care of yourself and do what Walt tells you to do for your own safety and well-being. I think we will be coming to Dallas in November, so maybe we will see each other then. Okay. I know. You too. Bye for now."

Later in the morning, as the friends were again on the same lounge chairs that almost seemed to be reserved for them, they relived the last week and a half. "Girls, our vacation will soon be over. This has been one for the books. What will we do next year to top this one?" asked Bernice.

Lucille said, "I don't know. What do you think about Texas? We haven't been there yet." She looked at Kathleen who gave her a sideways look and they nodded in agreement.

The last few days of their vacation, the three women browsed the museums, went to the dog track because Lucille wanted to go again, and enjoyed more sun on the beach.

As they prepared to head for home, they found it more difficult to get everything packed into the car. The backseat behind the driver contained the bags of gifts and souvenirs they had purchased. Lucille took the first driving shift. As they drove north, she stopped one last time to look at the beautiful gulf water.

"I'll be glad to get back home so I can get some rest. The grandkids have been missing me and wondering what I am bringing them. I really miss them when I am gone."

Lucille said, "I thought we went on vacations for a time of rest and relaxation. I think I wore you girls out and I do apologize again. Hopefully, our next vacation will be more laid-back and normal."

"If we are with you, it will not be more laid-back and certainly not normal," said Kathleen. "But we love being with you, Lucy." They all laughed together. Her cell phone rang and Kathleen saw Walt's name on the phone. "Good morning to you, Walt. How are you? (Silence) I am fine. We are just leaving Sarasota heading home. Tomorrow evening, we will be back in Indiana. (Silence) Yes, we will be very careful. Thanks for calling. Good-bye." She smiled out the window, wiped a happy tear from her eye, and said, "Walt."

"Really? We wouldn't have guessed, would we, Bernice?"

"Not at all. I don't mean to change the subject, but where are we having lunch?"

Lucille said, "Wherever you like, dear. Wherever you like."

The trip home seemed quite uneventful compared to the first week of their vacation. They were each glad to get back to their own abodes, even when it meant picking up the mail, paying the bills, buying the groceries, and doing two weeks' worth of laundry.

Chapter 9

Every day, Walt called Kathleen. She looked forward to his calls and planned her day around being there in the early evenings. She got back on her schedule of volunteering at the women's shelter and teaching an adult Sunday school class at her church. She had spent several weeks trying to figure out an appropriate gift for Walt when she went to his home in November. She had asked Lucille and Bernice to help her think of something creative she could make.

Bernice called and invited her out to her home for lunch on a Friday. After they had eaten, Bernice invited Kathleen into her workroom. Bernice had two dozen pictures in black and white and color that she had taken in Sarasota displayed on her worktable. "How about this, Katie? You make a collage of pictures in a beautiful frame for Walt to remind him of when he met you the first time. Look at this one of you two dancing, and there is one of you two walking down the beach in the sunset, or this one with the five of us that the waiter took at our table. On the other hand, if you want me to enlarge this one of you two dancing for a larger frame, we can do that. I really like this one of you two walking down the beach at sunset. What do you think?"

"I love that idea. He said he lives in a log home, so a rustic frame might be nice. Maybe I could do a small collage for his office and a larger frame of the two of us walking on the beach barefooted for his bedroom or living room. Let's go shopping. I will help you clear up the dishes and we can go. You can help me find the perfect frames."

Lucille had come over to have lunch with Kathleen before they went to a church bazaar. Lucille said she had heard from Shorty the day before. "He is in therapy and going to Gamblers' Anonymous meetings every day. He is trying hard to concentrate at work, and he says his nephew told him yesterday he could see an improvement in his work. Shorty seemed more content and happy with himself. Walt has started taking him to church with him. He said he had forgotten how good it felt to hear the music and even the sermon. There may be help for Shorty after all."

"Are you interested in keeping in touch with him?"

"Well, as friends. What do you hear from Walt? Has he suggested a week for all of us to go visit him?"

"Yes, he has. Check your calendar for the first or second week in November. He wants the three of us to stay at his home, although he said he would put us up in the hotel twenty minutes away if we prefer. At his home, we would each have our own bedroom and bath, have access to his heated swimming pool and his library, and he says he has a housekeeper and a great chef. I do not want to disappoint him by asking for the hotel. What do you think?"

Lucille answered dryly, "No, I wouldn't want to disappoint him either. Really, Katie, I think staying at his house sounds wonderful. It is nice of him to include Bernice and me. He really is an old dear. In addition, he is handsome, which is a plus. He looks like a great dancer. However, best of all, he is a Christian. That would have been a deal breaker. I am so happy for you."

"Next week, I think the three of us need to have lunch and discuss the date and details. I cannot imagine flying in a private airplane. He said he would send the plane, so that means he will not be the pilot. Maybe it is so small that there isn't room for him to fly out and back with us. I wonder how big the plane is. I guess we will find out soon enough. What does Lucinda think of you flying to Texas?"

"That girl is cheering us on. She knows I am happiest when I am in the midst of a crowd or getting into trouble. She doesn't worry as much when I am with the two of you. However, she doesn't know how much trouble you two can create." The two friends looked at one another before they burst out laughing.

"This shrimp reminds me of Sarasota, but it just doesn't stack up to the shrimp scampi I had there. How is your chicken?" asked Kathleen. The three friends were at their planning luncheon for their Texas trip. They only had three weeks to get organized and to discuss the details.

"My meal is fine and Bernice's must be too because she has eaten half of it already. Okay, tell us what the plans are. What does Walt have planned for us as entertainment?"

"Walt said the plane will land in Indianapolis on November 3 and the pilot will send a car for us in Columbus around nine o'clock on the fourth. Therefore, you two need to be at my house before that. You can come the night before and sleep over if you like. There will be lunch for us on the plane. He will meet us at the airport and drive us back to his home. We will have a quiet dinner that evening. The next day, he will take us on a tour of Dallas and surrounding areas. That evening, his family will all be over, including Shorty, for dinner so we can meet one another. That makes me nervous." Both of her friends indicated that she should not be worried.

"They will love you, sweetie," Bernice said.

"He wants to get us to an art museum and other highlights, but also wants us to have time around the pool just to visit. One day, he will take us to his office building to see what goes on there. Bernice, he knows you have horses at your farm, so he will be taking us horseback riding one afternoon."

"That helps us know what to pack. I guess my cowboy boots need to go with me."

"It sounds like he has a full schedule of entertainment for us. It will be fun."

"I hope I am not out of place with all the society people down there," Kathleen moaned.

"Kathleen, do you really think that Walt will let anything happen that would make you feel uncomfortable? Of course, he won't. Go buy something dressy for an evening out. Get a pair of heels, not too high, but classy. Let's all go shopping after lunch and find some glitzy stuff."

"I am not going glitzy, but I want to fit in. That will mean I can't wear the slacks and floral blouses like I do around here."

After lunch, the three friends went shopping for additions to their wardrobes for Dallas. Kathleen came out of the dressing room in a luscious pair of plum fitted slacks. With it, she had paired a light tan tank top with a muted floral long jacket that fitted her at the waist. The jacket had plum, tan, and white designs. Lucille ran back to the rack for a smaller size. Kathleen had been walking daily and following the Weight Watchers plan as she suddenly felt the need to be healthier and live a longer life. She had lost twenty pounds and her pants were baggy on her. Therefore, she tried on the smaller set and came out again. She could not believe how much better it looked. Bernice whistled at her.

"Bernice, stop it." Bernice just grinned at her and told her she looked great. "Here. Try this outfit also."

"And this one too." The girls helped Kathleen gather an entire new wardrobe for the weather in Dallas in November. She went home with shopping bags full of new clothes. As she hung them up and removed tags, she preened with pleasure. She looked in the mirror, decided she would get a rinse put on her hair next week, and have her hairdresser give her a new style. She needed something a little classier.

November 4 rolled around quickly, and the girls met at Kathleen's home to await their chariot to whisk them off to the airport. She offered them a cup of tea or coffee while they waited. Bernice turned it down because she did not want to have to take potty breaks along the way to the airport. Lucille thought that sounded like a good idea.

Kathleen had been praying for weeks that all would go well, that it would be a safe trip, and that Walt's children would not think of her as a country bumpkin. She had watched those shows like *Dallas* and *Dallas Housewives.* She did not fit that mold at all. She would avoid scolding herself for thinking she had to be someone she was not. Walt apparently liked her the way she is. If he wanted her to change to be some emaciated, overdressed, overly made-up, mean-spirited, angry woman, he could forget it. She liked who God made her to be, and if it was good enough for God, it had better be good enough for the Texans. She had decided against the hair rinse and just got a perkier haircut. She felt that Walt would not want her to be anything more or less than the woman he had met in Sarasota.

The doorbell rang and all three women stood up filled with anticipation. Bernice ran for the bathroom one last time. Lucille looked in the mirror and checked out her makeup and hair. Kathleen took a deep breath and answered the door. A uniformed chauffeur with his hat under his arm smiled at her.

"Ms. Keller? Your ride to the airport is here. Let me carry your bags," he said with a kind smile. He picked up two of the largest suitcases and said he would be right back. Kathleen walked quickly through her home, making sure all electrical appliances were unplugged and the faucets were not dripping. When Bernice came out of the bathroom, Kathleen ran in. When she came out, Lucille had the driver's attention as she flirted with him. Bernice held her smallest bag and waited for Kathleen inside the front door.

"Ready?" Bernice looked at Kathleen and nodded yes.

She stopped to lock her front door and looked at the car that waited. That is not a car. That is one big, black limousine. The driver held the door open, and Lucille took his hand as he helped her in. The other two women followed her. He told them there were soft drinks and hot coffee available in front of them.

"All that's missing are the doughnuts," Lucille said. They all grinned. The driver grinned also and pointed to the box with a pink bow around it.

"Mr. Alexander said to provide you ladies with doughnuts. The napkins are beside the box. Relax and enjoy. I will have you to the plane in no time. The music is behind you there." He gently closed the door and walked around the back of the limo.

The three friends looked at one another with their mouths hanging open. "I could get used to this," Lucille said.

"I am not sure I could," Kathleen said. This far exceeded her expectations of a ride to the airport. She was used to hatchbacks with broken locks.

"Break open the doughnut box. Walt apparently remembers me saying that our road trips always begin with a bag of doughnuts."

"That is one thoughtful man. I hope he proposes to you. I like this lifestyle. I think he loves you. Here is your chocolate doughnut. You marry him, and we can have doughnuts provided forever," Bernice kidded.

They chatted, and when Lucille pushed the button for music, they heard the song to which Walt and Kathleen danced their first dance. Kathleen thought, *Yes, he is thoughtful and has a good memory.*

As they pulled into the airport, the limousine went out on the tarmac and the driver stopped near a large jet. The Alexander Oil logo stood out on the side of the plane. Kathleen's heart started to pound. *This is too rich for my blood and I do not deserve this.* The driver opened the door and helped each woman out. They stared at the airplane. When they got their bearings and when their muscles and bones loosened up enough that they could walk without stiffness, they walked to the plane. A young steward met them at the bottom of the stairs and motioned them to board. The pilot, who met them at the doorway, shook their hands and introduced himself. He took them into the area where they would ride. A small living room with comfortable couch and chairs, a little library, and a dining table with four chairs welcomed them.

"I guess this will do," Bernice said with a giggle.

Kathleen grimaced at her and whispered, "I can't believe this. It is too rich for my blood. I am not sure I can be comfortable living like this. Not that he has asked me to marry him, but just visiting him is more than I ever expected."

"Of course, you can get used to it. You deserve some of the nicer things in life. Relax and enjoy it."

The driver delivered their suitcases to the bedroom and the half-empty box of doughnuts to the small dining table. The steward asked them to find a seat and fasten their seatbelts. They did so. After they were in the air, he told them that he would serve lunch in twenty minutes. They could freshen up in the bathroom to the back. They walked back to explore and found two small bedrooms and a bath. They took turns in the bathroom and went back to the living area of the plane. They looked at some of Walt's family pictures mounted on the wall. Kathleen had her first opportunity to see a picture of his deceased wife Delia and their three children without Walt present. She was a lovely woman. Kathleen noticed that she was not pencil thin nor was she dressed too fancy. She looked very comfortable with her children leaning on her. Kathleen felt quite reassured. The children were happy-looking munchkins, with the middle one smiling while missing her front teeth. The boys looked mischievous. The next picture showed the three children grown up with their spouses. She put her face closer to see his several grandchildren cavorting in a swimming pool.

The steward held their chairs while they sat down and took their drink orders. They chose iced water and coffee. He brought out plates of chicken salad surrounded with fresh fruit. He placed a basket of crackers and spreads in the middle of the small table. They enjoyed the meal and talked about whether Walt would meet them at the airport or not. After the steward cleared the table and refilled their beverages, he brought out a new deck of cards and a fancy notebook and pen for scorekeeping. "Guess Walt knows we like to play rummy also, eh, Kathleen?" asked Lucille.

"I guess he listened carefully to my ramblings," she said with a satisfied sigh. The girls played cards for a while and decided to move around a little. They did not want to be stiff when they got off the plane. There were current magazines in the rack for them. Some of the magazines were about photography, religion, education, horses, and gardening.

Kathleen pointed out a copy of the *National Geographic* with Bernice's story and pictures from Africa. Walt knew how to make an impression on the women. "What if this is the way he treats everyone? This is amazing. He is too good to be true. It just doesn't seem like an act, but who he really is."

"Don't forget how much he really likes you. You deserve the attention he is pouring out. Enjoy it, I tell you," Lucille said and Bernice agreed with her.

After a while, the steward asked them to fasten their seat belts in about ten minutes. They could freshen up now if they liked. They liked because they wanted to make a good impression on their host. They watched out the window as they landed and were amazed at the size of the airport. As they taxied to a stop, they unfastened their seat belts and stood up to get ready to look relaxed and well-put-together while disembarking. They stretched and walked around to get everything in their bodies gliding smoothly.

Kathleen stepped to the door first. She stopped and looked around for a familiar face. There, Walt stood next to Shorty and a driver. He waved at her and she waved back. "There he is," she exclaimed. She started down the steps gingerly. She did not want to embarrass herself by tripping and falling. She made it to the tarmac and walked toward him with a big smile on her face. He reached her, put his arms around her, and gave her a big hug.

"You are a sight for sore eyes, my dear. You look different. I like the colors in your outfit. Did you have a good flight?" Before she could answer, Bernice and Lucille chimed in, "Couldn't have been better." Shorty reached for Lucille and gave her a big hug. She kissed the top of his head.

"Shorty, I am so glad to see you. How are you? You look good," Lucille said. Shorty reached out and gave Bernice a big bear hug. He reached for Kathleen, and Walt allowed him to hug her as he gave the other two women a welcoming hug.

"Thanks. I am trying to get my life together. How are you, girls? Let's get in the car and we can visit on the way back to Buddy's house." As they walked to the limousine, the pilot and steward carried the women's bags to the trunk. Walt thanked them for the safe trip. Kathleen also thanked them for taking such good care of them. As they drove away from the airport, Kathleen looked at her watch and saw how early it was.

"Walt, I can't tell you what a wonderful day this has been. Everyone is so kind. We had those wonderful doughnuts on the way to the airport. We were served a wonderful lunch and even had playing cards available. Thank you. I hope you pay these people well," Kathleen said and then grinned at him. He took her hand and assured her that he tried to keep his staff happy.

He looked at Kathleen and said, "What is different? You look so serene. Have you lost weight? Your hair looks different. Whatever is different, I like it. But I sure liked what I saw in Sarasota too."

"I like the way you look also. You are as handsome as the first moment we met in that restaurant. As for me, I have been walking and watching my diet. I have decided to be healthier." She could feel her face getting warm again. She changed the subject. "How long does it take to get to your house? I am not in a hurry, just wondering."

"It will take about another thirty minutes if the traffic isn't too heavy. Have you girls been thinking about anything specific that you want to see or do while you are here in Dallas? I have cleared my calendar all except two mornings when I have standing meetings, so I am available to take you wherever you want to go."

Kathleen squeezed his hand. "That is wonderful. Anywhere you want to take us is fine, as long as you are the tour guide. This evening, I hope we can just relax and visit for a while. Who will be having dinner with us?"

Shorty said, "I've been invited. I think there will only be the five of us, right, Buddy?" Walt agreed with him. It would be a quiet, uneventful evening and early to bed if they chose.

Later, Kathleen looked out the window as they drove through large gates with the A emblem of the oil company on it. The gates closed behind them. They rode up a long gravel drive that turned into a concrete drive that led to the front door of a huge log home. The women saw to the left of the house a three-car garage and behind that a stable that had an upstairs apartment. The horses were standing at the fence as if they knew they were to be a welcoming committee for special people. The horses impressed Bernice. "Those are lovely horses, Walt. I look forward to seeing them up close tomorrow."

"Bernice, I want you to feel free to ride them every day. They need the exercise."

The limo stopped and the driver came around to open the door for them. The men got out and extended a hand to help the women step out. The women were gawking at the front of the house and the veranda on the second story that went across the front and down the right side. There were comfortable-looking chairs at intervals. Walt invited them in, and the front door opened before they got to it. "Ladies, I want you to meet Miriam. She is a wonder. She will try to meet your needs before you know you need it. Miriam, this is Kathleen, Bernice, and that is Lucille with her arm around Shorty. I will show them to their rooms if you will help Oliver carry in their bags." He led them to the second floor up an open staircase in the middle of the house. He pointed out the different rooms.

"My room is on the main floor. These are all guest rooms up here. Bernice, I think you will like this room. Some of my daughter's photos are on display. Lucille, this room is bright and cheerful just like you. Kathleen, this will be your room. It is serene and has a view of the city. You can see the city, but cannot hear any of the noise. Do you think you will be comfortable? You each have your own bathroom and plenty of closet space. There is a small refrigerator in each bathroom closet filled with water, juice, or soda. If you want hot tea or coffee in your rooms in the morning, just let Miriam know tonight and she will bring it to you. There is a great variety of books and magazines down in the library. Feel free to browse and bring up anything you would like to read. Dinner will be at six o'clock, so I will leave you to unpack and rest. I will be in the living room or out on the patio when you come down." He gave Kathleen a kiss on the temple and left the women to their own devices.

After Kathleen had her clothes unpacked and her items in the bathroom, she freshened up a bit and then sat down in the comfortable chair by the windows. "I feel like I've died and gone to heaven. This can't be me sitting here." She looked in the mirror and said to herself, "Yep, that's me all right." She grinned at herself and realized her heart was overflowing at seeing Walt in his own environment. *Why sit here alone, when Walt is just downstairs waiting for me?* She left her room, walked down the wide stairway, and found him out on the patio straining a few leaves out of the swimming pool. "Walt. Your home is beautiful. It is like a set for a movie."

"Delia delighted in decorating and planning. She did a great job. Kathleen, I am so happy to see you here in my home. Come here and let me give you another hug. I have missed you." She walked over to him and held out her arms. They hugged for quite some time, and then she pulled back and looked up at him.

"I have been wondering, even though you have called me every day and you stopped in to take me to dinner, if my life hadn't become a dream. I have to pinch myself to believe I am here. Would you show me the rest of your home?"

"Yes. We have time for a little tour inside before dinner." He walked her around the patio and pointed out bushes that the children had helped plant. They went back in the double doors, and he showed her the library, which had shelves up to the ceiling. She was amazed to see a sliding ladder to climb to the highest shelves. He ushered her out the door and they went into the TV room, which had rich-looking leather furniture that had to be very comfortable. A golden retriever stretched out on a rug in front of the fireplace. It snored and seemed totally oblivious of their presence.

"This is Taffy. She's been a part of the family for eight years now," Walt said. Taffy sat up and sniffed Kathleen's hand. She petted Taffy's head, and the dog leaned her head on Kathleen's knee. "She likes you."

"She is lovable. And who is that in the chair?"

"That old fluffy cat is cantankerous, so beware. Maggie is her name. She dominates and Taffy lets her. Maggie may end up on your bed some afternoon, or she may hide the entire week you are here."

He led her into the dining room, which could seat sixteen, and from there into the kitchen. He introduced her to the chef, Miriam's husband. She commented on how delicious the smells were. He smiled at her and said they were having steaks, fixings, and the best strawberry shortcake she would ever taste. She assured him that she believed it.

They walked out the back kitchen door down another hallway, and he led her to a small study that led into his bedroom. It did not look like a man's room, but a great blend of masculine/feminine looks that called out that this was a married couple's room. Kathleen told him it was gorgeous, while she felt uncomfortable in what was no doubt Delia's handiwork.

He pointed out that Miriam and her husband Maxim had an apartment behind the kitchen. She noticed they had their own screened-in porch. How nice. "They were very helpful when my wife got ill. I would not have made it and been able to keep her at home until the end without them. We had a full-time nurse for the last four months. Anyway, they are irreplaceable." They were back to the living room. A warm, crackling fire in the large stone fireplace invited them to relax. They sat down on the couch in front of it and began talking about her volunteer work. He asked about her family. While she talked, she could see Maggie out of the corner of her eye. The cat stood next to a chair watching this new person. Her tail swished back and forth. Suddenly, she took a few steps and jumped up into Kathleen's lap.

"Well, hello, Maggie. You are a pretty thing," Kathleen said as she gently petted the cat's back. Maggie purred and purred as she settled in for a nap.

Walt laughed and said, "Honey, you must be a pet magnet. Maggie does not usually like anyone. She hides when the family comes in. She owns the house but is not fond of most of the people who live here or who visit. The homeowner has accepted you. Good for you." He hugged his girl, and Maggie's eyes opened to tiny slits that said, "Hands off, she is mine." Walt chuckled and tickled Maggie under her chin.

As six o'clock rolled around, Shorty came back in the house from the stable. Bernice and Lucille came down the stairs and Shorty went into the guest bath to clean up. When he came out, Miriam announced, "Dinner is ready." As they sat down, Walt said grace and the meal began. Their conversations were as lively and entertaining as they had been in Sarasota. Of course, the conversation eventually turned to Shorty and Lucille hiding out in fear. Shorty said, "When we were at the dog track, I hoped that we would win big. We did not have time to place one bet before I spied this guy watching us. His jacket fell open and I saw his gun. I just knew I was in danger, and because I had Lucy with me, now I had endangered her. I told Lucille we had to high tail it out of there or I was a dead man. She is such a good sport. Even in those high heels, she ran with me."

"Good sport? It had nothing to do with being a good sport, Shorty. You put the fear of God in me. I am too young to die. We were using my car, so I had to get you to safety," Lucille said and then looked at everyone else at the table as they laughed.

"Neither of us knew our way around Sarasota that well. Lucy should drive in the Indy 500. She made it around corners on two wheels, getting us away from the black van that tailed us. She went through neighborhoods, down alleys, and hit the outskirts until we felt we had lost the black van."

"When you are being followed and you think your life is in danger, you do things you didn't think you ever could."

Walt said thoughtfully, "I am so glad you both made it through that dangerous escapade. Lucille, you have been a good influence on Shorty. Thanks."

Kathleen asked, "Shorty, exactly what is your given name?"

"My name is Albert Adams Alexander. Adams is our mother's maiden name, so all three of us got that middle name. Sis's name is Alicia Adams Alexander. Her surname now is Smith."

"Albert and Walter are strong masculine names. I like them both," Lucille said.

Later, after they had finished the scrumptious strawberry shortcake with the real whipped cream and cups of strong coffee, they walked out to the patio. "Wait until you see the sunset from these chairs. Have a seat," Walt invited.

They enjoyed a gorgeous sunset. Bernice went up to her room for a call to her daughter. Lucille and Shorty went into the library to play a game of canasta. That left Walt and Kathleen to sit in front of the fireplace and talk. Eventually, everyone had gone to bed, and Shorty had gone to his house down the road. Everyone had gone except Walt and Kathleen.

She said she had something for him and she would go get it. She hurried up the stairs and came back down with two beautiful packages with navy blue bows on them. She handed them to him and said, "I wanted to make you something, but I am not all that creative, so Bernice helped me out." She waited for him to open the smaller package. He held up the eight by ten framed picture of Walt and Kathleen dancing on the last night in Sarasota in her flowing dress. They both had idyllic smiles on their faces.

"Oh, Kathleen, this is just wonderful. I love it. I can look at you now morning and night. It is a perfect gift. I did not even know she had her camera on us. After this gift, what could be in the other box that could compare? Well, let's see." He opened the second box and smiled again with pleasure. This picture was a collage in black and white of the five of them in Sarasota.

"This one might work in your office," she suggested. He agreed and perused each picture with interest. She watched his face as he smiled at the pictures and then back at her.

"I love this one of us walking away down the beach. Yes, I will hang this one by my desk where I can see it all day." He placed the two frames where they could look at them. They watched the fire burn down, and she had to admit that she could not keep her eyes open any longer. Therefore, he walked her to the stairs and gave her a goodnight kiss. "Sleep in as late as you want in the morning. We will take an overview tour of Dallas before lunch. Good night, my dear. I am so happy you are here."

"Good night, Walt. I am happy to be here. Sweet dreams."

"They will be sweet because I'll be dreaming of you, dear."

Chapter 10

By nine o'clock the next morning, everyone gathered around the dining room table, finishing a Texas-sized breakfast. "Well, what is on the schedule today?" Lucille asked.

"We are taking an overview tour of Dallas, Walt told me last night. What should we wear?" said Kathleen.

"I think you need to wear flat shoes, slacks, and warm jackets. We'll meet at the front door in fifteen minutes, ladies," said Walt. The women trotted upstairs to make a last trip to their bathrooms, grab their jackets, and to let Lucille change from her high heels to flats. Fifteen minutes later, they were waiting for Walt at the front door when they heard a whirring sound. The door opened and Walt invited them outside. They walked around the side of the house and discovered the source of the sound. They were going in a helicopter for the overview tour promised.

Bernice smiled and said, "I swear, Walter, you just continue to amaze us. This is wonderful. I've never been in a helicopter before." They boarded the 'copter, the pilot started the engine, and off they went. Walt described the sights and the beauty from up above astounded them. For lunch, the pilot landed the helicopter on top of a tall building and they got out. Walt led them down a stairway to an elevator, which took them to the doors of a classy-looking restaurant. As they went through the double doors, they saw a round table with one man sitting alone.

"Oh, it's Shorty," Lucille cried. "Hon, I wondered if we would see you today." She hugged him and chose the chair next to his.

Bernice sat on his other side. After they had ordered their lunch, Shorty started asking Bernice about her horses. He offered to take them riding the next day. Lucille begged off, saying Bernice and Shorty could take the ride, and she would stay by the pool with a book. The unseasonably warm weather for November and the heated pool might entice her into the water.

Before they left the restaurant, they had a short list of places to see beginning with art museums. They arrived back at the house in time for everyone to rest a while before Walt's family began to show up. The women changed into dressier apparel to meet the family. They were standing around in the living room discussing their favorite artwork that they had seen that day. The front door opened and a rush of people and children came in the door. Nancy and her husband Kevin came in with their two. Walt introduced them all around. "And these little characters are Rick and Jane."

Nancy took Kathleen's hand, held it, and said, "I am so glad to finally meet you. Dad has been singing your praises ever since he got back from Sarasota."

Kathleen said it was a pleasure to meet Nancy and her family also. She had heard great things about them and she knew that Walt loved them very much.

The door opened and Nick and Carla pushed their brood into the foyer. Walt hugged Carla his daughter-in-law, tousled the hair of David and Adam, and picked up Crystal. The two-year-old angel had blonde curly hair and blue eyes. She patted her grandpa's cheek. She twisted around, looked at Kathleen, and then extended her arms. She obviously wanted to get acquainted with this new woman. Kathleen reached out and took her and little Crystal patted her cheek. After the introductions were finished, they made their way into the large living room. Nick told Kathleen it was a joy to meet her because she had his dad smiling. That bit of information warmed Kathleen's heart, and she felt her face flushing.

The doorbell rang, the front door opened, and a female voice with what sounded like a put-on southern accent called out, "We're here, ya'll."

Nancy whispered to Kathleen, "Prepare to be engulfed by my sister-in-law, Ms. Texas of a few years ago. Do not let her scare you. She is not as much as she thinks she is."

That comment took her aback, but later she realized Nancy was being quite upfront and honest with her. Ned and Tiffany came into the living room, and Walt put Crystal down on her daddy's lap, took Kathleen's elbow, and led her over to his youngest son and pregnant wife. He introduced them all around, and Ned said he was glad to meet her and Tiffany giggled and said, "My, my, Ms. Kathleen, you are not what I expected."

"Sorry. What did you expect, Tiffany?"

"Never mind, honey, it is not important. Nancy, how are you? Are those a few grey hairs I see? You really ought to get that covered up," Tiffany said. She turned and Walt introduced her to Bernice and Lucille.

Lucille had heard the comment by Tiffany to one of her best friends and so she said, "So you are Tiffany. My, you aren't what I expected." She smiled.

"Oh? What did you expect, honey?"

"It is not important. Nice to meet you, Tiff," Lucille said.

"Oh, no, I never go by Tiff, it is Tiffany, dear," she answered.

Lucille just smiled and thought, *Honey, don't mess with Kathleen or you will have double trouble. Pregnant or not, you better watch your manners.*

Tiffany, the skinny, bleached blonde, was used to being in the spotlight. Her four-month pregnancy barely showed. However, she wanted to be sure that everyone knew that she carried a baby out front and not too much dessert.

Kathleen sat down in a chair and began to get acquainted with some of the children. Before she knew it, Crystal was up in her lap. Jane was telling her about a spat she had with her friend

Stephanie at Sunday school the week before. Adam was showing her a plastic bug he had taken out of his pocket. He wanted to frighten her, but was impressed when she did not flinch. He liked that about her. Tiffany came over and told the children to run along so she could talk with Ms. Kathleen for a while.

"Kathleen, tell me about your family? Where are they from?" she asked.

"We are from southern Indiana. My great-grandparents came to Indiana from Virginia many years ago. They were all farmers. My parents are deceased, and I have one sister who is married and has two children."

"Have you never been married before? Why is that?" she asked condescendingly. Nancy and Shorty both overheard the inquisition at the same time and came to Kathleen's rescue. Nancy asked Kathleen to go with her to the library because she wanted to show her something. Shorty kept Tiffany from following them by asking about her aunt Paige. Tiffany told him her aunt was fine.

"And how are you getting along with your addiction problem?" she asked in a syrupy tone. Her husband came over when he heard that question and took her by the arm and maneuvered her out to the patio. Shorty grinned because he knew her husband Ned, usually a kind man, like his father, would chastise Tiffany. Shorty often wondered how Tiffany had roped poor Ned. She always behaved carefully in front of her father-in-law. She had liked Delia and planned to name her baby girl Delia Adams Alexander. She would do whatever she needed to do to ingratiate herself in her father-in-law's good graces. She did not want Kathleen to replace Delia. Even though she had been gone for some time and Walt deserved to be happy, she did not want any competition for the memory of Delia. Even after Delia in her last few weeks had told all the children that after she was gone, she wanted their dad to find another wife. He deserved to have a wife and she told the children to support him when the time came. Moreover, this woman from the hills of southern Indiana was not worthy of taking Delia's place, no matter what Delia had said. Perhaps her aunt Paige would be worthy of her father-in-law, but no one else. Also, if he married Aunt Paige, she would have a double claim in the family.

Nancy and Kathleen were having a conversation in the library when Walt found them. "Dad, Kathleen has been telling me how she met you. Your trip to Sarasota to get Uncle Shorty must have been even more eventful than you told me."

"Yes, it was eventful, and I am so glad of it. Are you ladies ready to go in to dinner?" He put one arm around his daughter and the other around Kathleen.

"Dad, you had better protect this lady. She is more precious than rubies and pearls," said Nancy, hoping he understood what she meant: protect her from Tiffany.

Walt got the family quiet, and he gave thanks for those around the table and for the meal. They had a delicious dinner, and with all the laughter and joy around the table, Kathleen felt so welcome. The youngest children were in high chairs and the others sat between adults who would help them.

Nicholas asked the three women about some of their other trips and escapades they had experienced. They took turns sharing the information and funny stories with them. Kathleen told about Bernice having to crawl through the hatchback to unlock the doors. They laughed about them cleaning out the wrong car in the parking lot. Everyone laughed with them. The little children even laughed loudly, not understanding the joke of course. Nancy asked Kathleen to share her call to the ministry with them. She gave them the brief story, and Lucille added the story of going to the seminary that her fiancé had attended until his death. Bernice told in a few words how Kathleen had helped the police find his killer. Walt's children were very impressed with the changes in careers she had experienced, including temporary detective.

They asked what she had liked most about the ministry. She told them about continuing with one of her favorite parts outside the usual worship and teaching. "I have had a heart for battered and abused women and children."

"Oh, my, Ms. Kathleen," Tiffany drawled, "that sounds like dreadful situations and really dangerous. It just sounds icky. You have to talk to all those people with such revolting problems? I don't know any people like that."

"Yes, dreadful situations, but when God leads people to make changes in their lives, it can be a beautiful thing. Seeing women escape with their children from batterers and begin a new life is wonderful. Seeing a wife beater come to Christ and turn his life around is equally wonderful, Tiffany. I've even dealt with a husband-batterer," she answered.

"Oh, no, women don't do that," exclaimed Tiffany.

"But they do. Sometimes abuse is physical, verbal, or emotional," Kathleen said.

"I suppose someone has to deal with those people, but I don't know any people like that," Tiffany drawled. Bernice looked at Walt and back at Kathleen to see their reaction. Walt tried not to give any reaction. Kathleen met Bernice's eyes and they knew what the other thought at that moment. *This girl is a case and could be trouble. She certainly doesn't have much empathy for others.*

After the meal, the family sat around the living room talking, and the children were in the television room playing with the toys that they pulled out of a chest in the corner. Walt had gone to his office to take an unexpected business call. Tiffany sidled over to Kathleen as she sat next to the fireplace. She pulled up a stool and started a conversation about fashion.

"Kathleen, we should go shopping while you are here. I could help you choose some appropriate fashions for Dallas. Delia always wore flowing gowns in the evening for dinner. She loved her horses and rode during the day. Then, she became a very feminine creature for her husband in the evenings. We could try to help you look more like a Dallas lady," Tiffany said.

"Actually, Tiffany, I am not a Dallas lady and I am content with the way I look. I would never try to fill Delia's shoes. You must have loved her very much. However, I am Kathleen, a retired pastor from southern Indiana, and that is who I will remain. My friends seem to like me this way," she said and patted Tiffany's hand. "And I am happy being me. Are you happy being you?"

Shorty had overheard the conversation and joined in with, "Kathleen, I think my brother is very impressed with you just the way you are. I don't think he would want you to change."

"Thanks, Shorty, that is very sweet. Have I told you since we have been here that I see a real change in you? You seem more self-assured and content. What has made the difference?" Kathleen asked.

"Walt started dragging me to church, and I found that it made a difference in my outlook. Now I go willingly. I had forgotten how good it feels to let Jesus back into my heart. Is that what you see?" Shorty said, with confidence.

"That is what I see. I am so glad you are turning your life around, or I should say I am glad you are letting God turn your life around," she answered.

"Excuse us, Tiffany, but I want to show Kathleen the pictures of our childhood in the library," Shorty said. He took Kathleen's elbow and guided her around the corner. "I guess we should have warned you about Tiff. She thinks she is upper-crust Texan and looks down on the rest of us. Her claim to fame is being a beauty queen, but her family is not as rich as she tries to make people think. When you go to church Sunday, beware of a tall redheaded woman who will swoop down on Walt and try to elbow you out of the way. She is Tiffany's divorced aunt who has had her sights on Walt for the past year. He obviously is not interested. By the way, you look lovely tonight. Walt is a lucky man."

"Shorty, you grow on a person. When we first met you, I thought you were a little nuisance, sorry, interfering with the girls' road trip. The better I get to know you, the more I appreciate you.

Lucille really likes you too," Kathleen said as she patted him on the arm.

"Hey, what is going on here?" said Walt gruffly. "I turn my back and my girl is going after my brother?" He laughed. "How are you doing? Did you figure out who the people are in these pictures?" They looked over the pictures and Shorty made an excuse to leave the room. "Sorry about the phone call. My kids really seem to like you. I hope you don't feel cross-examined by the women." They walked over to the TV room.

"No, I am enjoying your family. Your grandchildren are precious," she said as she watched them playing on the floor and the two older ones playing a board game on a table. "It must be nice to have them around so much."

He acknowledged that indeed he counted it a blessing. "We'd better get back to the living room or they will be wondering where we have gone." After the young folks had all gone home, Shorty had excused himself for the evening, and Bernice and Lucille went to their rooms. Walt and Kathleen sat on the patio, enjoying the cool night breeze. As the clock chimed midnight, they parted at the bottom of the wide staircase and kissed good night.

The next day, Shorty and Bernice went horseback riding while Lucille read beside the pool. Walt took Kathleen for a drive around his small ranch in his old red jeep. They saw Shorty's house near the other end of the property, which was also a log home, but a much smaller one. It had just three bedrooms and the guest rooms shared a connecting bathroom. It had a wonderful screened-in porch at the back facing the White Rock Creek, just as Walt's did. She asked him if he thought Shorty had made permanent improvements in his life. "I think this time that he wants to make a difference. All the times before, he seemed to try just to please me and get me to quit nagging. This time, he has let Jesus take the reins. That makes all the difference in the world, as you know," said Walt. He stopped the jeep on a small rise that faced White Rock Creek and turned off the engine. He put his arm on the back of her seat, and she felt his hand touching the back of her neck. She had a wonderful chill run down her spine.

"This part of the White Rock Creek is the prettiest in Texas. The trees give shade when you fish or just enjoy the beautiful view. Every season of the year is wonderful. When I have time, I'll come out here and catch a couple of largemouth bass and take them back for Maxim to fix up for supper. Nothing tastes better than that. Maybe we can do that sometime. Have you ever fished?"

"My dad took me fishing when I was a little girl. He taught me how to catch fish, and I admit that I was pretty darn good at it, if I do say so myself. We would sit out in the middle of the lake for hours in his old boat. He often let me rattle on about my little problems and ask him questions that he patiently answered. Those are some of the most precious memories I have of my daddy." She looked out toward the flowing water and smiled. "Can we walk over to the water's edge?"

He nodded and slowly hopped out and went around to her side of the jeep and took her hand as she stepped out. He continued to hold her hand as they walked toward the bank of the river. He said as they walked, "I'm sorry, dear. I am sure your daddy must have been proud as punch of you." Walt pointed out the volcano-shaped homes of the crayfish and a snapping turtle than moved into the water as they approached. He found an old log that had fallen some time ago that called for two older folks to come sit a spell. They answered the call and sat down next to one another. He continued to hold her hand.

He looked at her and said, "Kathleen, when I am with you, I feel whole again. Your spirit of kindness and contentment are a joy for me. Yet you have a spark of liveliness that I really enjoy. When we are apart, I think about you off and on all day. Mostly on. Are you enjoying being here? I hope so," he said.

She looked into his kind eyes and said, "Walt, since we met, my life has a new dimension that I thought it would never have again. You are so kind and thoughtful. I enjoy your company. But

I am not sure I am cut out to be a Dallas woman." She thought about Tiffany's comments the night before.

"Honey, I don't want you to become something you are not. You are not a Dallas woman. If you mean one of those skinny, overly made-up, self-centered women seen on TV, that is the last thing I want you to be. I love you just the way you are. You are a retired clergywoman from southern Indiana. You are kind and I enjoy being with you. You have a calmness about you that says you have no fear of the future where God is indeed in charge. Our hours of conversations over the past couple of months have been so enjoyable. We are not kids, you know. We can make decisions better and faster than young kids."

"Walt, what did you just say? Did you say you love me just the way I am?"

"Yes, and I meant every word. I love you," he said and kissed her. She pulled back and looked him in the eyes.

"I love you too, but we have such different lives. I am a country bumpkin and you are a Texas oilman. I can't imagine that I would fit in with your friends and associates out here," she said.

"You are not a country bumpkin. I started as a farmer's son who discovered oil on our land. I have not always lived like this. My friends are down-to-earth folks. Why are you suddenly so worried about fitting in? I want to marry you and spend the rest of our lives together. We are a good fit. I want to be your husband and spend every day with you. I want to make you happy and more content than the day I met you. You were happy, and in spite of my brother whisking away one of your friends, you had the aura about you that you were at ease. And you were lovely in my arms as we danced," he said.

"You know, don't you, that I hadn't danced for a long time? I was a little rusty, no, a lot rusty."

"No, I didn't think you were rusty, but I sure felt nervous and afraid I'd step on your toes and you'd run away. Can we get back to the talk about marrying me?" He chuckled.

She knew she could not tell him about Tiffany insinuating that she would never be up to par with Delia and other Dallas wives. She would not cause family problems for him. "I love you, Walt, but I need some time to think. I hope you understand. You are a most amazing man. Any woman would be lucky to be your wife. I have no experience being married, being a wife, living with someone. I do not know how good I would be at it. I don't deserve all the things that you have."

"Honey, you deserve more than I have. In addition, you ought to know that it is not about the things I have or you have. Nothing is more important than people are. Nothing is more important than people we love. I love you and I know I want to spend the rest of my days with you. Okay, I will give you some time, but I will not give up asking. I think Shorty became the catalyst to bring us together. God's plans are mightier than ours. I am a patient man, but remember, time is wasting. We are not spring chickens anymore. Shorty approves of you, and in spite of his problems with gambling and goofing up, he is a good judge of character. You, Lucille, and Bernice are good people. I cannot believe how blessed I am to have found you. Do not keep me waiting too long, sweetheart. I won't be looking around for anyone else. I just don't want to waste time being apart." He pulled her into his arms and held her closely.

Kathleen knew Walt to be the only man she had met since losing Tyler than stood a chance with her. He had some of Tyler's characteristics of being kind, solid, thoughtful, and loving. She knew her answer should be yes, but she still had to figure out how to deal with Tiffany. She did not want to cause him grief in his family. She would give up her happiness rather than cause family problems for him. She leaned back in his arms and looked into his face. He teased her with his lower lip out, begging her to say yes. She giggled at him, pulled his head down to her lips, and gave him a promising kiss that made his heart pound. She turned and leaned her back into his chest and pulled his hands around her waist. They sat like that for quite a while, watching the water flow by and wildlife flit in and out of view.

"Well, my pretty one, I guess we had better head back to the house. I could stay here all night with you, but the coyotes might scare you away." He took her hand, they stood up, and they waited a moment to let their joints loosen up. They walked casually back to the jeep. He turned the key to start the engine. It cranked, but did not start. He tried again without success.

Kathleen laughed and said, "You brought me out here all alone and intended to hold me captive, right?" She was referring to the time she had accidentally locked them out on the balcony in Sarasota.

"I am shocked that you would think such a thing, my dear. If I wanted to hold you captive, I would have brought a picnic basket and tent for overnight." They both laughed together. He tried once more, and this time, the engine started and sputtered. He gave it the gas and it smoothed out. He drove back to the house. "And if I wanted to hold you captive, I could. If you ever say yes, you will be my captive for life and I will be yours. Oh, Kathleen…" He took her hand, brought it to his lips, and kissed it. He felt the lack of a ring on her left hand and it pleased him. He felt she must be getting closer and would say yes. He prayed that his assessment might be true.

Kathleen watched his face and thought, *I feel like a teenager drooling over a boyfriend.* She felt her face turn red and she did not care. *I love Walt and will fight for him if need be. That little, skinny girl with the Texas drawl will not orchestrate her father-in-law's life or mine.* Could she take charge of the situation? She knew she would have to, but had to do it with love and care for all of them. She smiled to herself and felt that one skinny, little blonde girl would not change the course of her life when she so felt that God led her this way. Patience and love would solve the problem. She prayed that all would work out.

When Sunday rolled around, they were all up early for breakfast and ready for church. Shorty had joined them, and they were finishing their coffee when the phone rang.

Miriam came to the door of the dining room and said, "Mr. Alexander, it is for you."

"Who is it Miriam? Can it wait?" he asked.

She whispered, "It is Paige King. Shall I tell her you will call back later in the day?"

"No. I'll take it now." He got up and went to his study. Shorty said, "That is Tiffany's aunt. She has been chasing Buddy for a year now. She isn't getting anywhere, but doesn't give up."

It did not take long for Walt to come back in the room. He said to Shorty, "She knows I have guests this week, why would she invite me to her house for dinner today after church?"

Shorty guffawed. "Buddy, you are blind. She is trying to hog-tie you. Kathleen, you be careful at church today that she doesn't knock you down getting to my brother."

Walt chuckled with embarrassment. "You are right. She is after me. It sounds rather self-important to say that, doesn't it?"

Kathleen said, "I am surprised you don't have eligible women calling you all the time. I guess I do have competition. And these Dallas beauties are persuasive," she drawled the last sentence. Everyone laughed and Walt blushed.

"Remember, lady, I only want you. Did you all hear that? I only want this one," Walt said with authority as he walked over and put a kiss on the top of her head. Lucille and Bernice looked at Kathleen and grinned.

"Girlfriend, did you hear that?" said both friends at the same time.

Chapter 11

As the church service ended, some of Walt's friends gathered around him to meet Kathleen and her friends. She comfortably chatted with two of his business associates and their wives. She enjoyed their company and enjoyed hearing how Walt had been bragging on this wonderful Hoosier pastor he had met, yet she appeared somewhat embarrassed. She noticed that the women were dressed in similar outfits as hers and they were not overly skinny. The five women were talking about Shorty's adventure in Sarasota, and they were laughing when Kathleen told them about cleaning out the wrong rental car. She hoped she was not wearing out that story because it did make people laugh. The ladies had a touch of a southern Texas drawl, but seemed more like Kathleen and her friends than like any of the Texas women she had seen on the television shows.

Suddenly, they heard a southern drawl shrilly say, "Walt, honey, I wondered if I would see you here this mornin' and here you are." The two wives both chuckled and one whispered, "Here's Paige."

Walt turned and grabbed Kathleen's hand and pulled her gently toward him. "Paige, I want you to meet my very, very dear friend Kathleen Keller. She is visiting from Indiana with her friends.

"Hello, Paige. It is nice to meet you. I understand you are Tiffany's aunt."

"Well, hello. Tiffany said Walt had some folks visiting from up north. I didn't know what to expect," Paige said as she took

Kathleen's hand and checked out her manicure, which was well done but simple. Kathleen always wore clear polish. Paige compared her hand, which had red acrylic nails and several diamond rings on it. Kathleen shook hands with Paige and pulled her hand back quickly.

Walt said, "Paige, this is Lucille and this is Bernice. These three women have been best friends for a long time. Girls, get acquainted," he said and gently put his arm around Kathleen, and they backed out of the small circle. Bernice and Lucille took over.

"Well, Paige, is it? We have heard so much about you. You are Tiffany's aunt. You two look a lot alike," Lucille said as she put out her well-manicured hand with pink acrylic nails and a couple of very nice rings on her fingers.

"Oh, honey, some people have mistaken us for sisters," she cooed, as she noticed Lucille's hand and put her hand in Lucille's for a limp handshake.

Bernice said, "Is that right? My, my, what a pretty outfit. Sort of looks like the outfit Lucille wore to dinner the other night. Looks gorgeous on you also, Paige. Where do you live? Where do you shop?"

"I live in a condo not far from here, but I also have a home in Las Vegas so I can get away every so often. I shop here in Dallas, but prefer to go to Europe for most of my clothes."

"Tell me, dear, where can I find shoes like those? They would go with the dress I wore the other night. I think that they would match beautifully, right, Bernice?"

"Oh, my dears, these are one of a kind. You will not be able to find the exact pair anywhere. I found these in Paris," Paige said, putting her hand up to her chest aghast that Lucille might wear identical shoes or identical anything.

"Oh, yes, sweetie. Those look just like you. Yes, I know just the dress you mean. It is the one you found in Sarasota or the one you found in Rhode Island. That Goodwill store had so many pretty dresses, didn't it?"

"Paris? I've been to Paris, Kentucky, also," Bernice said, tongue in cheek.

"No, Paris, France. Goodwill? Oh, no, this came from a one-of-a-kind store," whined Paige. "My clothes do not end up at Goodwill. You must be mistaken. No one who shops at Goodwill could be small enough to fit into my clothes."

The friends looked down the hallway and saw that Walt and Kathleen were with his friends and were heading out the front door.

"Well, Paige, it was wonderful meeting you. Next time we are in town, we will look you up. Okay? We can go dress shopping together. We will help you get some great deals. Give our regards to Tiff," Lucille said as she took Bernice's elbow and directed her toward the front door as well. "Let's go, Bernie," she whispered and giggled as she swaggered down the hall. Paige stood alone with a confused look on her face, like 'what just happened?' She looked around for Walt, her target, and did not see him. She wondered what she was up against with these Hoosier women. Tiffany might be correct that Kathleen just was not right for Walter. She would have to work a little harder to get his attention back.

As they all got in the van to go back home, Walt thanked the girls for helping them escape. "I am sure she is a nice woman, but she is a little too persistent for me," Walt said apologetically.

Shorty laughed and said, "Nice woman? Buddy, you are excessively nice. She is a barracuda. However, Lucy and Bernie took care of her. If I did not know better, I would think you had been to barracuda training. You did a good job, ladies. You helped my brother protect his little lady."

"Believe me, definitely our pleasure," drawled Lucille.

"We have a date with her when we come back to take her shopping at Goodwill. We had her so confused, she probably would have gone with us today," Bernice added. Everyone laughed.

"Poor Paige," Kathleen said and clucked her tongue. "But she does have beautiful hands." Bernice rolled her eyes at Lucille who grinned in agreement that Kathleen seemed too benevolent.

That afternoon, Walt's children and their families were back for a barbeque. The warm weather allowed the children to play in the heated pool with their dads. Jane kept throwing a beach ball out of the pool for Kathleen to kick back at her. Shorty and Lucille were at the other end of the pool at a small table playing canasta again. Lucille won a second game, and Shorty was complaining about losing his mojo for winning at cards. She laughed at him.

At one point, Kathleen saw him pat Lucille's hand lovingly as she dealt him new cards. He stood up, leaned over the table, and kissed her on the cheek. Kathleen decided that maybe Lucille and Shorty were more than just platonic friends. Something romantic radiated in their faces.

Tiffany came out on the patio in a bright yellow bikini. The women thought that for a pregnant woman, she looked good, but thought a one-piece suit might have been more appropriate. She slowly walked down the steps into the shallow end of the pool. The kids were splashing and playing ball.

"Stop, don't get my hair wet, kids," she begged. Therefore, her husband splashed water at her and she pouted. "I said not to get my hair wet." She walked back up the steps and got out of the pool. Lucille quietly said to Shorty, "If you don't want to get wet, don't get in the pool, is my suggestion." He laughed and agreed. Tiffany wrapped herself in a large beach towel and sat down next to Kathleen. Walt had gone inside to get a fresh pitcher of lemonade for the crowd.

"Why don't you get in the pool, Kathleen? You don't have that much hair to get wet," and she giggled. "Did you not bring a bathing suit? We could go buy you one tomorrow."

"I brought a bathing suit, but I think the pool is full enough with all the little ones in there. I'll swim laps tomorrow morning," Kathleen answered.

"Oh, you swim laps? I wouldn't have guessed that at all," she drawled. Kathleen rolled her eyes.

"Did you meet my aunt Paige this morning at church? She thinks Walt is her next husband. She has a sixth sense about these things. Her first husband had been her high-school sweetheart who up and left her after their first anniversary. He seemed to always be a loose wheel and skittish. Her second husband, her daddy's age, loved her and left her all his wealth after being married just one week. He succumbed to a heart attack and was dead three days later. Her third husband married her for her wealth, so she dumped him good and proper. Walt will be her fourth husband and she thinks the last one. He is such a catch. He and Delia were so happy when they decided he should choose my aunt Paige for wife number 2." She looked at Kathleen and demurely fluttered her eyelashes. Her grin said it all. She let Kathleen know she needed to go back home and stay there. Aunt Paige had her sights on Walt and did not need any competition.

"Does Walt get a say in any of this, dear?" She changed the subject before Tiffany could answer. "When is your baby due, Tiffany? Do you know if it is a girl or a boy?"

"She is due in April. We have not had a test yet, but I just know it is a girl. I wouldn't know what to do with a little boy," cooed Tiffany. "I need a little girl to dress up and make her mama proud."

"Well, I hope you and Ned get what you want."

"I always do. I wanted Ned and I got him. I want a girl and I will get her. If not, it will be Ned's fault and he will live to regret it," she said with a giggle.

Ned pulled himself up on the edge of the pool and hung on his forearms. "Did I hear my name?"

"Honey, I just told Kathleen that our baby had to be a girl or it is your fault and you'd be sorry."

"One more thing to be sorry for, eh, Tiff?" he said and pushed off from the side of the pool and floated across it. Little Rick reached out and grabbed his uncle's hair, and Ned grabbed him and tickled him and pushed him away in his floatation ring.

Kathleen looked at Ned and then at Tiffany and wondered how this relationship would work out. Tiffany had to be her own worst enemy. Kathleen wondered how Tiffany had collared Ned, who seemed so kind and considerate.

Walt came back out with the tray of lemonade and fresh glasses and told everyone the barbeque would be ready in twenty minutes, so they needed to be getting out of the pool soon. Bernice came out from her nap upstairs. She looked very refreshed and happy. Her daughter had called and said that they had a new colt in the barn and the kids were excited.

Later that evening as everyone said their farewells to Kathleen and her two friends who would be leaving for home in a couple of days, Nancy gave Kathleen a big hug and said she approved of her dad's choice. "You are just what he needs. It is obvious you two enjoy one another's company. I approve and so do Nicholas and Ned. We hope you will be back for Christmas. That would be wonderful. Please disregard my sister-in-law Tiffany. She is a spoiled princess who needs to grow up. Do not let her influence your opinion of the rest of the family, and do not let Paige get under your skin. She has been chasing Dad for a year now to no avail. Uncle Shorty told me she accosted you after church, but your friends did a number on her. She deserved that teasing. I wish I'd been there."

Kathleen hugged Nancy again and thanked her for the kind words and advice. Again that evening, Walt and Kathleen snuggled on the couch in front of the fireplace. He said, "I hope you enjoyed the day with my family. Most of the time, things are rather smooth. Shorty told me Tiffany cornered you again. Please do not let her get under your skin. She is young and rather full of herself."

"I know. Nancy kindly warned me ahead of our encounter. I have dealt with young women like her before. It is okay, Walt," she patted his hand and tried to tell herself that everything would be okay.

On Monday, Shorty took the day off so he could take the women horseback riding. Bernice could not get her boots on fast enough, Lucille went under duress, and Kathleen begged off. She just did not think she would be ready to let them know how fearful she felt about getting on a horse. Maybe the next visit, she told herself. Maybe it would be easier without an audience. Kathleen changed into her bathing suit and walked into the pool. The water felt so comfortable. She began to swim laps, and she laughed to herself that Tiffany did not think she swam laps. What would she do with that girl? She wanted to be Walt's wife, but she did not want to bring strife among his children. She knew he did not want to marry Paige; he said as much to all of them. She kept swimming back and forth until she got exhausted. When she stopped and sat on the top step, she looked over at the door and saw Walt.

"Honey, I'm home," and he grinned. "I didn't want to break your rhythm. You are a good swimmer. I enjoyed watching you. You look like you are fifty years old."

"Yeah, right. Do you have your glasses on, my dear?" and she giggled. She got out of the pool, wrapped a huge towel around herself, and hugged Walt.

"Hey, you are getting me wet, woman," he exclaimed and just hugged her tighter. She excused herself to go change for dinner. The riders were coming back in and heading to their rooms to clean up.

Later, the women were coming down the stairs in flowing skirts for their last evening before returning to their Hoosier homes. Shorty came through the front door after cleaning up at his house. The five of them had a wonderful dinner, reliving the highlights of their first Dallas visit.

Lucille walked Shorty out onto the front porch when he told them good night. She did not come back in for a long time, and when she did, she had been crying. She waved good night and headed up the stairs.

"I wonder what brought that on."

"I don't know. I'll check with her before I go to bed," Kathleen said worriedly. Shortly thereafter, Walt walked her to the stairway, and they said their good nights with hugs and kisses.

When Kathleen got to Lucille's door, she knocked lightly and listened. She heard Lucille tell her to come in.

Kathleen opened the door and walked in. Lucille sat in her pajamas and took a few pins out of her hair. She no longer had red eyes, but looked somewhat overemotional. Her friend sat down in the chair and asked her how she was doing.

"Oh, Albert told me that he loved me and wanted me to come back soon. It just hit me that I really care for him. It does not matter that he is shorter than I am or that he does not have a thick head of hair or even that he is fighting his gambling addiction. He is such a dear, dear man. He is sweet and treats me with such respect and affection. Isn't he special? He likes me just the way I am. I want to come back soon, Kathleen. Will we?"

"Of course, we will. Well, I hope so," Kathleen said.

"Don't you dare let that little Tiff or Aunt Paige discourage you. Do you hear me?"

"Yes. I hear you. Well, I guess I will get myself ready for bed too. Good night, Lucy," Kathleen said with a big grin.

Tuesday morning, the women packed to go back to Indiana. The week had flown by. Maxim and Miriam helped the driver bring down the women's suitcases. Walt pulled Kathleen out to the patio for a few minutes' privacy.

"Kathleen, please think hard about it. Will you marry me? I love you." He held her close. She leaned back and looked into his eyes.

"Walt, I love you. Marriage is such a commitment and I do not take it lightly. I guess. We have known each other for such a short time and have not spent that much time together. I have always advised women to wait until they really know a man before making such a commitment. However, I will think about it and let you know as soon as I can. Is that good enough for now?"

"I will take whatever I can get, my girl," he said and kissed her passionately as he held her head in his hands. They pulled away from one another when they heard the doorknob turning. Shorty put his head in the door and turned to see them. "Excuse me. The car is packed."

The brothers accompanied the women to the airport. They went on board with them to get them settled, then after their good-byes, walked out and down the steps. As the plane began to taxi, Walt waved at her and she waved back with tears running down her face.

When Kathleen arrived back home, she called Walt and told him it had been a good, safe trip. She thanked him again for the wonderful week in Dallas and the transportation. He told her that he missed her already. They talked about her coming back for Christmas and bringing her friends. She told him that Bernice had already said she would be staying home with her family. Wild horses could not keep Lucille away.

The following day, the phone rang, and when Kathleen answered, she was surprised to hear Tiffany on the other end. "Kathleen, dear. I wanted to check and see that you made it home safely. We did not get to shop for new clothes for you while you were here. That is a shame. If there is a next time, maybe then. Did I tell you that Walt invited Aunt Paige to the Thanksgiving Ball? They make such a cute couple. I understand she saw you at church. I told her you weren't what I expected and she said you weren't what she expected either."

"Thanks for your concern, Tiffany. We got home just fine. How are you feeling? Oh, yes, I met your aunt Paige after church. We really did not get to visit and get acquainted. But Bernice and Lucille enjoyed their visit with her, they said."

"Aunt Paige and Delia were best friends after my aunt moved to Dallas a few years ago. They had so much in common. I am sure Delia is looking down from heaven, hoping that Walt will marry her best friend now that she is gone. Well, have to go. Bye for now," and she hung up.

Kathleen did not get a chance to say, "Good-bye or even kiss my grits, little girl." She tried not to seethe. She fixed herself a cup of tea and sat down to think through the situation. If she married Walt, would she have to listen to Tiffany belittle her for the rest of her life or compare her to Delia and Paige? She did not need that. She did not want that. She could straighten Tiffany out, but what about the fallout? In addition, the girl was pregnant, so this would not be a good time.

She called Bernice and asked if she could come out for a while. Of course, the answer was yes. When she pulled up in front of Bernice's house, she saw her out at the fence, watching Bethany feed the horses. Bethany saw her and yelled, "Hey, Aunt Kathleen." Her mother turned and headed toward Kathleen and waved. Kathleen waved to both of them. They hugged, and Bernice put her arm through her friend's arm and walked her around to the back steps.

"What is going on? You look terrible. Spill the beans, Katie."

"Guess who called me this morning?"

"Walt? That would be my guess, but I would think that would put a smile on your face."

"No. His daughter-in-law, Tiffany. You remember Tiff? She was sorry we had not had time to go shopping because I sure need her help. Walt invited Aunt Paige to the Thanksgiving Ball and I was not what Paige expected when she saw me at church either. Apparently, I looked a lot worse. In addition, Delia is looking down from heaven, expecting Walt to ask Paige to marry him, since she was Delia's best friend. Can you believe that girl? Am I going to be able to deal with her?"

"Don't pay any attention to that little sniveling, simpering Ms. Dallas. You know she is lying. Walt would not invite Paige to walk across the street with him. You looked great in Dallas. You are not looking so good today. You are letting her get to you. Shorty told you she was a menace. Tiff the trouble maker, the menace. You know that Walt loves only you and wants to marry you. I really doubt that Delia would want Walt to marry Paige. I doubt that Delia and Paige were ever best friends. From what we have heard about Delia, she would not put up with such bad behavior in a friend. I also wonder about the relationship Delia and Tiffany had. Chill out, as the kids say," Bernice coached.

"I know I am being silly. I do not think I can deal with Tiffany. She is pregnant, so it is not the time to confront her. She can cause a lot of trouble for Walt and upset the family dynamics. You know that. I am not jealous of Paige, am I? I called Lucille and she is coming over too. I need both of my best friends for this pity party."

Bernice looked out the window and said, "And here she is. Come in, come in. How are you doing?"

Lucille walked in when she heard Bernice say to come in. She hugged both of her friends. "What's going on, girlfriends? Katie, you look awful today. Did your dandelions die in your front yard or what?"

Kathleen told her about Tiffany's phone call. Lucille echoed what Bernice had said. "You have nothing to worry about with Walt. He loves you and does not want anything to do with Paige. You know he did not invite her to a ball. He'd rather beat himself with a ball bat." They laughed.

"I am upset because Tiffany is a troublemaker. She wants Walt to marry her aunt Paige. I am not classy enough to be her new mother-in-law. She will not give up. I cannot say anything to Walt. It will just cause him distress and I will look like a whiner," Kathleen said.

"Honey, he runs a billion-dollar business. I think he can deal with a little family duress. Let me talk to him. No, let me talk to Tiff," said Lucille. "She needs a little encouragement to become a lady. I would love to take her under my wing and straighten her out. She is a little thing, but she has no manners. She acts as if she is still a junior in high school and is a valley girl. I know how to deal with those little snooty things. I've done it before and I can do it again."

"No, Lucille, you are too eager. Before I retired, I would not hesitate to work with someone like this and help him or her become a better person. It is different when it is family or could-be family. Maybe I need to confront her and help her become more Christ-like. However, she may be right about me. Maybe I am not the one for Walter Alexander. I cannot believe I am such a marshmallow about this. This is not who I am. You have seen me stand up against wrong before, against mean-spirited people, and bullies."

"Yes, I've seen you stand up against evil and meanness. It is different when it is about you, when it is personal. Do you think you do not deserve respect? Money has nothing to do with it. You know Walt would have a fit if he knew any of his children disrespected you. Just because Tiffany has some money, is skinny and cute and dresses to kill, and won a beauty contest does not mean she is better than anyone else is. Let me call Walt and have a chat, okay?" said Lucille.

"No. I need to take care of this myself. If Tiffany is going to respect me, I need to talk to her. Next time I go, if I go, I'll sit her down for a talk," Kathleen said.

"What do you mean—if you go? We are going for Christmas and don't you forget it," Lucille said. "You don't want to cheat me out of another trip on that airplane, do you?"

The three of them sat eating Bernice's famous date cookies and drinking hot tea. Bernice talked about her kids and horses. They made plans to go to Indianapolis the following week for some Christmas shopping and to go see a play. After an overnight stay, they would enjoy walking in the snow around Monument Circle in the middle of town. This was an annual trip for Bernice and Kathleen since they were in college, and then Lucille had joined them. Traditions were wonderful. It was nice to have special events to look forward to throughout the year, especially with best friends.

Walt continued to call Kathleen daily. She had yet to accept his proposal. She kept putting him off, unable to make a decision.

When she told him she was not sure she could come out for Christmas, she felt guilty for hurting his feelings. It was just such a big decision to make. She could not try marriage, and if it did not work out, back out. It was forever or not at all. Lucille tried to convince her that they needed to go.

"Don't you dare let that skinny little snob get the better of you. Pregnant or not, she cannot continue to get away with being Miss Meanness of 2012. Hey, I want to see Shorty. I have been looking forward to this trip. Does that encourage you at all?"

"Oh, Lucille, you do know how to put on the pressure. Let me pray about it some more and I'll make a decision soon."

Kathleen spent the next few days reading her Bible, praying, and contemplating what God had planned for her. She did not go out of her home for a couple of days. She thought that maybe she would get a cat or a dog to keep her company. She listened to Beethoven, Mozart, and Sandi Patty, all the while worrying about the decision she had before her. She could not keep Walt dangling with no answer from her. "After all, Paige was waiting in the wings to grab him," she thought with a grimace. She was lying on the couch unable to make a decision.

Chapter 12

Her doorbell rang. She thought it must be Lucille trying to push her to make a decision about the trip. She opened the door and the snow was blowing in her face. She looked down and started to say, "Come in, Lucille," when she saw men's boots on her porch. She looked up the pant legs and up to the face. Her mouth dropped open. "Come in, Walt," she said with a shaky voice. She stepped back, and he came inside, pulling the storm door closed. She took his coat, and he bent down to pull off his boots and put them in the boot tray by her front door. "What are you doing here? What a surprise."

"Well, first may I kiss you hello?" He did. "I was very concerned about your indecision to come out for Christmas. I hoped that we could talk and you could tell me what is really bothering you. I was really hopeful that you would decide to say yes to my proposal."

"Come in and sit down. Can I get you something to drink? Coffee or tea?"

"No, I need answers, not coffee. I am concerned. I thought you loved me. Dear, please be honest with me." He sat down on one end of the couch and looked around her living room. "Nice home, Kathleen. It looks like you. It is cozy, warm, and pretty."

"Thank you. I am comfortable here. Walt, I really cannot give you an answer about why I am so afraid to say yes. I wish I could tell you."

"Well, let me tell you. Last night, Shorty told me about a phone call he overheard between Tiffany and you. She called from my study and he heard her end of the conversation. He debated whether to tell me because he knew it would cause a problem between Tiffany and Ned and me. However, when he saw that you might back out of our relationship and your trip at Christmas, he told me. I could not believe the bad manners she exhibited. Shorty said she had been equally rude to you in November behind my back. I went to their home and sat down with them. Tiffany loved Delia very much. She wanted to be like her, but Tiffany has not grown up enough to be like Delia. She tried to copy her. Delia was as you are, kind, generous, thoughtful, and forgiving. You do not want to say or do anything to hurt others. You do not judge people by how they look or what they own. I respect that very much in you. But this is not fair."

"Oh, Walt, I didn't want to interfere in your family and cause problems for you." Kathleen continued to look from Walt's face to her lap.

"Tiffany at first tried to deny she had called you. She said we could look at their phone bill. I said someone heard her using my phone and she remembered that she had called you to be sure you made it home safely. I told her what I knew she had said. Ned was furious, of course. I told her that she knew I had not invited her aunt Paige to go anywhere. I told her that she knew I loved you and I think you are beautiful just as you are. I told her she owes you an apology and she needs to get off her high horse if she wants to be welcome to our home. Ned told his wife that he could take her to a Texas manners class. Ned said, 'Tiff, I love you, but I don't like the way you treat people. You are beautiful on the outside, but when you treat others badly, it is ugly. I want our child to have a kind mother who is not judging others, especially family members. In addition, if we have a boy, you will know how to deal with him. Not everything is about fashion and ostentatious snobbery. Tiffany, I love you, but at times I don't like you.'"

"Oh, my, that must have hurt her feelings." Kathleen was surprised that the truth had emerged without her saying anything.

"It was an intervention that had to happen. We have hope that this will make a difference and she will change and become a nicer girl. Quite honestly, I think she needs you to help her become a kinder, gentler woman and a good mother. Delia just got too weak and tired to work with her the last few months before she died. She told me that Tiffany was her own worst enemy and hoped that someone else would be able to help her."

"Me? I have never been a mother. I am not a Dallas woman."

"No. However, you are a kind, gentle, Christian woman that most young women respect and would want to emulate. If Tiffany does not change, she is going to be a miserable woman all her life and could ruin any children she and Ned have. I need you and want you in my life for the time we have left. Not because of what I think you can do to help my family, but because I love you and miss you too much when we are apart." Walt stood up, stretched, and rubbed his knees. He grabbed a pillow and put it on the floor beside Kathleen. He slowly got on one knee and looked into her eyes. Again, her mouth was hanging open in disbelief that Walt was really in her living room.

"Kathleen Keller, I love you and want you to be my wife. Will you marry me?" He pulled a little white box out of his jacket pocket. It was stuck and he had to twist his hand to get it out. He succeeded and opened the box. Inside was a diamond solitaire that shone. It was not ostentatious; it was just the right size diamond for Kathleen's finger. Her hands were beautiful for a woman her age. Her niece had told her they were gorgeous hands with slim fingers because she played the piano and they got exercise. She was not sure about that. At this point, it did not matter. Walt had a ring for her finger. Walt pulled the ring from the box and looked into her eyes.

Kathleen's hand went to her mouth and she inhaled, "Oh, Walt. It is beautiful. Yes. I will marry you. I cannot believe you showed up on my doorstep. However, I am so glad you did. I have so wanted to say yes since you first asked me, but I did not want to be a thorn in your side with your family. I see now that you indeed are in charge, as it should be. You protect and care for each one of them. You have insight that every man should have for his family. You are what I have been waiting for. I have waited forty years for you. Yes, yes. I can't believe…" He slipped the ring on her finger, struggled up off his arthritic knee, and pulled her up with him.

He put a gentle index finger to her lips and whispered, "Shhh," and kissed her passionately. "Oh, at last you said yes. I was not dreaming, was I? You did say yes you would marry me, didn't you?" he said and chuckled.

"Yes, my dear Walter. I said yes. In addition, I will come to your home for Christmas. Lucille has been twisting my arm for weeks now. She will be glad. She and Shorty have been communicating, and I think she is falling for him. She wants to spend Christmas with him. But it couldn't be as much as I want to spend Christmas with you."

Just then, the doorbell rang. "Who can that be?" she said. She stepped back out of Walt's arms and went to the front door.

"Well, I saw that car in your driveway and hesitated to come to the door. You have company. That is a rental car, isn't it? You didn't tell me you had company coming," Lucille said breathlessly.

"Come in, Lucille. You are letting all the cold weather inside," she said as she shut the door behind her friend. "Look who is here. See who my company is?"

Lucille saw Walt, scurried to him, hugged him, and said, "Oh, Walt, you are amazing. I have been praying that you would get up here and help Kathleen make up her mind finally. You are, as they say, 'a sight for sore eyes.' Have you convinced her yet?"

Kathleen held out her left hand and let Lucille see the beautiful engagement ring on her finger. "Oh my goodness. That is beautiful. I told you he did not want Paige what's-her-name. He wants you," and she laughed giddily.

"For heaven's sake, Lucille. I knew he did not want Paige. You are embarrassing me."

Walt laughed aloud. "Well, ladies, when do you want the plane to pick you up for Christmas? The sooner the better, as far as I am concerned. How long can you stay this time?"

Lucille said, "Honey, I am going out to your kitchen to put on a pot of coffee. Do you have any muffins in your freezer? I will look and warm them up. We need to celebrate, and you two need to stay in here and decide when the big day will be." She scurried out of the living room and waved her hand at them as she went through the door.

Walt pulled his intended over to the couch and they sat down together. "She has a point. We need to decide when, where, and how we are going to have this wedding. This long-distance relationship is hard on us. Time flies, and at our age, we don't need to be wasting time, do we?"

"No, we don't, dear. What are you suggesting?"

"Well, I think the first of the year would be good. I do not want to rip you away from where you have lived your entire life. Do you want to keep your home here, and we can stay here when we come back to visit family and friends? We can spend most of our time in Dallas, since I am still working. What are you thinking?"

"Most of my thinking lately has been about my answer. I need a little more time to think about plans for the future. By Christmas, we should have our thoughts together."

They heard Lucille calling from the kitchen, "Kiddos, the coffee is ready."

Chapter 13

As the plane landed at the Dallas airport, Kathleen and Lucille were looking out the window searching for Walt and Shorty.

"There they are," shouted Lucille. She waved, and Kathleen told her they probably could not see her, even though they were waving at the plane. They unhooked their seat belts and stood up. They stretched and moved around to loosen the muscles and joints. The steward opened the plane door and the steps came into place. The friends gathered their bags and special gifts they had carried on. When they got to the door, the brothers stepped in to greet them. The girls dropped their armloads of bags so they could hug the men. Kathleen walked into Walt's arms, he kissed her, and Shorty hugged Lucille. The driver stood back waiting to help with their bags.

On the drive to the house, the women chattered about the trip. Kathleen told about the terrible snowstorm in Indiana. If the snowplow had not come through when it did, the car would not have been able to pick them up.

Lucille looked at Shorty and said, "Albert, you look different. What have you done to yourself?" Kathleen and Walt looked at one another and silently mouthed, "Albert?"

Shorty said, "I've been working out, lost some weight, and have a new attitude. Lucy, you like?" He grinned at Lucille.

"I like. You even looked taller when I saw you next to your brother."

"Well," he held up his foot and they all looked at his new cowboy boots with a higher heel. "Whatever it takes to improve my image, Lucy."

Lucille took his hand and held it. "You are full of surprises, aren't you, Albie? You Alexander brothers are something else." Kathleen decided that Lucy and Albie must have been having some long-distance conversations of some depth lately. No wonder she wanted to come here for Christmas.

When they arrived at the house, it was getting dark because they had stopped for dinner. Miriam had turned on the Christmas lights, and the house was beautiful with all the white lights on the trees and in the windows. Kathleen inhaled and was oohing and aahing because it was breathtaking. "Walt, it is beautiful."

"I hoped you would like it. It is easier for us to decorate outside here than back in Indiana. I think you may get more snow than we do." He helped her out of the car and the other two followed them. The driver got the bags out of the trunk and followed them in. Kathleen noticed how beautiful the living room was. The Christmas tree was almost as tall as the ceiling, which was two stories high. Miriam had put out the cranberry red throws, candles, and pillows. The fireplace was crackling and it looked like a magazine cover. Shorty took the women's coats and hung them in the guest closet at the front door. Walt escorted Kathleen and Lucille up to their rooms and left them to get unpacked. Kathleen looked around the beautiful room and noticed a lump of fur in the chair by the window. "Maggie, there you are." The cat jumped out of the chair, went over, and rubbed against her legs. She jumped up on the bed, walked in a circle, and plopped down beside the fluffy pillows. Kathleen sat on the bed and Maggie purred when she stroked her back.

Lucille called her niece Lucinda to tell her she had arrived safely. She also called Bernice, whose family was glad she had not gone to Texas. She said to tell everyone there Merry Christmas. When the women unpacked and freshened up, they met in the hallway outside their rooms. They linked arms and headed down the stairs. The brothers were waiting in the living room with spiced cider, cheese, and crackers for the women. "It is so good to have you both here again. Sorry Bernice could not be with us, but I know her children would miss her for Christmas. Have a seat, ladies," Walt said.

They relaxed, and Walt noticed that Maggie had followed the women down and she was curled up next to his fiancee. Kathleen pulled her feet up under her and covered them and the cat with one of the throws. When the women started to yawn, Shorty decided it was time for him to go home, but he would be back to have breakfast with them. The day after tomorrow, all of the family would be in early for Christmas Day. Ned and Tiffany would come the night before and stay in the room Bernice had on the last visit. The other two young families would be coming in from home in the morning. The children needed to be in their own beds for Santa's visit.

Next morning, when the girls came downstairs for breakfast, Shorty stood in the kitchen chatting with Maxim. When he heard Lucille laugh, he came out to the dining room and gave her a hug. "You look wonderful this morning, Lucy. You do too, Katie. Did you sleep well? You both look rested." They agreed that it had been a restful night. They slept well.

Walt came into the dining room and smiled at his loving fiancée. He gave her a hug and a kiss on the cheek. "You do look lovely. I am so glad you are here."

"Me too, Walter. Me too," she answered with a smile as she put her hand in his.

Later in the day, the women were putting their Christmas gifts under the big tree in the living room. "Just look at the wrapping on these gifts," said Lucille. "He obviously doesn't wrap his own. These are professionally gift-wrapped. Here is one with your name on it, one for Shorty, and here is one with my name on it."

"Lucille, quit rifling through the gifts. You are like a kid the day before Christmas."

Lucille grinned at her and said, "I feel like a kid. Isn't this just too perfect—the decorations, the meals prepared, the gifts under the tree, and the men?"

Miriam came in and asked them if they would like to have a cup of coffee or tea and a few Christmas cookies. They said it sounded wonderful and they would like tea. Before long, she brought in a tray for them in front of the fireplace. On a little plate, there were gingerbread men, Christmas trees beautifully decorated, and filled date cookies. "Thank you, Miriam, those look delicious. Did Maxim make those?" said Kathleen. The housekeeper grinned and nodded yes.

"He is amazing. The little gingerbread men are so tasty. Enjoy." Miriam told the truth. All the cookies were scrumptious.

"This is strange to know that Christmas is tomorrow and we don't have to get any food ready. I do not have to clean house or drive to Adrienne's house. Lucille, will I be able to get used to this?"

"Are you kidding? Of course, you can get used to it. You will be able to read more, do some writing, and you can start gardening again. You will find things to do. You will probably do some traveling with Walt."

"I wonder why I am worried about it. Just being with Walt will bring me more joy than I have had in a while. Maybe I will learn how to ride one of the horses. Bernice always tried to get me on old Brownie at her house. I could surprise her next time she visits. How about a game of rummy?" They spent a leisurely afternoon in the TV room with cards and tea.

On Christmas Eve, Shorty had invited Lucille to his house for dinner, just the two of them alone. Shorty had prepared the meal himself and that impressed Lucille. They worked together to clean up after the meal and load the dishwasher. Shorty put a couple of logs on the fire while Lucille brought in their coffee and dessert to the living room. They snuggled on the couch together, and finally, Shorty got up enough nerve to say, "Lucy, I haven't been an upstanding citizen my entire life. However, Jesus has made a change in my life recently. I once said to you that I am not a marrying man. That has changed. I am not any kind of great catch. However, I have fallen in love for the first time in my life. I love you and would consider it a real honor if you would marry me." He reached into the drawer in the coffee table and pulled out a white box.

"Albert, I am so surprised. I had no idea…I really like you. I think I love you, Albie. You know I have been single my entire life. I have had hundreds of children that I taught. I did not think I would ever find someone I wanted to marry. I want to say yes, but I am afraid to make a quick decision. Let me see that ring," she said with a giggle. The ring had a yellow gold band with three diamonds arranged in a curved design.

"Oh, it is beautiful. Still, I have to think about it. Can you wait just a little bit to get my answer?" She handed it back to him and held both of his hands in hers. "I thought it ought to be a no-brainer, as the kids would say, for Kathleen to marry Walt, but I see what a big life-time decision this really is." She grabbed his shoulders and hugged him.

"Lucy, I will wait. Let us just not wait too long. The old clock is ticking. I will not pressure you, but I love you more than you can imagine. In addition, one of your best friends would be living next door. That is a plus. I'll try to be patient, okay?" They settled down and put their feet up on the coffee table to enjoy the fire and the Christmas lights.

Early Christmas morning, Kathleen awoke to a light knocking on her bedroom door. "Come in," she called. Walt walked in with a small tray topped with a cup of hot chocolate with whipped cream standing up out of the Christmas mug. Next to it, he had put a small gingerbread muffin. He set the tray down beside her bed, went to the window, and opened the curtains.

"Look, honey. I brought you some snow for our first Christmas together," he said lovingly and grinned at her. "Okay,

I had nothing to do with the snow, but it is our first Christmas together. There is snow, which will be gone by noon. So have your hot chocolate, enjoy the snow quickly, and get ready for a big day with the family. Merry Christmas, my darling." He kissed her and left the room.

"Merry Christmas," she finally said as he closed the door. She thought, *That man is one of a kind. This will be the best Christmas I have had in a long, long time.* She had her beverage and muffin before going to the shower. She stepped out of her room, looking very festive in her hunter green dress with hunter green and cranberry long scarf draped around her neck. She knocked on Lucille's door and walked in when she heard the invitation to enter.

"Merry Christmas!" they both said. "Let's call Bernice and wish her the same," Kathleen said. They called their missing vacation friend, and when they were ending the conversation, Lucille said, "Girlfriend, you are gorgeous in that outfit. Walt is going to drool."

"For heaven's sake, Lucille. You are embarrassing me. You look very festive yourself. Albie is going to love your silver sweater."

"By the way, your husband-to-be brought me a mug of hot chocolate to start my day. It will be an exciting day to open our own gifts. He is such a thoughtful guy." They walked down the stairs and everyone called out Merry Christmas to one another.

Tiffany and Ned came into the dining room after the others had begun eating. They all greeted one another with a Merry Christmas.

Kathleen said, "Tiffany, you are glowing. Being pregnant looks good on you." She smiled at the young woman. Tiffany thanked her and patted her belly. Everyone seemed surprised that she did not have an answer.

After breakfast, they put on their coats and went for a walk in the light covering of snow. Walt told them if they waited too long, it would melt. They checked out the horses, and Walt gave his driver/stableman an envelope and wished him a Merry Christmas.

Before noon, the two young families with rambunctious children arrived. Little Crystal ran over to Kathleen begging to be picked up.

"She remembers me," Kathleen said with excitement, and she picked up the little blonde angel. Crystal patted Kathleen's cheek and said, "Grandma." Everyone applauded the little girl for her welcome to Grandpa's intended. Jane hugged Kathleen's legs.

Nancy gave her a hug and said, "Welcome to this noisy family, Kathleen. We are glad you are here for your first Christmas with Dad and all of us." She turned to Lucille and said, "And welcome to you also, Lucille. We are glad you are here." Nancy took Lucille's left hand unobtrusively, pulled it up, and looked at it, and said, "Hmmm."

Lucille whispered, "Nancy, you know something. Did Albert tell you about the ring?" Nancy nodded yes. "He asked me to marry him last night, but it surprised me. I asked for a little time to make a decision. Don't tell anyone else, okay?"

"Your secret is safe with me, Lucy," Nancy said with a wink and a smile. "But don't make ole' Shorty wait too long." Lucille nodded yes. They all visited and listened to the children tell what Santa had put under their trees. When the older children started touching the gifts under the tree looking for ones with their names on it, Grandpa Walt said, "We can't make these children wait any longer. Everyone find a seat and let us allow Ned to play Santa's helper." Shorty took Lucille over to a loveseat next to the fireplace and they sat down together. Tiffany sat on a footstool next to the tree and watched her husband hand out gift after gift. He made sure that all the children had their gifts from Grandpa before he gave any adult a gift. *He is thoughtful, just like his dad is,* Kathleen thought. The children were thrilled with their gifts and the older ones remembered to thank Grandpa. The little ones observed and did the same. The children opened gifts from Kathleen. Each one had a handmade hat with a matching scarf and a book. Crystal's hat had snowmen for the earflaps. Each hat had a different look to fit each child. They modeled their hats, kept them on as the older ones sat in front of the welcoming fire in the fireplace to read their books.

Ned started handing a gift to each of the ladies in the room. Kathleen watched until Ned handed Tiffany her gift. Tiffany looked at the gift card and read Kathleen's name. She looked up at her future mother-in-law, and her face turned red. "Oh, how nice, Kathleen." She slowly opened the box and pulled back the tissue paper.

She said, "Look, Ned." She held up a beautiful baby baptismal dress in white. It had lace and tiny white bows. She held up a matching hat. Under the dress, she discovered a lacy crocheted baby blanket.

Ned said, "Isn't that beautiful. Kathleen, did you make that for our baby?" Tiffany felt the softness of the little blanket.

"Yes, I made them with love for your little one," she said. Walt took her hand and kissed it. The adults, especially the women, were admiring the baby things.

Tiffany said, "My, my, you made it? Wow. I have already ordered a set from Ireland for our little one." She put it back in the box and replaced the lid.

Before she could continue, Ned interrupted her and said, "Kathleen, it is gorgeous and we will use it. Tiffany, I need to see you in the TV room." He gently took her elbow, lifted her up, and guided her out of the room as she clutched the gift box to her belly.

Nicholas said, "Well, let me be Santa's second helper." He continued handing out the gifts.

Walt said, "Kathleen, that is a beautiful, thoughtful gift. Thank you. I see we still have some work to do." He nodded toward the TV room. Nicholas handed his dad the gift that she had put under the tree for her fiancé. He looked at the gift tag and saw her name. He smiled at her. He began to open it slowly as she watched. When he got to the top of the box, he stopped and smiled at her. He lifted the lid up and pulled back the red and white tissue paper. He held up a beautiful cashmere neck scarf with his initials embroidered tastefully in one corner. "Kathleen, this is a handsome scarf and it will keep me warm in the winter." As he pulled it out, he noticed something else wrapped in white tissue paper under the scarf. He removed the wrapping and saw his beautiful girl in a silver frame. She had let Bernice take her picture in the dress she had worn on his second night in Sarasota. Her hands were under her chin with her engagement ring showing. She had had her hair done and a makeup job as well as a manicure. "Wow," he said. "How did I get so lucky? You are a stunner. This is just the right size for traveling. But I hope that after we are married, you will always travel with me." He kissed her and thanked her again.

As Kathleen opened her gift, Tiffany and Ned came back in the room. Obviously, Tiff had been crying because her eyes were red. She went over to Kathleen and scooted little Jane over so she could sit next to Kathleen. Without looking up at her, she said, "Kathleen, I am sorry. It was very unkind of me. I have been a snob and rude to you. I want to do better and want you to feel welcome in our family. I promise to try harder, and Ned said that you have permission to correct me when I am wrong."

Kathleen took her hands and said, "Tiffany, thank you. I accept your apology. I want you to know that if you want to use a different baptismal gown for your baby, that is fine with me. I should have asked before I made it to see if you had one picked out. If your first baby already has a baptismal set, you could save the one I made for the second or third child. It is okay. You do not have to use it at all, if you have something else in mind. If this baby is a boy, the set I made might be too feminine."

"Oh, no. This one is a girl. I feel it in my bones. We will be getting a test soon, and I'll let you all know that we are having a little Delia Adams Alexander."

Nancy and Carla both laughed and said, "Good luck, Tiff."

The rest of the day went well. Dinner was a masterpiece, and Walt asked Miriam to bring Maxim out before dessert. "Miriam and Maxim, you have been with us almost twenty years. We love you like family. Maxim, we enjoyed the Christmas dinner as usual. This year, we decided not to buy you gifts."

Miriam had a strange look on her face. "Mr. Alexander, have we displeased you in some way?"

"Oh no, my dear. We decided not to buy you a gift that had to be wrapped up in a box." He stood up. "We are giving you an envelope. In this envelope is our gift. Please open it." He handed the envelope to Maxim who opened it, looked at it, and handed it to his wife.

"Two tickets to see our family in Vermont. We leave on December 30 and return January 14. Oh, this is too wonderful. But what will you do without us, sir?" She and Maxim hugged one another.

"Well, these two ladies are staying with me and have agreed that we will hire a cook while you are gone just for those two weeks, mind you. That will give us time to make plans for the wedding." The entire family applauded their beloved staff as Maxim and Miriam both shook hands with their boss.

Miriam sidled over toward Kathleen and said, "Ms. Kathleen, we are glad to hear that you and Mr. Walter are getting married. We like you very much."

"Thank you, Miriam. I am glad that he has had the two of you to take care of him all these years. You too, Maxim. In addition, I like both of you very much. I look forward to your meals and care."

The chef and his wife went back in the kitchen, and the family could hear her squealing in delight at the gift they had received. Taffy pushed through the swinging door from the kitchen to escape the squealing Miriam and headed over to the table, hoping someone had dropped a tidbit on the floor. Rick's hand went from his plate down to his side, and Taffy hurried over to get the piece of roast beef secretly offered to her. Kathleen met Rick's eye and winked at him. They had a secret now. Walt noticed the look between them and pretended not to notice the look of love Rick had for his soon-to-be grandma.

They filled the afternoon with toys and games, naps, football games, and Christmas carols sung by all. Kathleen sat down at the grand piano in the corner and began to play the Christmas songs beautifully. Walt exclaimed that he had no idea she could play the piano. Kathleen and Lucille could not remember enjoying a family Christmas Day this much in a long time. Walt thought the same. It had been a few years since his house had been this full of fun and love. Since Delia's death, it had been a challenge for him to pretend that all was well when the children and grandchildren were there. It had not been the same. However, having Kathleen here made all the difference and it felt wonderful. He felt a new chapter beginning in his life.

The children and their families were preparing to go home after the buffet supper. The gifts were organized, and the men carried them out to their vehicles. They came back in to say good-bye, Merry Christmas, and thank you while gathering their children. They carried the sleeping youngsters out and fastened them into their car seats. They gave final hugs, and suddenly, the house was quiet. Shorty and Lucille went to the TV room for their favorite game of canasta. Walt and Kathleen sat down in front of the fireplace after they had gathered up the last of the gift-wrap and ribbons. Maggie, the cat, finally came out of hiding and went for a long piece of ribbon. Walt took it away from her before she could eat it. She swished her tail in protest, walked over, and jumped up in Kathleen's lap.

"There you are, pretty thing," she said as she petted the furry old cat. Taffy came in from the kitchen after having been outside and plopped down in front of the fireplace. They felt so comfortable. Walt went to his study, came back with a new ivory leather notebook, and handed it to Kathleen.

"This is for our wedding plans," he said. She opened the front cover and in beautiful calligraphy, it had "Wedding of Walter and Kathleen Alexander" and a space on the last line for the date.

"This is very nice. Who printed our names? We will have to get him or her to put the date in later."

"That would be Nancy. She is very artistic. Calligraphy is just one of the sidelines she picked up in high school. She is good. When we go to her house, you will see the beautiful paintings she has done. The one in my office of the skyline is one of Nancy's. That little picture of Maggie on the bed that she gave you today surprised me. She does not give her work to just anyone. She made an exception with you. I am glad you showed so much appreciation. She is somewhat self-conscious about her work."

"It is a beautiful piece. I felt her telling me that Maggie would be my cat now. In addition, it looks like my hand petting her, doesn't it. I am really touched."

Walt pulled a small calendar out of his shirt pocket and said, "Let's pick a date. Do you have to go home before we tie the knot? We could get married, and then I could go back with you and help you pack up what you need out here. We would have an opportunity for me to meet your other friends and see your family again. Actually, I would like to fly your sister and her family out for the wedding. Is there anyone else you want to invite from Indiana? We can get them here with no problem."

Kathleen looked at him and bent her head sideways in thought, "That would be wonderful. I hope they can all come. I want Bernice here, of course. Bethany and her children are like family also. However, the kids will be in school. We need to wait until Miriam and Maxim get back from their trip. So that means maybe January 20, Saturday afternoon?"

"That looks good. We can send the plane back for Bernice and any of your family who can come. I look forward to meeting your sister and her family."

"I know they want to meet you also. How many can we bring on the plane? I imagine Bernice's daughter Bethany would like to come. Her husband will stay home and take care of the children. Where will we get married? I want it to be in a church. We need to talk to your pastor tomorrow. I hope he is available for the twentieth."

After more discussion and note taking, she put down the notebook and pen. "Enough for tonight. Let's join Lucille and Albert." Just then, the two of them walked out into the living room. Shorty said he felt very tired and needed to head home. Lucille walked him to the door and then she headed up to her room.

Chapter 14

Several days later, Walt took the two women out for lunch, and Shorty, who looked tired, met them. Lucille asked him if Walt worked him too hard.

"No," he chuckled. "Guess I need to take a day or two off, Buddy. What do you think?"

"From the look on your face, I think you are right. Maybe you need to take the rest of the week off. See your doctor for a checkup. This is not a busy week. Even if it were, take the rest of the week off. In fact, go home with the ladies after lunch. Get some rest and make that appointment with Dr. Benson."

Following lunch, the ladies took Shorty back to his house, and Lucille decided to stay with him. She made sure he called for a doctor appointment the next day. The driver took Kathleen back to Walt's house. She let Maxim know that Shorty would be down for dinner with them. She went to her room to read a book she had pulled off the library shelves. She fell asleep on the bed while she read one of Delia's books. Sometime later, she heard a knock on her door. Walt opened her door and walked in. He sat down next to her on the bed and asked if she felt all right.

"Yes. I just got drowsy with the book and the quiet house. When did you get home?"

"About ten minutes ago. Do you want to come downstairs and have a cup of tea with me?"

"I would love that. How did the rest of your day go? Did you get everything done so you can have the day off tomorrow?"

"Yes, I did. It will be a restful day for us." Kathleen put her book aside, sat up, and slipped into her shoes. They walked down the stairs together. Miriam put a tray of tea and cookies on the coffee table for them. He thanked her.

"Miriam, how is the packing coming along? Will you and Maxim be ready to leave on time?" She assured him that they would be ready and were looking forward to the trip. Their families were excited about the visit as well.

Later in the day, Shorty and Lucille came in the front door. He looked a little better, but the others thought he still looked pale. They sat down and Kathleen went to the kitchen to ask for another pot of tea. Lucille asked how the wedding plans were progressing.

"We have the date set, the church and pastor, and the place for the reception dinner. It is going to be a small wedding party with you two, Bernice, and Frank who is Walt's best friend since college."

"I am honored that you have asked me to be a maid of honor. An old maid of honor," Lucille said and laughed.

"Well, if you would say yes to me, you would be a matron, not an old maid. And if anyone does not look like an old maid, it is the two of you ladies." Walt agreed with him.

"Lucille, I hope you will say yes to my brother. He has become such a better man in the past few months and he deserves someone good in his life. You have been good for him."

"You can say that again. Lucy, you are the best."

"Are you two trying to wear me down? I really am thinking hard about this decision," Lucille said as she got up, walked to the Christmas tree, and examined an ornament. "I am working on it." She kept her back turned.

"Dinner is served," Miriam said from the doorway. The two couples headed into the dining room and sat down to a light supper. Following supper, they decided to play a game in the TV room. After just an hour, Shorty decided he needed to go home. "I wonder if I am getting the flu. I just don't feel my old self."

Walt suggested that he stay in the extra room upstairs in case he was ill. "That sounds like a wonderful idea," Lucille added. "I can look in on you and take care of you, Albert."

"With that offer, I think I will. Do you still have the extra pajamas in the bottom drawer, Buddy?"

"Yes. Get into bed and let Lucille take your temperature and tuck you in. You know where everything is. There are new toothbrushes in the cabinet beside the mirror." Shorty stood up, pushed his chair in under the table, and walked out of the room to prepare for bed. The three remaining at the table were concerned about him.

"He has his doctor appointment at ten o'clock in the morning. I want to go with him. I'll go get clean clothes from his house in the morning and get him there," Lucille said. Walt suggested that instead, he would go down to the house right now and get what he would need to clean up the next morning. He stood up and went to the front closet, grabbed his coat, and went to the garage for the Jeep.

When he returned with clean clothes and a bag, he took it up to Shorty's room. Lucille fussed around his room, got him a glass of water, took his temperature, and adjusted the curtains. Walt hung up the clothes and put the bag on the floor of the walk-in closet.

"All this attention is sure spoiling me. Is this what it would be like to be married to this beautiful woman? I like it. Here," he handed the thermometer to her, "tell me what it is. Do I have a fever?" She took it and read it.

"No, you don't have a fever. What else do you need, my dear?"

"Well, how about reading from the New Testament to me? I like having you next to me. Even when I feel better tomorrow, I may not tell you. I want you to keep pampering me."

Lucille pulled up a chair next to the bed and picked up the Bible from the nightstand. Walt and Kathleen told them good night and went back downstairs.

"I am tempted to go along with him to the doctor with Lucille tomorrow. Maybe we all could go along."

Kathleen agreed that it would be a good idea. "What time will we need to leave the house?" He told her they would leave by nine o'clock. She went back to the TV room, straightened up the room, and took the tray of cups and saucers back to the kitchen. She rinsed out the cups and looked around at the fantastic kitchen that Maxim used to create the meals they so enjoyed. It was very impressive. Walt had told her that Maxim had designed the kitchen before they built the house. He had done a good job. Walt followed her into the kitchen and watched her explore.

"What do you think?" he asked. She looked at him and nodded.

"He did a good job. This must be a joyful room when he is creating our meals. He keeps a clean, neat kitchen. I am impressed."

"By the way, Maxim suggested a friend of his from his church could come and cook for us while they are gone. Another husband and wife combination will take care of us. Is that all right with you?" Walt said. Kathleen said it would be wonderful.

After they spent some time talking about their wedding guest list, they decided to turn in for the night. He walked her to the stairs, kissed her good night, and watched her trudge up to her room. He stood at the bottom of the steps with a goofy grin on his face. He had not been this happy in a long time. At the top of the stairs, she turned and saw he still watched her. Therefore, she turned around and walked back down the long staircase and he met her halfway. He hugged her tight, gave her another kiss, and as she turned, he smacked her backside lovingly. She giggled, as she moved quicker than she thought she could. At the top of the stairs, she turned and looked at him again and waved good night. He turned and walked down the stairs, wishing she were not having to sleep in a different room. It would not be long and she would be sharing his bed.

The next morning, Kathleen got up early and checked on Lucille. She did not find her in her room, so she peeked in

Shorty's room. Through the open door, she saw Lucille sitting up in the comfortable chair with her head leaning back on a small pillow. She slept and snored softly. She had apparently slept the entire night in the chair. Lucille opened her eyes and looked at Kathleen and at her Albert. She signaled for her best friend to come on in.

"He slept fitfully all night. He got up once and went right back to sleep. I feel like I have a stiff neck. I wonder why?" she said and laughed quietly. "Is it time for him to get up? He probably should not eat breakfast if he is going to have blood work. Therefore, he does not need to get up yet. I will go take a shower and come down for breakfast."

Both women left the room and went to their own rooms to shower. When Kathleen came out of her room dressed and ready to go, she noticed that Walt nudged Shorty to get him up and ready for his doctor appointment. They said good morning to one another.

"I think I am feeling better this morning, Buddy. I will get a warm shower and get dressed. I cannot eat breakfast until after my appointment. I'll be down later."

Walt walked Kathleen downstairs, and they went in for a buffet breakfast. Lucille came in, served herself, and sat down. They talked sporadically, as they all were worried about Shorty.

By nine o'clock, they were heading out the driveway with Walt driving. Shorty and Lucille sat in the backseat holding hands. His silence made them all uneasy. Walt let the three of them out at the door to the medical building. When he joined them in the waiting room of the doctor's office, the nurse had already taken Shorty back to the examining room. The women flipped through magazine after magazine while Walt tapped his foot and watched folks come in and go out. After about twenty minutes, the nurse came out and said, "The doctor has called for an ambulance to take Shorty to the hospital. Shorty started complaining of pain in his chest during the testing. We gave him an aspirin and hooked him up to oxygen. They are checking his vitals as they go. You might want to go on across the street to the emergency room because he will be there within five minutes."

They thanked her and hurried out the door. When they arrived, Walt asked about his brother. The young woman at the desk said she would check and came back quickly saying the doctors were with him and would be out to talk to them when they were done. She told them to have a seat.

The women sat down and Lucille cried. "I can't believe this is happening. On Christmas Eve, I should have said I would marry him. I love him. Why did I put him off? Oh, Kathleen, please pray right now." Walt came over and sat down and she prayed and prayed.

Eventually, a doctor came out and said that they had gotten Mr. Alexander stabilized for the moment. He gave the details and said the patient would need surgery very soon. Lucille asked if she could go in and see him. When she got the nod, she walked quickly through the double door and found Albert in the third room on her left. She took his hand and put her left hand on his forehead.

"Oh, Albie," she cried. She carefully kissed him on the lips.

He opened his eyes and whispered, "Hello, dolly. I love you."

"I love you too, Albie."

"Go over there to my pants and reach in the pocket and pull out the box." She did so and brought the ring box back to him. "Have you made up your mind? Even if you don't want to marry me, I want you to have the diamond ring."

Tears were running down her face, and she took the ring out of the box and slipped it on her finger. To her amazement, it fit perfectly. "Albie, I will marry you. You get through this surgery, and when you are well enough, I will marry you." She kissed him again. He closed his eyes, smiled, and rested. Walt and Kathleen came into the room and Lucille held up her left hand. They saw the diamonds sparkling and grinned at her. "I said yes."

The nurse told them they needed to let him rest, so they left the room. They were waiting around until Lucille could go back in the room to sit with Shorty. Throughout the day, they took turns going in and sitting with him for a few minutes at a time. They had an operating room available and ready for the heart surgeon, so they had a few moments to pray with him and then watched him being wheeled down the hallway. Walt insisted that the women go with him to the cafeteria for dinner. None of them seemed hungry, but they obviously needed some nourishment.

Every couple of hours, the family received a message about the patient. Late into the night, the surgeon finally came into the waiting room. His news brought a smile to Lucille's face. He had come through, and they were expecting him to be fine after some recuperation. They decided that they would go to the hotel down the block for the night and be back early in the morning. After they got to see Shorty, they walked down to the hotel and found their rooms. Lucille and Kathleen shared a room, as Kathleen did not want her friend to be alone during the night.

The next morning, Walt called them and asked if they were ready to head back to the hospital. When they arrived at the intensive care unit, they were not too surprised to see that the patient still slept. Lucille had tears in her eyes as she watched her Albie lying so still. Kathleen suggested that they pray. They gathered around the bed, and she prayed for strength that Shorty could heal quickly. As she prayed, she felt him squeeze her hand. She opened her eyes and grinned at him and closed her eyes as she finished praying. When the others opened their eyes, they were pleased to see Shorty looking at them. He smiled at them, although weakly. Lucille leaned down and put a kiss on his forehead. "Oh, Albie, how are you?"

"I've been better. What are y'all doing here? What am I doing here? I am ready to go home. Will you take me, doll?"

"Shorty, you aren't going anywhere for a while. After your heart surgery, you will stay put here until they say you are ready to go home," Walt said.

The nurse indicated that only one person should be in the room at a time, so Walt and Kathleen waved and left Lucille to sit with him. They sat in the waiting room for a while and Lucille came out. The nurses needed to do a procedure, so she had to step out. Lucille reassured herself that Shorty looked better. It would just be a matter of time before he would be back home again. They waited with Lucille and checked in on Shorty a few minutes every hour. By evening, Lucille suggested that they go home and come back the next day. "I will be fine here. I can check on him throughout the night. Tomorrow, you two can come and be with him, and I promise to go to the hotel and get rest."

They agreed to that and left for the night. When they returned home, they went to the kitchen and fixed omelets and decaffeinated tea. They were both so tired, that they rinsed off the dishes and left them in the sink. They kissed good night at the bottom of the stairs.

It seemed like Kathleen had been asleep but a short time when Walt called her name softly and patted her arm. "What is it, Walt?"

"We have to go back to the hospital. Shorty has taken a turn for the worse. Lucille called and said the doctor told her to call us back. Can you get dressed in a hurry? We need to go as soon as we can. I'll have the car at the front door in a few minutes."

"Yes, I'll be ready. Hurry, dear."

Walt drove as fast as he could in spite of the wet roads. Kathleen kept her hand on his knee. She wanted him to know that she would stay by his side. When they arrived, he parked the car in the drive next to the emergency room. They rushed up to the intensive care unit and saw Lucille in the waiting room. She had been crying and ran to them and hugged them. Walt said, "How is he? Can we go in?" All three of them went into the room. Shorty looked much worse than he had a few hours earlier. Walt went over to the bed and took his brother's hand.

"Shorty, Albert, you need to rest and get stronger. Lucille has said she would marry you. That is what you want, so let's see you perk up a little."

Shorty did not open his eyes. Lucille continued to hold his hand and she rubbed his forehead. Kathleen began to pray for Shorty to regain strength and heal. When she finished, he opened his eyes and said, "Thanks, Buddy, for being a great big brother. Katie-did, thanks for the prayers. You take care of Buddy." He turned his head towards his fiancée, "Hello, dolly. Where have you been all of my life?" His eyes closed again. The nurse shooed them out so she could take care of him.

They filed out of the room to the waiting area. Walt stood and held both women as they put their heads on his shoulders. They were in a group hug and Lucille sobbed when the pastor came in. They sat down and told him what had happened with Shorty. He prayed with them. When the nurse said that two of them could go back in, Walt suggested that Pastor Rod and Lucille go in together. Walt and Kathleen sat side by side and held hands. She asked if he wanted a cup of coffee or tea. He opted for the coffee and she got it for him. He took a sip and made a face. She tasted it and took it back to the table. She went to the desk and asked if they could make a fresh pot of coffee. "No problem," the clerk said.

A short time later, Lucille and Pastor Rod joined them. Kathleen got both of them coffee. Lucille said Shorty looked like his sleep seemed normal. The machines were not beeping and ringing as much as they had been.

"I am so glad that all of you are here," she said. Ned and Nicholas walked into the room and Walt stood up to hug them. He told them the latest news. Following within a few minutes were Nancy and Kevin. Walt hugged them both and asked about the children.

"Kevin's parents came over right away to stay with them. Oh, Dad, is he going to make it?" Nancy asked with tears in her eyes. Kathleen hugged them all and invited them to come over and sit down with them. Walt suggested that his children go in by themselves for the next visit. When they came out within a few minutes, Lucille asked Walt to go in with her.

Nancy said, "He looks so vulnerable. He did not know we were there. When I held his hand, he squeezed my hand, but did not open his eyes. Maybe they have him sedated too much."

Kathleen pulled her over to the chairs and offered her coffee or hot chocolate. She wanted nothing. Kevin talked softly to Ned and Nicholas over by the entrance. They came over and sat down with Nancy and the pastor. Kathleen decided to go back into Shorty's room again. When she walked in, Walt reached out and put his arm around her shoulder. Lucille talked softly to her Albert. "Honey, when you get better, we will set a date. I promise. Do not try to talk, just get better. Save your strength. I love you. I am so glad we found each other. We have better times ahead." She sobbed and made herself stop. He squeezed her hand. She kissed his lips and felt his lips move. Walt and Kathleen left the room and Lucille sat down in the chair next to Shorty's bed.

She continued to hold his hand as she thought about the high points of her life. Finishing college had put her into a classroom teaching high school English, which had been her dream since she had Mrs. French for eighth-grade English. Mrs. French always started the year telling her classes that she might be French, but she loved English and hoped they all would by the year's end. Lucille indeed had been so obsessed with literature and poetry and by Mrs. French's ability to lead unsuspecting students to want to study, that she knew that she wanted to do that for the rest of her life. She had been amazed at her own ability to make the literature come alive for her students. She had heard a few of her students talk about getting high, but they would never believe that she felt a high when she saw the lightbulb go on for a student as he finally understood what she was teaching. She thought about Marcus, who had taught down the hall from her. They had dated for a couple of years, talked about getting married, but he wanted a stay-at-home wife. She had loved him, but could not give up what she considered her ministry. Teaching was her call in life. His expectations were too old school for her. She wanted a husband who would not want to change her.

One of the machines attached to Shorty with a thin wire started beeping. She jumped up just as one of the nurses rushed in to check on her patient. She pushed a button and the noise stopped. Lucille backed up from the bed, hoping the nurse would not ask her to leave. The nurse smiled at her and left the room. Lucille sat back down and took Albert's hand again. "Albert, I want you to listen to me very carefully. I love you and want to marry you. I have waited a long time to find a kind, gentle man to marry. Now that I have found you, I am hanging on. I said yes, so I want to see you perk up. Sleep now and I'll be right back." She stood up and kissed his lips, and she thought she saw the corners of his lips turn up into a smile when she pulled away from him. She smiled and felt more optimistic than she had in a couple of days.

When she got to the waiting room, she went to Kathleen and hugged her. "I think he is doing better. He smiled at me after I kissed him."

"That must have been some kiss," Walt teased. The three of them sat down, and Nancy suggested they think about getting a bite of lunch. Lucille begged off and asked that they bring her a sandwich and a cold soda. Kathleen said she would wait with Lucille, and they could bring them each a sandwich. Walt gathered up his family and pastor and led them to the elevator that would take them to the cafeteria. Kathleen took Lucille's left hand and looked at the diamond ring.

"Lucille, that is a beautiful ring. Albert outdid himself finding you the perfect ring for your finger. He really loves you."

"I know and I love him. He honestly just grew on me. He behaved so gentlemanly when we went underground. That is what he calls our little hiding game in Sarasota. He is not the tough guy he would like to be. He is a pussycat, a sweetheart. Kathleen, do you think he is going to get through this?"

"I don't know, but we can only leave it in God's hands. If prayer can bring him strength, he is getting plenty of that. I called

Lucinda and asked her to get her prayer circle busy on this one. She wants you to call when you can."

"That was sweet of you and her. Kathleen, I have turned down two men in my life and then Albert came along. I am glad I had turned down the first two because otherwise, I would not be free to date Albert. However, this seems like a bad dream. Albert is finally getting his life together, he has recommitted his life to Jesus, and he has found love for the first time. Why would it be cut short now?" Lucille wiped tears from her eyes, took a deep breath, and sat up straighter. "Let's go back in to see Albie." She stood up and took Kathleen's arm as they walked together through the double doors into the critical care unit.

They stood side by side at Shorty's bed and watched his chest move up and down. Lucille rubbed his forehead gently and she saw a smile beginning. He opened his eyes partway and whispered, "Hello, dolly." His eyes closed again.

"Hello, Albie dear. I am here. I love you." She continued to rub his forehead as if she was pushing hair back off his forehead, but he had no hair there. She did not care because she loved him.

The nurse came in and said Walt had delivered their lunch, so they patted Shorty's hands and quietly left his room. Walt and Nancy were carrying the sandwiches and drinks. Kathleen and Lucille decided to go to the ladies' room before eating. When they returned, Nancy had cleared off a side table and had their small meal set up for them. Kathleen hugged her soon-to-be daughter-in-law and thanked her. She gave a short blessing for their food and they began to eat. After a couple of bites, Lucille had eaten all she thought she could eat. Kathleen did not do much better. Walt and Nicholas had gone back in to check on Shorty.

Chapter 15

Lucille said to Kathleen and Nancy, "Did I tell you about the first night that Albie and I were hiding out in Sarasota?" The listeners shook their heads no. "Well, we found this awful little row of motel rooms out in the country. We walked into this room after Albie finally got the door unlocked, and we saw it only had one double bed. I looked at him, and he immediately turned red in the face. He stammered that he had not thought to ask about the number of beds. He immediately told me the bed would be mine. There were no other rooms available, which confounded me considering the disrepair of the place. There were four other little cabins. We were the only customers. Shorty had gone back into the office and asked for another.

The owner told him that the other four had no running water and were unusable. Therefore, we had to share the one room. I told him he could sleep above the covers with a blanket and I would sleep under the covers. He would not hear of it. Would you believe he made a pallet on the floor in front of the door. He did not want to jeopardize my reputation, he said. Such a sweetie." She began to cry and Kathleen put her arm around her and patted her shoulder while Nancy held one of her hands.

Ned came back in the waiting room from his phone conversation with Tiffany. Kathleen asked about Tiffany. Ned said, "Oh, yes, she is all right. Just complaining about my being gone so long and how her clothes aren't fitting properly."

Kathleen walked over to him and put her arm around his waist and he said, "Kathleen, she didn't even ask about Shorty. What is wrong with her?"

"Ned, she is just very immature. She will grow up soon. Having a baby usually brings a girl to her senses to become a woman and no longer be so self-absorbed. With time, I believe she will grow up. You just have to remain as patient with her now during pregnancy as your dad says you have been."

"Thank you, Kathleen. I will try to be patient. I have told Tiffany she needs to be kinder to others. She says she tries. Her aunt Paige has been too much of an influence on her. You know Aunt Paige," he said petulantly.

"Ned, don't worry about that right now. Why don't you go in and check on your uncle." Ned appreciated having a task set before him. He needed something to think about besides himself and his wife now. He turned and walked toward the double doors. As he went in, his dad and brother came out.

A few hours later, Walt suggested the kids go home for the day. He would call them if anything changed with Shorty. They said their good-byes, gave hugs all around, and walked out together. Lucille had been with Albert for the last ten minutes. Walt and Kathleen went back in to check on both Shorty and Lucille.

"Don't you think his color looks better? He seems to be breathing easier," Lucille said. Walt could not see any difference, but did not say so. He wanted to let Lucille have hope. Kathleen had her hands on Lucille's shoulders as she sat near Shorty.

Suddenly, the machine by his head began to beep. The nurse rushed in and asked them to step out. The crash cart came with a group of staff people. The three of them stood outside of the room and watched through the glass wall. They worked on Shorty for some time. The small room filled up with uniformed doctors and nurses all at work. Finally, one of the doctors reached around, turned off the machine, and shook his head. Lucille turned around and Walt held her as she cried. Kathleen held them both and wondered why. There were so many questions always left unanswered with death. The staff had adjusted the covers, removed the tubes from Shorty's face, and invited them back into the room. They went in and said their good-byes. Kathleen prayed once again, but this time, she thanked God that Shorty had recently found his way back to Jesus. She prayed for his loved ones. Later, Walt took care of the paperwork and details that followed a death in the hospital.

They left Lucille alone for a few minutes with Shorty. "Oh, Albert, I am so sorry I didn't say yes the first time you asked. I wish we had met years ago. You have touched my heart in ways I could not explain to you. I love you, Albie. You are with Jesus now. I thank God for that. We will see each other again, my love." She kissed him on the lips, squeezed his hand, rubbed his forehead, and then she left the room. When she got out to where Kathleen stood next to Walt as he made the phone calls to his children, she leaned on Kathleen and cried again.

"Honey, you made his last days very happy. I am sorry you did not have more time, but you made his life better. He found his way back to God. You two have had four wonderful months. That is not long enough, I know. You made each other's lives enjoyable and full of love and excitement."

"I know. He made me happy too. He made me laugh. He made me scared. He made me run in high-heeled sandals." She smiled at Kathleen. "He wants me to keep the engagement ring. I guess I will wear Albie's ring as you wore Tyler's ring for years. I now know how you felt."

Walt turned to them and said, "Let's go home. We have an appointment at the funeral home later today. We have done all we can do right now. Lucille, I thank you for bringing Albert so much happiness in the past few months. I had not seen him that happy or content, since I…I do not think I have ever seen him that content. Thank you, dear." He hugged her and wiped tears from his eyes.

Kathleen and their pastor shared the funeral service. When they came back from the cemetery, the family and old friends gathered with them at Walt's home. The couple filling in for Maxim and Miriam had a buffet set up and folks sat around and reminisced about Shorty's life. In spite of his gambling issues and in spite of his abrasive personality in his earlier years, family and friends loved him. He had some endearing qualities that several people mentioned. Lucille knew many would miss him. Friends and neighbors had said such complimentary things about him. They told about ways he had helped them that Walt did not even know. It warmed his heart to know that others saw the value of his brother as he did.

As Tiffany and Ned sat on a swing on the patio, Kathleen went out to see if they needed anything. Tiffany said they were fine. "By the way, Kathleen, we found out we are having a boy. I guess I will figure out how to love a little boy without putting bows in his hair. I know you have not had children of your own, but maybe you can help me become a good mother."

"Tiffany, that is exciting. I would be happy to help all I can. You have two sisters-in-law close by who can help you also. I do look forward to being a grandmother. It will be a new experience for me. Will you let me baby-sit for you once in a while?"

"That would be wonderful," Ned said. He stood up, hugged Kathleen, and had her sit next to Tiffany. Kathleen took Tiffany's hand and they swung in silence, while Ned went in to get some coffee.

By evening, the crowd had thinned and left Walt, Kathleen, Lucille, and Bernice to tie up the evening. Walt had sent his plane to pick up Bernice the day after Shorty's death. Walt knew that the girls needed to be together at this time.

They talked about where they all first met in Sarasota and how Shorty had made such an impression on them. Lucille told them again the details of Shorty taking her along while he hid out from the killers. She laughed as she told how Shorty had tried to keep her safe and how he had helped her run in her high heels at the dog track. Walt told the story of when Shorty decided to run away at the old age of four and how their mom watched him sitting behind a tree in the front yard with his little suitcase filled with baseball cards, a peanut butter sandwich, and one pair of clean underwear. They enjoyed sharing stories into the late-night hours.

New Year's Eve came quickly. Walt's children had planned to go to a ball and leave the grandchildren with Walt and Kathleen. They were thinking they ought to cancel. Walt suggested that they keep their plans. Shorty would want them to go and bring in the New Year, just the six of them. He also suggested that he wanted the grandchildren as planned. They would have a good time with Grandpa and soon-to-be Grandma. Bernice and Lucille were looking forward to it also. Walt set up a couple of cribs that were kept in the storage area on the second floor and put one in Kathleen's room and one in his room. They had bought hot dogs, ice cream, jell-o, cupcakes, and pretzels. They thought they were ready.

The kids came in excitedly and shouted that they were prepared to stay up all night to see the fireworks. Lucille and Bernice looked at one another and mouthed, "All night?" Kathleen looked at Walt and he seemed to have not heard the proclamation. She said, "Grandpa, all night?"

"What did you say, dear?" he answered as he carried Crystal into the living room. The other children swarmed in with some of their Christmas toys and games. They herded the children into the TV room. Kathleen grabbed Walt's shirt and stopped him as he followed the children.

"They said they were staying up all night, dear. Who is staying up with them?" He looked at her with a startled expression.

"Uh, no one said all night to me. We will get this straightened out after a while. They will get tired, and the little ones will be in bed by nine o'clock. Trust me, Kathleen." She sighed and turned to look at her two best friends who were giggling at her.

The children had not seen each other since Christmas Day, so the older ones were ready to play games. Nicholas had hooked up a game player, as Walt had called it, to his TV and the kids knew how to make it work. The quickest two made it to the TV and the other one played a hand-held game. The two littlest were playing with toys on the floor.

Walt and Kathleen sat down to watch them. He took her hand and told her it would all be okay. After an hour, Walt suggested that they all go out to see the horses. The older ones would get to ride. They put their boots and jackets on and headed out to the stables. Bernice led the pack like one of the kids. She missed her horses and was overjoyed as they headed to the stable. Jane asked Grandma Kathleen which horse she would ride.

"Not today, dear. I will leave the horses to you and Aunt Bernice," she begged off.

Bernice and Walt began helping Miguel, the driver/stableman, who had the apartment atop the stable. Rick and Jane were jumping with excitement as they watched the men saddle the horses. Grandpa helped the two get in the saddles and he led them out to the training ring. He walked them around once and asked if they were ready to walk on their own. They both had some experience, so he handed them the reins and they walked the horses themselves. Bernice sat in Lady's saddle and Crystal begged to ride. Kathleen put a helmet on her and handed her up to sit in front of Bernice. When Crystal sat in front of Aunt Bernice, she reached down, patted Kathleen on the head, and gave her a smile that could get the entire bag of cookies from a cookie monster. Bernice trotted Lady, and Crystal held on tightly. Walt held little Adam in front of him in the saddle, and Miguel had David on the pony and walked him around the large circle. Kathleen said, "One of these days, I am going to have to be brave enough to get in a saddle. It looks like fun, and I want to share Walt's love of riding with him."

"Well, I suggest you do it when you don't have this audience of little Alexanders," answered Lucille and smiled at her friend.

Kathleen agreed with her. When Walt saw the children were getting tired of riding, he called them back to the stable. Walt, Bernice, and Miguel took care of the horses while Lucille and Kathleen steered the children back to the house. They got them out of their boots and jackets, washed up, and ready for dinner.

Lucille pulled Kathleen and Bernice aside and with a straight face said, "Well, I feel bad that if we all weren't here, Walt could have taken Paige to the ball. I know he hates missing that big date." They all laughed and Kathleen elbowed Lucille.

By the time Walt and Bernice came back in, the kids were complaining about being hungry. The housekeeper had the meal ready to set on the table. The adults helped the children into their seats and high chairs. The children were very hungry and the meal became rather quiet for the first five minutes. However, as their little tummies were getting full, they started talking. Rick and Jane began to argue over who could ride better. Bernice told them they were both good. They would each be a great cowboy and cowgirl. They grinned at her and preened with pride. Little Crystal began whining. She laid her head down next to her plate. Kathleen helped her eat a few more bites by spooning the food into her little mouth before she held up her arms indicating she wanted out of the high chair. Kathleen accommodated her. They went upstairs to get her cleaned up and ready for bed. Crystal allowed Kathleen to put her cute little pink and yellow plaid pajamas on her. She snuggled down in her crib with her teddy bear. Kathleen sat down in her chair, hummed a little tune for her, and prayed for her and all the other children. In her prayer, she included the rest of her family, friends, and the world as a new year approached in a few hours. She had forgotten about the baby monitor in her room and had no idea that Walt listened to her from the library as she sang to his precious little granddaughter and prayed. *Oh, how he loved this woman.* When Kathleen saw that Crystal slept, she tiptoed out of the room and turned off the light.

Downstairs, the older children were back at the video games. Bernice had challenged Rick to a game her grandchildren had taught her. Rick showed frustration and excitement as the game progressed. Lucille, David, and Jane were playing rummy. Jane was winning. Walt had just taken Adam to his room to get him in the other crib. Adam cried and cried. The baby monitor from Walt's room picked up the fussy little guy. Finally, Kathleen went into the room to see if she could help. When Adam saw her, he stuck out his lower lip and wailed some more. Kathleen went to him and asked what he needed.

"I want my mommy. Reads book and holds me," Adam said, then stuck out his lower lip again. She looked through his little suitcase and found a book.

"How about this one? Would you like Grandpa to read it to you?"

"No. You read. Please?" Adam looked at her again with his lower lip stuck out and she melted.

"I can do that." She sat down in the comfortable rocker, and Walt put the little guy in her lap and kissed her on the head. "Sorry, Grandpa, I think he wants someone maternal right now. Do you mind?"

"Not at all. Anything to help him quit crying. I'll be in the other room if you need me." He walked over to the door, stopped, and looked back at them and winked at her.

Adam fell asleep halfway through the book, so she managed to get him into his crib. She covered him up, put his stuffed bear next to him, and left the room. When she walked into the TV room, Rick got louder and louder as he talked to himself trying to win the game. Walt had joined the rummy game. Lucille moved over and said, "Pull up a chair and you are in on the next hand. These kids are good. Who taught you kids to play rummy?"

"Dad and Mom. We play games every Sunday evening. It is family night at our house. On Sunday nights, we do not play video games. We play games with Mom and Dad, eat popcorn, and we have to get ready for school the next day," said Jane. "I like it. We can always count on Mom and Daddy both being home on Sunday nights."

"Sunday night is game night at our house too." Walt enjoyed hearing that his children were carrying on the family traditions. Nicholas and Nancy were both carrying on Delia's tradition of Sunday night being family night. Bernice laughed loudly and hugged Rick. "Okay, guy, you finally beat me. You are good."

"So are you, Aunt Bernice. I did not know old people could play video games. Maybe you could teach Grandpa so we can beat him sometime."

"I heard that Richard," said Grandpa. "First, it is not polite to call your elders old people. I would have to retire and stay home practicing for a long time to ever defeat you at one of your games, Rick." He chuckled. "Actually, maybe I ought to just retire."

Rick's face got red and he apologized to Aunt Bernice. She laughed and said, "The truth is the truth, kiddo."

Kathleen thought she heard Walt say that maybe he ought to retire. Really? She put it on her list of conversations to have with him later.

Walt said, "Hey, gang, how about some popcorn?"

"Yeah," they shouted together. He got up and went to the kitchen where the chef put the finishing touches to a large tray of caramel corn, popcorn, sliced apples, and hot chocolate.

"Thank you, Jock. This is an amazing spread. I will hold the door while you carry it in. You and Mildred take the rest of the New Year's Eve time for yourselves. We have appreciated your help during this time," Walt said.

"No problem, Mr. Alexander. We are happy to help and we are glad that Maxim recommended us. Happy New Year, sir."

Jock carried the tray to the TV room where he got a standing ovation for the spread of snacks. He laughed and backed out of the room. The kids were ready for a snack. They decided to settle in and watch *It's a Wonderful Life*. When "The End" appeared on the screen, the kids were nodding off.

"All right," thought Kathleen, "it won't be all night. Good." She and Walt directed the kids upstairs to get ready for bed and hurry back. They were going to sleep in sleeping bags in the TV room. Lucille and Bernice said good night and headed to their own rooms. When the children were settled in and falling asleep, Kathleen hugged Walt and told him Happy New Year. He did the same.

"It won't be long now when we will not have to say good night at the bottom of the stairs. I love you. Good night, sweetheart." She nodded and they went to their own beds to wake up to a new year.

Chapter 16

January 20 came quickly. Bernice and Lucille both stayed for the wedding. They were a big help in getting the details done at the last minute. They had decided not to postpone the wedding. Lucille told them that Albert would not want them to wait. When it neared the time to depart for the church, the driver brought the limousine to the front door.

Kathleen and her friends walked down the stairs and Walt waited for them. Along with Walt were his best man and Nicholas, who filled in for Shorty. Kathleen had on a white satin dress with a straight skirt. It had a matching jacket with lace trim. She had let her hair grow a little longer and pulled it back on one side. She planned to carry a single white rose. Her friends also wore long dresses but in navy blue, and they carried a single white rose with navy blue ribbons.

Walt and the men had small white rosebuds in their lapels. They escorted the women to the limousine.

When they arrived at the church, the pastor's wife met them and led the women to a room reserved for bridal party preparation. They received a message that they would be starting a little late. Ned and Tiffany had not arrived yet. Ned had called and said they had a little problem. The women decided to sit down and relax a few moments. They talked a while wondering if the young couple might be stuck in traffic. Fifteen minutes after the service was to start, they wondered if the young pregnant woman had a medical issue. Twenty minutes after the service should have started, Walt sent the pastor's wife to tell the ladies they were going to start, even though the couple had not arrived. Walt now knew where they were, but did not share.

Shortly thereafter, the piano music began and the women walked down the aisle. Lucille wished that Shorty were alive and standing next to his brother. However, Kathleen had not been this happy in years, so she smiled contentedly. Bernice and Lucille looked lovely in their beautiful long, dark blue dresses that had jackets similar to the bride's dress. Lucille, of course, had on the highest heels while the bride and Bernice had chosen medium height heels. Family and special friends filled the first five pews. They had about forty guests. The grandchildren were all in their best dresses and suits. Crystal waved at Kathleen when she walked by and received a wink from her soon-to-be grandmother. Walt escorted his bride to the front where they stood in front of the pastor, Walt held out his hand and she took it. She smiled at him and he whispered, "You are beautiful."

As they stood facing one another, the pastor said, "Dearly beloved, we are gathered together to join this man and woman in holy matrimony…" It was a beautiful wedding.

As the bride and groom kissed at the end of the service, the back door opened and Ned and Tiffany rushed in and came up the aisle. When Ned saw they had missed the entire wedding, he took Tiffany by the arm and led her to an empty seat near the middle of the sanctuary. The pastor said, "May I present Mr. and Mrs. Walter Alexander. The guests applauded and the couple started down the aisle. Kathleen noticed that Tiffany had red eyes and mascara stains under those eyes, but she looked healthy. In the limousine on the way to their reception, Walt started to laugh.

"Can you guess why Ned and Tiffany were late?"

"Not an idea. Did they get stuck in traffic? Did she get sick?" guessed the new Mrs. Alexander.

"No, you are not even close. Tiffany had a brand-new dress to wear to our wedding. She wanted to be the best-dressed woman.

She had bragged to Nancy that she and her dress would steal the show from the bride and bridesmaids. Well, she bought the dress two months ago, and when she put on the dress today, she and the baby would not fit. She had not tried it on since she bought it. Ned said she could not get the dress zipped. He could not get it zipped for her. He tried to get her to pick something else. She said she did not have anything appropriate or pretty enough. She made him take her to the store to buy a new dress. She did not find one, so she came in her inappropriate (her words) maternity dress that she had bought for church. She felt humiliated. She is sorrier for not finding a dress than she is for missing our wedding. Oh my, Tiffany is so self-absorbed. I hope this new baby helps her grow up. Does that ever happen?"

"Poor Tiffany. I have seen cases where an adult finally grows up with the responsibility of a new baby. At least, the wedding went on without her. I do not know how much longer our guests would have waited. Do you think she will stop at Neiman-Marcus before coming to dinner? I thought she looked fine," Kathleen said with a little grin.

"Darling, you are so beautiful today. At last, you are my wife. Tomorrow, we will take off for Europe. For three weeks, we will see the sights and enjoy one another's company. No way would Tiffany get Ned to take her shopping before our dinner. I just don't think that would happen."

The limo pulled up to the restaurant and the newlyweds stepped out. The guests stood and applauded as they walked into their private party. They took their place at the head table. Walt thanked everyone for sharing this special day with him and his bride. Their pastor stood and had prayer for them and the meal. The servers began bringing out the meals. As they began to eat, Lucille turned to the bride and said, "Tiff is missing. You don't suppose she went shopping, do you?"

"Poor Tiffany. Walt said no way she could get Ned to stop and shop on the way over here. Maybe he misjudged." They changed the subject and enjoyed their meal. Several folks stopped by their table to offer their congratulations. After the meal, the best man gave a fitting toast to the bride and groom. As they started to cut the wedding cake, the main door opened and in walked Tiffany and Ned. Those in the know looked at one another and could not help but giggle. Tiffany had on a gorgeous, long, formal maternity dress. A waiter showed them to their table. As she walked toward her seat, she stopped to kiss a few of her friends on the cheek. As she sat down, Bernice elbowed Lucille. She nodded toward the pregnant daughter-in-law. "Check out the armpit." The price tag hung out from under her armpit. She was unaware that a number of people had noticed. She preened in her beautiful dress, which was fancier than the dresses the bridesmaids were wearing. It was fancier than any dress in the room, including the bride's gown.

As Walt and Kathleen returned to their seats, they stopped at the table to say a word to the late couple. Ned apologized profusely. "Dad, she wouldn't come until she had a new dress. I did not know pregnant women could be so wacky. I am so sorry. If I hadn't stopped to shop, she would have sat in the car instead of coming in with me."

"It is okay, Ned. Some pregnant women do get a little weird. We will pray that she gets over this in a few months." He patted his son's shoulder and kissed his daughter-in-law on the cheek.

Kathleen told Tiffany what a beautiful dress she had and noticed the price tag. She unobtrusively pulled it off and handed it to Tiffany under the table. When Tiffany looked down at her hand, she burst out crying. Kathleen tried to console her and suggest she not attract any more attention to herself. "Eat your dinner, dear, and forget it. You look lovely pregnant, and you do have the most beautiful dress in the room. Let Ned enjoy his meal. It will all be forgotten before you know it."

The newlyweds went back to their seats and began to eat their wedding cake. The string quartet played beautiful music, and Walt asked Kathleen to dance with him when he heard their song played.

Folks were watching them, and Lucille leaned over to Bernice and said, "I am so glad that they found one another. If it had not been for Albert, they would not have met. I remember the first time I found Shorty. He came out of the water, looked up at me, and said, 'Hello, dolly. Where have you been all of my life?'" Bernice nodded that she remembered. "I wish his life could have been longer for both of us. We made each other so happy."

"I know, dear," said Bernice, patting Lucille's hand. She noticed that Lucille still wore the engagement ring Shorty had given her. They watched the couple continue their dance. A tall man of their age came up behind Lucille and asked her if she would dance with him. He introduced himself as Dave, one of Walt's employees and golf buddies.

"Actually, I would prefer to watch you dance with my friend, Bernice. Thank you for asking though," she said and encouraged Bernice to dance with the stranger. Rather than cause a fuss, Bernice agreed to the dance. Lucille watched the couples who were dancing. Little Crystal left her mom's lap and walked around the table to see Lucille.

"Aunt Cille, why are you crying?" she said as she crawled up on her lap. Crystal patted her cheek and gave her a hug.

"Oh, baby, these are tears of joy. I am happy that Grandpa Walt married Grandma Kathleen today and that they look so happy together. Isn't that nice?"

"Yes, they are pretty. Oh, look. Mommy and Daddy are going to dance. They are pretty too," said Crystal. She put her head on Lucille's bosom, put her thumb in her mouth, and watched the dancers.

"What a pretty little girl you are and so loving," said Lucille. She looked down and saw that she had fallen asleep. Her mom stopped by on the way off the dance floor to pick up her little blonde angel. She carried her back to her table and held her while she ate her wedding cake. The other children were getting tired and leaning on their elbows, waiting for someone to take them home.

The evening was waning. The guests stopped by to congratulate the couple before leaving, thanking them for the wonderful meal, and wishing them many years of happiness. When the majority of the guests were gone, Nicholas told his dad he would take the bridesmaids back to the house. The newlyweds told all their attendants thanks and said they would see them in three weeks. The two friends were going home to Indiana in a few days, so they would not be at the house when they returned from their honeymoon.

Walt's family gave them hugs and kisses and Rick said, "I speak for all us kids. Grandpa Walt, we congratulate you on finding such a pretty wife at your age."

Rick's dad said, "I think that he meant that to be a compliment. Welcome to the family, Kathleen." She acknowledged the welcome and said she had never been happier.

The limousine took Walt and his bride to a hotel close to the airport. Their honeymoon and new life together had begun. When they got to the honeymoon suite, Walt unlocked the door. Someone had the room prepared with dim lights and a beautiful bouquet of white roses. Their suitcases were waiting for them.

Walt said, "This is the time when I am supposed to carry you across the threshold. Could we not and say we did? I am not sure my back or my knees can take it. I am not saying you are too heavy, dear, I am saying I am older than I look."

They looked at one another and burst out laughing. Kathleen said, "I had not imagined that you would carry me anywhere. I want you to be able to stroll with me down the streets of London and Paris. I will not push you in a wheelchair yet, my love, because you damaged your back due to an overload. After all, your grandson did tell you he was glad you could get such a pretty wife at your old age. We dare not take any chances at our age."

He shut the door, locked it, and turned to his bride. "Very funny, my love. My grandkids are cute, aren't they? Hope he does not take after his Aunt Tiffany. Let's get out of our wedding gear, get comfortable, and I'll pour us a little glass of champagne to celebrate our wedding night." She agreed and carried her little bag into the bathroom. When she came out in her pretty nightgown with her perfume refreshed, he had taken off his black suit and put on black satin pajamas with a long top.

She took the champagne glass he offered her and he said, "To my beautiful bride. May we have many wonderful years as man and wife." Their glasses clinked together; they took a sip, put their glasses down on the table, and walked into each other's arms. As they hugged, Walt said a prayer of thanksgiving that they had found one another. After they both said Amen, he led her to the bed. She slipped out of her slippers and sat down on the bed, pulled her feet up under the covers, and scooted over to the middle of the king-sized bed. Walt crawled in beside her, pulled the cover up to his waist, and turned out the light. He lay down, rolled over on his side, looked his bride in the eye, and said, "Hello, my love. This is the beginning of a beautiful marriage."

She smiled and felt her face turn red. "I love you, Walt, my husband." She put her hand on his cheek and caressed it, thanking God for sending her new husband into her life. He put the palm of his hand over her hand, moved his face so he could kiss her palm.

The soft light radiating from the bathroom put a glow on their faces. Kathleen reveled in her good fortune to have found Walter Alexander.

"What a lucky man I am." He began to sing softly, "You are my sunshine."

"Oh, Walter, that is so sweet. You are making me cry tears of joy," said his bride as she cuddled up next to him and he leaned over to give her a long, passionate kiss.

"Oh, Kathleen." He thought he heard her purring.

Chapter 17

Three weeks later, Kathleen and Walt stepped into her condo and were surprised to see it dust-free and a bouquet of flowers in the middle of the dining room table. Lucille and Bernice had come in the day before and freshened up the place for the newlyweds. There was a note on the kitchen counter welcoming home the Alexanders and telling them to look for the fresh milk, eggs, and cream in the refrigerator and frozen homemade cinnamon rolls in the freezer for their breakfast the next morning.

Walt said, "What thoughtful friends you have, my dear. We will definitely take them out for dinner before we head back home. Back home to Dallas, I mean."

She giggled "Honey, Dallas is now my home too. Anywhere you are will be home to me." She put her arms around his waist and looked into his eyes with love.

"I am the luckiest man in the whole wide world," he answered and gave her a kiss.

The telephone rang and Kathleen stepped away from him to answer it. Bernice said, "Welcome home, lovebirds. Did you have a good honeymoon? As if I needed to ask."

"Each day just gets better and better. How are things in the neighborhood?"

Bernice told her that they were good. She and Lucille could not wait to see her. Kathleen put her hand over the phone and said to Walt, "Do you want to take the girls out to dinner tonight?"

He nodded yes with a smile. "Bernice, Walt wants to take us all out for dinner so we can catch up with one another. Are you available? Oh, good. We will pick you up at six o'clock. Good. I cannot wait to see you either. Bye for now."

She turned to her husband and said, "I'd better call Lucille before she makes other plans." The call succeeded. The three friends and Walt had a wonderful evening over a scrumptious meal and shared their lives over the past few weeks with one another.

"Girls, we are going to Dallas in a couple of days. Next time we come back, I think I will put my home up for sale. It will just be sitting idle. When I come back to visit, surely I could stay with one of you?" Kathleen asked.

"Well, I guess that could be arranged," Bernice said slowly, and she laughed and agreed that it would be a wonderful idea." When they drove back to her house, she invited them in for a cup of coffee so they could see the wedding pictures she had taken. The official photographer had not sent them the pictures yet, but Bernice's pictures were ready for a perusal. As they looked through them, there were many oohs and aahs.

When they got to the family picture taken at the reception, Bernice said with a straight face, "I am sorry I couldn't have gotten the price tag still on Tiffany's dress in a picture. I thought of Minnie Pearl. However, she is too young to know about Minnie Pearl. Minnie always had a price tag hanging down from the brim of her hat on *The Grand Old Opry Show* way back when. Tiffany's price tag did not make nearly as big a hit at your reception. I'm sorry, Walt, I shouldn't make sport of your daughter-in-law," said Bernice as she realized she might be causing him a little embarrassment.

"Oh, Bernice, that girl needed to be knocked down a peg or two, and the price tag was just what that pretty girl needed. It embarrassed her at the time, but I hope she learned a lesson. She is going to need lots of direction and help when her baby is born. My Ned has his hands full."

"I think she will grow up a lot after she goes through childbirth. I haven't experienced it, but I've been in enough delivery rooms after the babies have been born and I've seen a distinct growing up in many young mothers," Kathleen said.

Bernice said, "Labor pains will do that for you. Did I tell you I suffered through thirty-six hours of labor with Bethany?"

Lucille and Kathleen chimed in, "Yes, many times, dear. In addition, you have reminded her often enough of the pain she caused you. For years, you have reminded her." Walt chuckled as he watched the three friends have so much fun together.

Lucille pointed at a tall man in one of the pictures and asked, "Walt, who is this man? He asked me to dance, but I pushed him on Bernice. I wasn't really in the mood."

Walt bent down and looked at the picture. "Hmm, that is my general manager. Dave Vincent. Nice guy. He lost his wife about three years ago. When I called back to the office while we were in Paris, Nancy said Paige, Tiffany's aunt, tried to pin him down to a dinner date. He hid in the closet of his office one day to avoid her. Lucille, I think you or Bernice need to meet him. He needs to get out and get on with life as I have done. Next time you are down, I'll invite him out to the house for dinner."

Bernice said, "I keep telling you people I don't want a date. He is all yours, Lucille."

"He is a handsome guy. Is he anywhere near being as much fun as Albie?"

"Well, no. Shorty tops them all, honey," Walt answered. After they decided which pictures they would like to take with them, they headed home and dropped Lucille off on the way.

Kathleen spent the next couple of days deciding which of her possessions she wanted to take with her and incorporate into their Dallas home. Walt worked with her and helped her carefully wrap the breakables. The evening before they were to fly out, Walt asked her to sit down so they could talk.

"Sure, dear. Is there a problem?"

"No problem. I have been ruminating for a few days now about the possibility of my retirement soon. The kids have a good handle on the business. Frank is doing a good job taking over for Shorty, according to Nicholas. If we move Glenda up to Nicholas's position and Nicholas takes over for me, I think the company will run just fine. What would you think about having me home day and night? I know you thought you would have the days to yourself while I worked, but these past three weeks have been great."

"Why would you even ask? Of course, I would love to have you all to myself day and night. However, what would we do? You are used to traveling some on business and working hard. Will you get bored being at home…with me?"

"I don't think so. There are many things we can do and see together. We can travel and go places neither of us have ever been. We can get more involved in church. I would like to do more work with the horses, and I hope you will get comfortable around them and learn to enjoy riding."

She leaned into his shoulder and admitted she would like to try riding. "I can't live in Texas and not ride a horse, right?" she said with a giggle. "When would you retire? Have you talked to the kids about it? What do they think?"

"I have mentioned it to them, and they think I deserve some relaxation, especially since I am married again. When we get back, we will all sit down together and discuss it. That means you also, dear."

"That sounds wonderful. It is getting late, and if we are going to get out of here by noon tomorrow, we'd better get some rest." He stood up and gently pulled her up beside him.

Chapter 18

Walt's family arrived early for dinner the day that he and Kathleen returned to their Dallas home. Maxim and Miriam had flowers in their bedroom, the living room, and on the dining room table. The smells of the beef roast mixed with the garlic potatoes and the rhubarb pie had Walt almost salivating. He was glad to be home with the familiar foods that his favorite chef prepared every day. Kathleen felt very comfortable and looked forward to unpacking some of her prize possessions to make the home feel like hers as well. She had pulled out a picture of the three musketeers with Walt and Shorty taken in Sarasota and put it on a side table. One of the wedding photos of the wedding party and family sat on the opposite table. The children hugged their grandparents and called Kathleen their Gram K. She liked it fine. They made her feel very much a part of the family.

Then Ned and Tiffany came in. She hugged Walt and welcomed him home. She took Kathleen's hand and shook it and said Aunt Paige said to tell you hello. Ned said, "Tiffany, why do I doubt that? Your Aunt Paige is already chasing Dave Vincent. I think dad is out of the running, so knock it off." Tiffany stuck out her tongue at him behind Walt's back. Ned gave Kathleen a warm hug and welcomed her home.

Kathleen invited them into the living room where a crackling fire made them feel at home.

The grown-ups wanted to hear all about their tour of Europe, and after a few minutes, the children wandered off to the TV room to pull out some games and toys. Walt admitted that there is no place like home because all that foreign food had caused him to lose five pounds.

Miriam stepped into the room and invited them in to dinner. The children heard her from the next room and ran in to grab their parents' hands to draw them into the dining room. Little Crystal put her arms up asking Grandpa Walt to pick her up, which he did. They sat at the table and Walt prayed, "Father, we thank you for the bounty you have given, for safe travel, for family, friends, and for home. We are grateful to have the entire family around this table, and I feel blessed to have my dear Kathleen across the table from me. Bless this food, Lord, and those who have prepared it and served it. Bless us all, in Jesus's name. Amen."

Several adult children around the table said amen; Little Crystal shouted, "Amen, Jesus."

They passed the large platters and bowls around the table. Nancy asked about Bernice and Lucille. Rick asked about her horses. The family dinner was relaxed and enjoyable. Kathleen asked Tiffany how her pregnancy felt and what the doctor reported on her progress.

Tiffany said, "I am so tired, honey. We hired Mabel full time now so I do not have to do any housekeeping chores. All the shopping and decorating to get the nursery ready is just wearing me out. Carla, I do not know how you do it on your own. I guess it explains why your house tends to be messy when I drop in. Nicholas, why don't you get her some help?"

Nicholas answered bluntly, "Well, Tiffany, Carla likes being home with the children and she doesn't want help. Secondly, our house is not messy. It is lived in with toys on the floor during the day. Children cannot play very well if you make them leave the toys in the toy box. Right? Carla is a good mother and has her priorities in order. Our home is happy."

Carla looked at her husband with love and pride. It had been a couple of weeks since they had seen Tiffany, and she seemed to be back at her hardnosed critiques of everyone but Walt.

She hoped that her new stepmother-in-law would hold her own with that sister-in-law. Kathleen looked at Nancy who gave her a wink and a smile.

After dinner, the children went back to their play. Walt and his sons went out to look at the horses. Walt had missed his horses.

The women sat down in front of the fireplace with a cup of tea and settled in. Nancy noticed the box of wedding pictures that were on the coffee table and asked if they could look at them.

"Of course you can, dear. Help yourselves. Bernice sent those, but we are still waiting for the hired photographer's album to arrive." Nancy and Carla sat down next to one another and started looking at each picture. Tiffany disinterestedly picked up a magazine and flipped through the pages.

"Oh look, Tiff, here you are in your new dress. I guess it was worth our wait to have you come in wearing that beauty," Nancy said.

"Yes, I had the most beautiful dress in the room, didn't I? If I had not found that at the last minute, we would have missed the entire meal. However, you should have seen the original. It would have outshone every dress there," Tiffany bragged.

"Well, I think Kathleen's wedding dress outshone them all," Carla said.

"Thank you, dear. I sure loved it, and it made me feel so special. Walt thought I looked beautiful and that is what mattered most to me."

"You are kidding, right? We do not need to care about what the men like or think looks good on us. It is what we women like to see on one another. We are the ones with the fashion style, not those ole' men. I don't care what Ned thinks about what I am wearing. His opinion doesn't matter, does it?" Tiffany said with disgust.

"Tiff, you have such a fine husband. My brother is a jewel of a man. I hope you learn to appreciate him. He deserves appreciation and respect," Nancy said as she bit her lip.

"Oh, honey, don't get your panties in a knot. I appreciate Ned." Just then, before anyone could give her a response, the men came back into the room talking about the new horse.

Walt looked around the room and could almost cut the tension with a knife. He looked at Kathleen and she looked at him and mouthed, "It's okay, dear." She winked and smiled at him.

"Come sit beside me, dear. You have a new horse?"

"Well, I had Ned go to the auction last week and buy a filly that I think will be your pride and joy. At least I hope so. She is a beauty."

"Really? My own horse? Wow. I guess I am going to have to learn to ride, aren't I?"

"And you'll have to learn to muck out her stable also," he said with quiet laughter as he looked at her. Her excitement pleased him. That was another reason he loved her. She had an amazing way of being open to new experiences.

"Why, Ms. Kathleen, don't you know how to ride?" Tiffany giggled.

Walt looked at Kathleen who smiled but obviously held back her irritation, and he looked at Tiffany who looked at Kathleen with derision. "Tiffany, not everyone in Indiana lives on a farm or ranch. Not everyone in Indiana owns a horse. This will be a new delight for Kathleen. Have you ever parasailed, Tiffany?"

"Well, no, that looks rather scary to me," she said, realizing she had stepped on toes again.

"It is scary, but Kathleen and I parasailed off the coast of France and we enjoyed it. After you have this baby, maybe Kathleen can take you parasailing for your first time."

"Oh my, no. I couldn't take a chance on dying when I will have a newborn baby," she said as she wrinkled up her nose.

Ned said, "Tiffany, not everyone has grown up in Texas. Kathleen will find what things she likes to do out here and what she doesn't like. I think it is time I took you home." He stood up, took her hand, pulled her up, and pushed her gently out the door.

They all said their good-byes and Walt walked them to the door. He had his arm around his new wife.

As Ned and Tiffany walked to their SUV, the couple standing at the front door noticed that he gave her yet another upbraiding for her bad manners.

"She will learn with time, dear," Kathleen said and looked up into Walt's face and smiled.

"You are one of a kind, my love. Let us get back to the kids. Want to play a game of rummy with them?" She agreed and they set up a second game table and the five adults mixed with the older children for a rousing game of rummy that Walt would lose.

The next few days, Kathleen carefully unpacked her belongings from the boxes. They walked around the house to find just the perfect places for her pieces. It amazed them that her items blended so well with Walt's. She and Delia had similar taste in decorating. They also spent some time in the stable, letting Kathleen get acquainted with her horse. It did not have a name yet, so she had to choose. After a few days, she awoke with the name on the tip of her tongue.

"Walt, I know what to name that beautiful horse you gave me. I want to name her Sara, you know, for Sarasota where we first met. What do you think?"

"I think that is perfect. I'll ask Nancy to make a sign to hang over her stall in the stable with her name on it." She was getting to like the horse and enjoyed the stable. They had already gotten her a pair of riding boots and a hat. She too had lost a few pounds on their honeymoon and she liked what she saw in her three-way mirror when she had on her fitted jeans, leather jacket, and boots. She felt so satisfied with life and happier than she thought she ever could be again without being a pastor.

The next day, they had an appointment at the company office with his children and with Dave Vincent. They were discussing how they would work out the new division of labor. Kathleen shook hands with Dave, the guy Walt wanted to introduce to

Lucille. He was somewhat shy, but very knowledgeable about the business. When they had finished their meeting and were leaving the boardroom, Kathleen chatted with Dave and he looked down the hall. Aunt Paige strode toward them waving at Dave.

"Oh, oh," Dave whispered. "I've got to get out of here. I am sorry, but the barracuda is on my trail." He backed into the boardroom and left the rest of the family chatting in the doorway.

"I thought I saw Davie here talking with you. Did I miss him?" Paige saw Kathleen and said, "Oh, Katherine, is it? It is nice to see you."

"Kathleen, it is. How are you, Peggy, is it?"

"Paige. My name is Paige. How am I? I am brokenhearted since you stole my beau," she whispered into Kathleen's ear.

Kathleen could not believe what she had just heard. "What? You are brokenhearted since I stole your beau? I didn't realize that, Paige," she said loudly enough that Nicholas heard her. "I had no idea."

Nicholas said, "Paige, can I help you? Did you need something here?"

"Well, I hoped I could take Davie out for lunch. Can you tell him I am here?" she said, turning on her Texas accent.

"I think he is busy and I think he has plans for lunch. This is not a good day. We have him very busy. Work, work, work. He is busy. Another day maybe. I'll tell him you were here," Nancy said. Paige turned around disappointedly and walked back toward the front door of the office.

When she had gone out the door, Ned opened the boardroom door and said, "Dave, it's safe to come out now." Everyone laughed as he came out with a red face.

"How am I going to escape from her the next time? I heard Nancy say maybe another day. I have had a few widows call me in the past couple of years, but none has been as persistent as that woman is. What am I going to do?"

"You are going out to lunch with us to celebrate my retirement decision," Walt said as he put his arm around Dave's shoulder and gave him a little shake. He turned to Kathleen and took her arm as he led the entire group out the door to the van that would take them to a restaurant. They all would celebrate the phenomenal day that Walt had turned over the family business.

Spring days had brought exceptional weather for riding. Kathleen amazed Walt with her prowess in learning how to ride. She had not thought she could ever love a big animal as much as she loved Sara. She and Walt took daily rides and occasionally took a thermos of coffee and sweet treats with them to the river and sat and daydreamed together. They thought the time had come to invite Lucille and Bernice back for another visit. When they returned to the house, she called them and they set a date for Walt's plane to pick them up in Indiana.

When Kathleen put the phone down, she announced that the date chosen worked for all of them. She turned to tell Walt and the phone rang. When she picked it up, she heard Tiffany's drawl saying, "Hi, Ms. Kathleen, it's Tiffany. How are you, dear? Good. I wondered if you would like to meet me for lunch downtown tomorrow. You could go shopping with me afterwards. I am an excellent shopper, you know."

"That sounds fine, dear. I do not need to shop but would love to watch you try on a few things. Or are you shopping for the nursery?"

"No, ma'am. I want us to go to the dress shops. Well, never you mind, we will have a fun day. See you at noon, dear." The phone went dead and so Kathleen hung up.

"Oh my, Walt. I just said yes to lunch and shopping with Tiffany. What have I done?"

"You can hold your own, my dear. Do not let her get uppity with you. If it gets to be too much, just excuse yourself and come home. Leave her standing in the store. It has happened to her before, I daresay."

She responded that she would not want to do that. Walt just raised an eyebrow at her.

Lunch the next day seemed quite pleasant until the meal's end.

Tiffany was talking about how she felt, what the doctor had told her, and how she planned to decorate the nursery.

"Well, I invited you here because I want to help you dress appropriately for my father-in-law. Dad deserves the best. I don't want him to feel embarrassed to take you out, so I am going to take you shopping and buy you a couple of outfits to get you started. Let's go, Kathy."

"My name is Kathleen, Katie, Pastor Kathleen, or Mrs. Alexander. Sit down, dear."

"What? I am ready to buy you some nice clothes. My treat today."

More firmly, Kathleen said, "Sit down, dear." Tiffany sat down. "Tiffany, I told you some time ago that I am very capable of dressing myself. My husband likes the way I look. He loves me just the way he found me. I am not Delia and will never be Delia. I know how much you admired and loved her, but I cannot and will not try to be Delia the Second. I am Kathleen, Walt's second wife. I am a retired Hoosier pastor. He chose me in spite of the fact that I am not a Texan. I am not going shopping with you unless you want to shop for baby things. Tiffany, you may think you are being helpful, but the insinuation you are giving is that I do not meet your standards. You will have to change your standards. I don't think that we are going to have fun shopping together today."

"Yes, we will, Kathleen."

"No, we won't…I won't have fun. You are being passive-aggressive telling me that you do not approve of me for your mother-in-law and you are going to fix me and make me somewhat presentable. I do not need fixing. Do you get my point, Tiffany? I am trying to help you. These comments hurt feelings. It makes people angry with you. I hope this is not what you want to happen. Tiffany, you are such a pretty girl, but I want to help you here. Do you want a suggestion?"

Tiffany got tears in her eyes as she whined, "I am only trying to help you look like the rest of us. I did not mean to hurt your feelings. Why do people take offense when I try to help them? Yes, give me an ole' suggestion." She dabbed at her eyes with a tissue and pouted.

"It is the way you do it. Tiffany, you are not the only woman who can choose clothes or hairstyles. When you say things, there is always a twist in it that is offensive. Do you know what I mean?"

"No. I do not know what you mean. I think you are trying to hurt my little feelings."

"Well, let's go back to what you said a few minutes ago. You said you wanted to buy me some things so Walt would not be embarrassed by me. That is hurtful and not true. I do not embarrass Walt. You take a nice idea like wanting to go shopping and turn it into an insult. Do you understand? You are very pretty, but it is important that your inside person is also pretty. Enough said."

"I guess I know what you mean. Ned says I say mean things all the time. I do not want to hurt your feelings or his. I just want to help you."

"Dear, just think before you talk. It is best to be sure someone wants your help before you try to change them. We all have to be careful how we say things. Thank you for the good lunch, Tiffany. I think I'll go home now and work in the garden." Kathleen stood up, kissed Tiffany on the cheek, and walked out of the restaurant.

"Hey, you can't leave," Tiffany said too loudly. She sat in her chair, looking at her mother-in-law walk out on her. She thought, *Why does everyone walk out on me? I do not get it.* She looked around her and saw two young women her age at the next table grinning at her, and she went by their table and said angrily, "What are you staring at, bimbos?"

They looked at one another and one said, "Tiffany, you haven't changed. You are still a spoiled brat." They went back to their meals. Tiffany realized the girls knew her from high school. *Why are girls always so mean to me? I do not get it.*

Tiffany made up her mind to shop for Kathleen and take the outfits to her. She just knew Walt would appreciate the better changes in his wife. Kathleen just did not know that she needed help.

On the day that Lucille and Bernice arrived, Kathleen and Walt met them at the airport. When the two friends came down the steps of the airplane, Kathleen noticed that Lucille had on flat-heeled shoes. Interesting. They met halfway to the SUV and shared hugs and laughter. The plane trip had been wonderful, they reported, and appreciated the doughnuts. They did miss Kathleen, however. When they arrived at the house, the women settled into their usual rooms. They sat around the pool and visited until Walt finally said he needed to retire and let the hens have some time to themselves. They all said good night, he kissed his wife good night, and went to their bedroom. Miriam brought out tea and cookies for them.

"Lucille, it sounds like Walt has someone he wants you to meet, doesn't it?" said Bernice. "I appreciate that he isn't including me in his matchmaking profession."

"I don't know, Bernice. You know me. I love people and like to meet new people, but it seems strange that Albert's brother would try to fix me up with someone. But it is the guy who asked us to dance at the reception."

Kathleen said, "Well, I have met Dave and he is a very nice man. When I met him the first time, Paige chased him down the hall at the company office. He hid in the boardroom so she could not find him. Paige told me I had stolen her beau, can you believe that?" She explained how she had handled the situation and they cheered her on. She said, "Well, Paige is trying to get her claws into shy Dave and hopes she can rope him in. We have to save him. Don't you think?"

"Well, if I can help save any man from the clutches or claws of fancy Paige, I am game. Did you really call her Peggy? Yes, let's have him out for dinner. Bernice, are you sure you don't want a dinner partner? I am sure Walt could find a nice man to make it six," answered Lucille.

"No thanks, dear. I like being the fifth wheel and watching you two enjoy yourselves."

The following evening, Dave Vincent came for dinner, and Kathleen introduced him again to her friends from Indiana. They seated him between Lucille and Bernice, and he enjoyed the company of both equally. The friends decided to save him from Aunt Paige's snare. They would protect him while they were in town, if for no other reason than to aggravate Tiff's Aunt Paige.

The next day, Kathleen and Bernice wanted to go ride and talked Lucille into going with them. Her friends were very pleased to meet Sara and to know that Walt pampered and spoiled their Kathleen. Lucille surprised them by riding better than they thought she could.

"You have been keeping secrets, friend," Kathleen said. She led them around the ranch and down to the river where they sat on the old log that she and Walt enjoyed.

"I am so glad you and Walt found one another, but Bernice and I were saying on the plane how much we are going to miss our road trips." Kathleen whipped her head around and said, "What do you mean, miss our road trips? We are not going to miss our road trips. I told Walt that I would not give up our annual treks and he agreed that I shouldn't. Where shall we go this June?" She smiled at her friends as they started to celebrate that the road trip trio was not retired.

"Well, if we left from here, we could go to Las Vegas or California. Mexico is out for me. We could go to the Grand Canyon," Lucille bubbled. "I am so excited that we can go on the road again." She started singing a few bars of "On the Road Again," and the other women joined in.

"Willie Nelson has nothing to worry about from us," Bernice said with a giggle.

"Did you girls really think that just because I got married that our road trip days are over?"

"Well, it looked like you and your handsome hubby had grown together at the hip, and you looked so happy, we didn't think you'd want to be apart," Bernice said teasingly.

"I love that man and never get tired of him. However, you, my friends, are too important to me to dump for a man. What were you thinking? Would you dump me for a man?"

"Perhaps not, well, I guess I have a time or two," said Lucille with a giggle. Bernice elbowed her and said, "Of course you would, you did. But not me."

That evening as the four of them played canasta, they shared their plan with Walt. He seemed happy to see them planning another road trip, even though he would miss his sweetie. They listed the places they were considering, and after some discussion, they decided to choose the Grand Canyon. When they finished their game, which Walt and Kathleen had lost, the girls went to the computer to search for information about travel plans. Walt said good night and left them to their excitement in planning another trip. As he left the room, he turned and came back in. "Ladies, one request."

"What, dear?"

"On your last trip, one of you disappeared and one of you found a husband. No disappearing and only Bernice and Lucille are now free to find a husband," he said and laughed as he left the room again. The girls continued to explore the Internet looking for vacation ideas.

The following morning as the girls were comparing vacation spots, the doorbell rang and they heard a voice, "Yoohoo. Kathleen, are you there?" All three women recognized the voice and moaned. The young pregnant blonde came rushing out to the pool area with two large shopping bags. "Oh, hello. I forgot your down-home friends are here. I did not realize you had company. How are you, Lucy? And Beatrice, is it?" She turned from the two friends she had misnamed to her mother-in-law. "When you were too tired to shop with me the other day, I just decided to pick out some outfits that I thought Walt would like on you."

Kathleen stood up, took Tiffany's elbow, and led her out of the room. She stopped in the living room and said, "Tiffany, I thought I made myself very clear that I don't want you choosing my wardrobe. I thought I had made it clear that you need to work on your social skills. Don't you realize that you hurt people's feelings when you try to help them when they do not want your help? Sit down here." She gently backed Tiffany to the couch and helped her sit. Kathleen sat down beside her. "Tell me what part of 'I don't need you to fix me' you don't understand. I will not let you push me into being someone I am not. You are getting into my business."

"Honey, I am only trying to help you." Bernice and Lucille were now standing beside the door where they could hear better, but not be in the way. Walt walked in, and he obviously had been listening from the hallway.

"Tiffany, I didn't realize you were coming out today. What brings you out?"

"Dad, the other day, Kathleen seemed too tired and testy to shop, so I decided to shop for her. I brought your lovely wife a couple of outfits that I thought she would look better in. They are pretty and I thought you'd like to see her in them," Tiffany said with a sugary smile.

"Dear, I have tried to tell Tiffany that I prefer to shop for myself and don't need her help to be more presentable here in Texas."

"I know. I heard her. Tiffany, my wife just said no thanks, so I think you need to take those back to the store and get a refund. I love the way she looks every day. Please do not try to change people. You have your hands full getting ready for a baby and taking care of yourself. You owe your mother-in-law an apology."

Kathleen started to say it was not necessary, but Walt put his hand on her arm. Tiffany got tears in her eyes and said she was sorry. "Sorry for…" Walt questioned.

"Sorry I hurt your feelings. I only want to help people, but everyone gets upset with me. Oh, Dad, I didn't mean to hurt her little ole feelings," Tiffany whined.

Walt took Tiffany's arm in one hand and her shopping bags in the other and gently led her to the front door. "Tiffany, take these clothes back to the store and don't shop for people when they have asked you not to do so. I will not have you insulting my wife. Understand? You explain this to Ned. Good-bye, dear. Drive carefully." He handed her the shopping bags and waved as she walked slowly to her Mercedes. Walt shut the door when he saw she had gotten into the car. He turned and hugged Kathleen and said, "Honey, I am so sorry. I can't say that she means well because I don't think she does. Is there any hope? After you told me about your conversation at lunch, I hoped that you might have made a dent in her attitude. It does not look like it has helped yet. But I know you tried."

Lucille and Bernice came into the living room and Kathleen said, "I suppose you heard all that." They admitted they had been eavesdropping.

"That little valley girl is a handful," added Lucille. "I don't see much hope in her changing unless something dramatic happens to her. How about we get another pot of tea from the kitchen?" The girls went for the tea and Walt headed out to the stables.

"Well, let's get back to our vacation planning. When we get back, I still have quite a lot of work to do to help that little girl."

Lucille begged, "Oh, please let us help you." Bernice laughed.

"Absolutely not. You almost did in her aunt Paige. Remember, she is pregnant right now. Let's be gentle."

Chapter 19

Two weeks later, the girls were packing Walt's SUV for their trip to Arizona. He had asked Maxim to make them a dozen doughnuts to take on their trip to go with the big thermos of coffee they needed. They were dressed in jeans and going casual. Before pulling out of the driveway, they made their last trip to the bathroom before leaving. Walt held Kathleen in his arms and told her to have a wonderful time, but he would be missing her every day. They would talk at least twice a day. He reminded them of the trouble they had in Sarasota and to be very, very careful. He kissed both of her friends on their cheeks and knocked on the driver's door as they started to pull away. She looked out the rearview mirror and saw him waving at them as they drove off. She rolled down her window and waved her arm at him.

Bernice said from the backseat, "Lucille, haul out those doughnuts and pour the coffee."

"We aren't even out the front gate yet," Lucille said and yelled, "The musketeers ride again. Road trip."

Kathleen chuckled and seemed glad to be going on the trip, but knew she would miss Walt. How many years had she been single? Sixty-nine. Now it seemed like she had always been with Walt. She thanked God for putting him in her path. She told herself to buck up and not become maudlin and homesick. They had only been gone for half an hour. She realized she had been missing the conversation about where they would stop for lunch. In addition, she needed to pay attention to her driving. She would talk to Walt in just a few hours. The three girls were going to have a good time on this road trip. She chimed in about restaurants and remembered a special place Nicholas had mentioned on this route west. They could stop there in two hours, if they liked. They made it their next stop.

As they came close to where the restaurant should be located, they started watching for signs. Suddenly, Bernice pointed at a large sign advertising the restaurant, "There it is. It says three miles on the left. All right. We have found the first target on our list of places to see on this trip."

Kathleen slowed down when she saw the restaurant on the left and noticed the parking lot was nearly full. "This must be a good place to eat. Well, let's go try it for ourselves. We'll find out what kind of eating places Nicholas thinks are top of the line."

They walked into a cowboy's dream. The waitresses wore cowboy boots, short leather skirts, hot pink satin blouses, and cowboy hats. Their cute little blonde waitress stopped at their table and said, "Howdy, ladies. What can I do for ya today?"

"What are your specialties? We were told this was the best place in the area to eat," Bernice said as she silently read the waitress's nametag.

"Well, the barbeque ribs are to die for, the big burgers are the best in the state, and everything on the menu is delicious," Bambi said. "Do you need a few more minutes to decide? I can take your drink orders and get back to ya."

They chose their Texas-size sodas and starting perusing the menu. By the time Bambi came back with their drinks, they had all decided to have the Texas burgers and fries. They were looking at their itinerary when the little blonde cowgirl came back with their orders. The meal surpassed Nicholas's promise. None of them could finish the burger or the fries. They were full and felt like they needed a nap, but one of them had to drive. They decided that the one in the backseat could sleep while the two in the front had to stay awake, especially the driver.

They drove all day across the great state of Texas. At one point, they came upon a camper with a flat tire. Lucille started to slow down to see if they could help. "Maybe they have some small children and it is so hot out here," she said.

Kathleen argued that if they had a camper, they had beverages and what could three old ladies do to help in changing a flat tire. Most people had cell phones these days. As they got about thirty feet beyond the camper, Bernice looked out the back window and saw that there were four college-aged guys coming out of the camper with beers and tools for changing the tire. "I don't think they need our help, but Lucille could probably make friends with them. In fact, one of them is probably one of her former students. It has happened before." They all laughed. Lucille hit the brake and acted as if she might go back to meet the guys, and then she giggled and sped up again.

Farther down the road, they saw an old man had his thumb out hoping for a ride. He had a big cowboy hat, jeans, and cowboy boots with run-over heels. Lucille slowed down again to get a better look. When he gave them a lascivious look by wagging his tongue at them and waving for them to stop, she sped up again. "Sorry, cowpoke. You are too scary for me."

"Lucille, how could you even consider picking up a hitchhiker? Walt would have a fit if he thought we would ever do that. And that cowpoke looked disgusting," Kathleen said.

"That old guy was like the stupid semi driver in the movie *Thelma and Louise* flirting with the girls. Do you remember what happened to his truck? They blew it up. Hey, that sounds like fun. We haven't done that trick yet on a road trip," Bernice said and they all giggled.

"Well, I didn't stop, did I? I was just looking," Lucille said with a peeved grin. Bernice and Kathleen looked at each other and grinned. What would they ever do with their Lucy? At dinnertime, they found a motel with a restaurant nearby. After checking in and taking the minimum baggage in, they freshened up and decided to walk next door for dinner. It felt so good to be out of a moving vehicle. Following a light dinner, they walked back to the motel. Kathleen had not forgotten the deck of cards and scorecard tablet. They had finished the second hand when Kathleen's cell phone rang and she jumped up to answer it. She knew Walt's ringtone and she had missed him all day. She went outside the room and talked in the hallway. Bernice's phone rang and she had a conversation with her daughter Bethany. "All is well, dear. If we can keep Aunt Lucille from picking up college boys, we will be fine. We are very tired tonight and we have another day of driving tomorrow, but we are having a good time. I am winning the first card game tonight." Lucille sat back and listened to Bernice's end of the conversation. "Tell that girl that I am behaving myself," she joked.

When Kathleen came back in the room, she sniffled. "I'm fine. Everything is okay at home. I just miss my husband. He said to tell you girls to behave and stay away from the college boys and cowboys, Lucille." They laughed and decided to finish the card game. Kathleen wondered how Lucille felt about being the only one who had not received a phone call. As they were in the middle of the next hand of rummy, Lucille's cell phone rang. She looked surprised, as she did not expect any calls. Kathleen had a big smile on her face and mouthed the words Dave Vincent to Bernice behind Lucille's back.

"Hello? Oh, Dave, what a surprise. Yes, we are having a great trip." She got up and walked out of the room to talk with some privacy. Kathleen told Bernice that Dave had asked for her phone number from Walt that morning. He wanted to make a date with Lucille before she headed back to Indiana.

"Oh, oh. There goes Paige's possible conquest again. First, you steal her beau, now it looks like Lucille is going to steal her Davie-pooh," Bernice said. They were laughing when Lucille came back into their room. She did not even ask why there were laughing.

"What a surprise. I did not give Dave my phone number, did you?"

"He asked Walt this morning for your cell phone number, and Walt said he asked a few questions about my blonde Hoosier friend. You have charmed another one, my dear."

"He is a nice, shy man. He wants to take me to dinner when we get back to Dallas before we head for home, Bernice. Do you mind?"

"I would mind if you didn't go," said Bernice. "Whose turn is it?" and they were back involved in the game.

The next day, the scenery became more mundane without the excitement of broken-down campers or hitchhikers. By evening, they had reached the Grand Canyon National Park. Walt had called to get them rooms in an inn, knowing it was a long shot. He managed to be the first caller after there had been a cancellation. They got one room that a family had to cancel because the children had gotten chicken pox back in Illinois and would not be able to make it. They felt they had unbelievable luck. They would all be in the same room and would have to endure Bernice's snoring, but they were willing. After all, many people had made their reservations last year to get a room like theirs and they could tolerate Bernice's snoring.

The beauty of the Grand Canyon had not changed since Bernice and her husband had been there a couple of years before he died. It took her breath away, and she walked away from the other girls with her camera and began shooting. She had only a few minutes of good light left.

When she finished, they got back in the car and Bernice drove to the inn. They were tired from the travel, so they stopped for coffee and a sandwich before going to their room. Again, they were on their own dragging their luggage to their room. What a relief to have a room on the first floor. They unpacked and took turns getting hot showers and relaxing their sore muscles. Lucille had gone for ice and back to the car for some snacks they had brought along. She thought they might want snacks if they played cards. By the time she had her turn in the shower, Bernice had fallen asleep on the far side of one of the queen-sized beds. Kathleen sat up in bed reading her evening devotions when her cell phone rang.

"Hi, Walt. How are you, dear? Yes, I miss you too. We are at the inn and the room is very nice. The view out our window is spectacular. Bernice got some pictures with the sun setting. Lucille is in the shower and Bernice has fallen asleep already. The snoring has not started yet. We will be very careful. I promise. Love you too. Good-bye." As she shut her phone, Lucille said, "How is he doing without his loving wife? I know he misses you."

"Yes, he misses me. He said we are to be very careful. So let's remember to do that."

They turned off the lights and both friends were asleep within five minutes before the snoring began. Kathleen and Lucille were so tired that the snoring did not keep them awake. In the middle of the night, Bernice woke up and went to the window to look at God's masterpiece under a full moon. She remembered the trip she and Zackary had made when they had stayed in this same inn, but they were on the top floor. They celebrated their fortieth wedding anniversary while they were here. The chef had heard about their anniversary, so he had made a small cake for them with four candles, one for each decade of their life together. They had spent the rest of the evening sitting on a bench, observing the Canyon and reminiscing about their wonderful years together. However, Zack had held his back and told her he had back pain. He managed to wait until they got home to get to the doctor for the agonizing diagnosis. From that point on, life changed for the worse. There were too many trips to doctors and cancer hospitals. The kids rallied around and helped all they could. Each day that they had together from that point became so poignant and precious. *Oh, Zack, I miss you so much.*

Kathleen had been watching Bernice, and when she saw her shoulders shaking, she got out of bed and went over to console her. She held her in her arms and let her cry, knowing she thought about the last trip she and her husband had taken. Kathleen had wondered if this destination had been a good choice. Bernice finally pulled away and said, "Kathleen, I miss him so much. We had such a wonderful life together and I have so many memories. But I miss him."

"I know, dear. You two were quite a couple. He had such a wry sense of humor and kept us laughing all the time. I miss him too. However, we will see him again. He shared a wonderful gift with all of us…his faith in God. He shared it with strangers also. Not every Christian has that ability."

Lucille woke up and asked why they were up. Bernice said they were reminiscing about Zack and their trip to this same inn on their fortieth anniversary. "Let's go back to bed, girls. We are tired, remember?" They lay back on their pillows and continued to talk about their memories of Zack.

"Remember your wedding? I especially liked the part where he almost fainted because the church got so hot and had no air conditioning back then. His brother grabbed him when he started swaying back and forth. You got the giggles and he bent over and took a few deep breaths and the ceremony continued," Lucille said and they all giggled.

"I had almost forgotten that. That little church was like an oven. A lot of sweating in that sacred space that day. Thanks, girlfriends, for those memories. Tomorrow, I am going to take some special pictures in memory of Zack. Let's go back to sleep. Good night." The three friends lay quietly after Lucille extinguished the light as they tried to go back to sleep. Before long, Kathleen sat up, nudged Lucille, and they both started snickering because the snoring had begun. They were glad that Bernice could get some sleep. However, what about them? Eventually, Lucille got up and went to her makeup case and came back to bed with two sets of earplugs. What a great invention those things were.

The next morning, Bernice got out of the shower and made noise to awaken her friends. When they stirred, she said, "Wake up, sleepyheads. It's a new day, so let's get moving." Kathleen put her feet on the floor and looked at Bernice with a frown.

"You are chipper this morning. Glad you slept well."

"How do you know I slept well, dear?"

"If snoring is any indication of deep sleep, you slept well."

"I am sorry, girls. Did I do it again? I may have to try some of those new-fangled objects to help me stop snoring."

Lucille put in her two-cents' worth, "Sounds like a good idea. We love you, girlfriend, but it is hard to share a bedroom with you. Sorry." She gave Bernice a hug and headed for the shower.

"We have time for a leisurely breakfast before we head out for the bus tour. I am looking forward to today. Aren't you?" Bernice asked.

"Yes, all three of us are in agreement on that one. What kind of coffee have you made there?" Bernice poured a cup and handed it to Kathleen. By the time Lucille came out of the bathroom dressed and ready to go, Kathleen had finished her coffee.

Later, the three musketeers headed out for the dining room. Over breakfast, they reviewed their plans for the next couple of days before they would head back for Kathleen's home near Dallas. Bernice started shooting pictures of her two friends who put their heads together and gave her beautiful smiles before they made funny faces. "Let's get out of here and go somewhere where I can get some good shots while the light is good." They followed her out and watched from a distance as she moved from here to there using her artistic flair to get her prize-winning pictures. Bernice noticed a young man with a similar camera and decided he would be the guy to ask to take a picture of the trio with the Grand Canyon in the background. He took half a dozen pictures from different angles until Bernice signaled enough. She thought one of those would become a great Christmas gift when framed for her friends.

In the midst of the tour around the Canyon, Bernice took a chance to get a better shot by stepping over the railing. There were signs giving instructions not to go beyond the railing, but she had always taken chances with her camera. The tour guide yelled for her to get behind the railing. The shouts startled many of the people, including Bernice. She started to slide down the steep incline. She held up her camera to protect it as she slid quickly down the slope until her foot hit a stump. She lay very quietly in the same spot so she would not start the slide again. The tour guide had called for help and a man appeared in climbing gear with a rope and tackle.

Kathleen yelled for Bernice not to move, but they could not hear if Bernice answered them. The rugged man got the rope set up around a nearby tree and began the descent. As he got near her, he called out, "Ma'am, can you hear me?"

"Yes, I'm all right. I think I sprained my ankle."

"Don't move until I get there," he said as he continued down the incline. When he reached her, he called up that he had her. He put her in a harness and helped her up on her good foot and his assistant at the top helped to pull them both up. When he had her on the right side of the railing, he laid her down on the ground and checked her ankle. Her foot had already started to swell badly. An ambulance arrived, and they put Bernice on a gurney and transferred her to the vehicle. Lucille and Kathleen told her that they would follow and meet her at the hospital as soon as the bus got them back to the inn. They were at the last stop, so it would not be too long. Lucille called Bethany, Bernice's daughter, while Kathleen drove so she would know that her mother had an accident.

"Bethany, we are so sorry. She got on the wrong side of the railing and slid down until she caught herself on a tree. They will be getting x-rays and probably fitting her with a cast. She said she thought she had a sprain, but we think it is broken. Yes, we will call you as soon as we know something and let you talk to her. I know, she thinks she is twenty-nine, instead of sixty-nine. Good-bye, dear."

Lucille pulled Walt's SUV into the hospital parking lot. Kathleen said, "We are here. This does not look like a very big hospital. I guess they will know what they are doing. They probably see lots of broken bones and sprains." They got out and had a short distance to walk to get to the door, and then they were in the emergency area. They waited in an area with a few chairs and a pop machine. Finally, a young, red-headed doctor came out and told them Bernice required surgery and that she would do it. They went in to see Bernice quickly before the surgery. She seemed drowsy because they had given her pain medication, but she managed to say, "I am so sorry to ruin our vacation like this."

"You haven't ruined our vacation, Bernice. When we get you fixed up, we can drive you back to Dallas and we will get you home eventually," Kathleen said.

"At least I am not responsible for slowing down our vacation this time," Lucille said with a grin. Kathleen took Bernice's hand and reached for Lucille's as she said, "Let's pray before they shoo us out of here."

As the friends were waiting during surgery, they heard a call for a crash cart, and they both jumped up out of their uncomfortable chairs. This could not be for Bernice because she had just broken an ankle. They were anxiously waiting in front of the double doors to the operating area.

A man in a black shirt and pants with white tie came over to them and introduced himself. "I am Pastor Jim. I work here part-time as their chaplain. They called for me to sit with you because it seems your friend's heart stopped for a few moments, but she seems to be doing better now. Let me go check again for you."

Lucille introduced herself and Kathleen and added that Kathleen was a retired pastor. They made some small talk before he left to go through the double doors to get more information. He returned in about ten minutes, and he shared good news.

Bernice's surgery was finished and the doctor would be out to talk to them soon. The ladies thanked Pastor Jim and he prayed with them.

The friends made a quick trip to the ladies' room, and as they came back to the waiting area, the doctor came through the double doors on the opposite wall. They sat down with her and she shared that Bernice had scared them for a few minutes there. The doctor said, "I got her heart going again very quickly. She needs to see her doctor when she returns home for a good checkup and some tests. Her ankle has a pin in it and a cast. She needs to use crutches for a while. They could see her in a couple of hours, so the doctor suggested that they go down the street to get dinner while they waited.

When they finally got to see Bernice, she opened her eyes briefly and saw they were there. "Well, I guess I won't be taking any long walks for a while. Thanks for taking care of me. I saw you come down the mountain after me, Lucille. I did not know you were so strong. You carried me up on your back and I do appreciate it."

Lucille started to laugh, "Bernice, thanks for the vote of confidence, but I did not come down the mountain after you. A park ranger rescued you, and he was darn handsome, by the way. You are feeling no pain, are you?" Bernice shook her head in agreement. She felt no pain, and she had a happy grin on her face for her two friends.

"Well, I guess I'm ready to get out of here. Pull that log off my leg and I can get up and we'll go get some dinner," Bernice slurred.

Kathleen put her hand on Bernice's arm and said, "You aren't going anywhere tonight. That log on your leg is actually a cast. Your leg is broken and they had to pin it together. You rest tonight and we will be back to see you tomorrow. I hope that we can get you out of here, if not we will try to sneak you out the next day. Rest well, dear. We will call Bethany and let her know how you are now." Bernice closed her eyes, and as they watched her sleeping, they decided they would go back to the inn and come back tomorrow. As they walked out the door, they heard their friend snoring.

"She is back to normal," Lucille said. They looked at one another and were pleased. Before they left the area, Kathleen gave the nurse her cell phone number. On the way back to the inn, they stopped at a gas station to fill up the tank and to pick up a snack for later in the evening.

Chapter 20

As they walked by the check-in desk at the inn, the clerk called them over. "Ladies, the park ranger who rescued your friend came in earlier asking about her. How is she?"

The women took turns telling the story of the condition of her ankle and the apprehensive time during surgery when her heart quit beating. However, they told the clerk that she would be all right after some recuperation.

A couple of older men who had been sitting in lobby chairs stood up and came toward Lucille and Kathleen. *Oh, no,* Kathleen thought.

The taller of the two introduced themselves as twin brothers who were traveling from national park to national park for the summer. The more talkative one said, "We watched your friend fall and get rescued. That certainly made for an exciting day. We would like to hear more of the story. Can we take you ladies out for a drink and some conversation? How about dinner?"

"No, thank you," Kathleen said. "I am married and we both are tired. It has been a stressful day." Lucille surprised her as she spoke up in agreement.

"Thank you, but we'll take a rain check." She took Kathleen's arm. "Let's go, dear. We are both so tired." As they got to their room, Lucille said, "If those guys were twin brothers, we are monkey's uncles. Something felt sleazy about them. One is at least five years older than the other is. They are not twins. Something is wrong. Didn't you feel it?"

"Lucille, I am so tired that all I feel right now are my aching arches and a backache. What did you feel? What is wrong with them? They do not look alike, I agree. They do not even look the same age. You are right. Something is different about their story. I get the shower first."

While Kathleen eased her sore muscles in the hot shower, Lucille removed her makeup and brushed out her hair. She could not get the two men out of her mind. She knew herself to be a good judge of character and those guys were suspicious. Kathleen walked out into the bedroom with wet hair and steam followed her.

"That certainly felt good. Now it is your turn." She noticed that Lucille looked puzzled and had sketched in the notebook they used for score-keeping. "What is it, dear?"

"There is something about one of those men that looked so familiar. Did you notice it? Look at this face. Doesn't he look strangely familiar?" Kathleen looked at the sketch. Besides being amazed at how quickly her friend had drawn the man's face, she agreed that the face seemed eerily familiar. However, she could not place the face.

Lucille got up to take her shower and Kathleen kept looking at the picture. She had chills running up and down her spine, but she could not put a name or a situation to the face. She pushed it aside and called Walt. He had been waiting to hear from her and get the update on Bernice. She also told him about the two men posing as twin brothers who had introduced themselves to Lucille and her in the lobby and their response to the men. He told her to be careful. After some other chitchat and love talk, they hung up. She called Bethany again with the latest update and told her she did not need to fly out because she and Lucille would take good care of her. Bernice would be upset if Bethany left her family to come to baby her mother. Bethany agreed and said she would call tomorrow. Lucille came out of the bathroom and heard Kathleen talking to Bernice's daughter. She reached out for the phone.

"Bethany, dear, we will take good care of your mama. By the way, do not bother to call her tonight. She is so full of medication that she thanked me for climbing down the mountain to rescue her," Lucille said with a laugh. "We'll talk to you tomorrow. Good night, Beth."

The girls were not sleepy, so Kathleen suggested a card game. As they started playing, Lucille's sketch continued to draw Kathleen to think about why this man's face looked familiar. By the end of the game, she still could not put a name to the face. Kathleen led them in scripture reading and prayer before they turned off the lights and crawled into their beds.

The ringing phone on the table between their beds woke both women. Kathleen reached over and picked up the receiver. "Hello," she said sleepily. She waited for a voice.

"Hey, old lady, you don't remember me, do you? You better watch your step. I have a beef with you. You fingered me once, never again. What luck running into you out here. Like I said, watch your step or you'll end up like your short friend."

"What? Who is this? Don't call here again," Kathleen shouted. She dropped the receiver and jumped out of bed. She went to the door to be sure that all the locks and chains were in place.

"Kathleen, what is it? Who called?" Lucille got out of bed and followed her to the bathroom door where she turned on the light. She had not seen her friend this upset in quite a while. "What is it?"

"A raspy voice said he had a beef with me, I apparently didn't remember him and my luck had run out. He said to watch my step or I would end up like Bernice. I wish I knew who he is," Kathleen said, as she walked over to her bed and sat down. "What time is it?" She looked at the alarm and saw it was three o'clock. She got up and walked over to the table where the cards, notebook, pen, and Lucille's sketch laid. "He called me an old lady. That makes me mad." She picked up the sketch and a curtain lifted from her memory.

"Lucille, one of the men in the lobby is the big guy on the beach who negotiated with the skinny guy named Slim to kill Shorty and you if you got in the way. He must have recognized us from when we went to the police station to point him out in the line-up. Remember, he accidentally saw us as we were leaving the area and yelled at us, calling us something a lot worse than old lady. To make it worse, he must have seen our picture in the newspaper."

"So what's his deal now? How is he out of jail so soon? Did he escape? When morning comes, we need to call Walt and the police. I do not think I can go back to sleep now, and I do not want to turn out the light. What about you?"

"No. I am going to wait two hours and call Walt. Want to play canasta?" They turned on more lights, took turns in the bathroom, and sat down to play. They discarded each card with a slap, slap, slap. Neither talked nor concentrated on the game. When the clock showed five o'clock, Kathleen got up and called Walt. He sounded sleepy but glad to hear her voice so early, until he heard the reason why. He sat up in bed, turned on the light, and listened carefully.

He said, "Honey, I don't like the sound of this at all. I am flying out as soon as I can get the arrangements made for the helicopter. I will call the police station out there, talk with them, and have them check to see if the Goodings character has escaped or gotten out of jail sooner than expected. Please do not leave your room, get room service for breakfast, and call the hospital and have them watch out for Bernice. Neither of you should leave your room to go anywhere. I do not mean to scare you, but better to be safe than sorry. I'll call you soon and let you know when to expect me."

Kathleen repeated Walt's message and decided they should get dressed and call for room service to deliver their breakfast and a pot of coffee. When they were both ready for the day, Lucille had made their beds to have something to do. They were each silently praying for protection. Kathleen had called the hospital and told them to keep a close eye on visitors to Bernice's room because they had received a threat. When she assured herself that they took her seriously, she hung up the phone. Within thirty seconds, her cell phone rang. She hesitated to answer it, but recognized Walt's ringtone.

"Kathleen, I will be there this afternoon. The police in Sarasota say that Everett Goodings, the man you identified as the man telling Slim to kill Shorty is still in jail. I do not know who that guy is out there. Are you sure you are remembering his face correctly? I am sending you his picture from the wanted poster. Is it the same guy?"

She looked at the picture, held it out for Lucille to see, and they both agreed it was the guy in the lobby last night. "Yes, Walt, we both agree it is the guy. How can that be? We are scared and we are glad you will be here to rescue us soon. We will call Bernice and tell her to hide out in her hospital room until you get here. Yes, dear, I love you too. We will be careful and lay low as you say. Good-bye."

"Lucille, please call Bernice and tell her about the threat and to stay in her room until we get there. Not that she is going anyplace too far by herself in that cast." Kathleen pulled her laptop in front of her on the table. She started digging for information about Everett Goodings. They had him in jail last year for conspiracy to commit murder. That she knew. He should still be in jail. Walt said he was. As Lucille talked to Bernice, the room phone rang and Kathleen picked it up.

A malicious male voice said, "Hey, little ladies, we know where you are. You cannot get away from us. You hurt us, now we are going to hurt you." Kathleen hung up the phone as if it were a hot coal in her hand. She called the town police and told them about the men making the threatening calls who had approached them in their hotel lobby last night. They agreed to come check it out. She went back to her computer. She checked on a people-finder site and typed in his name. After some work and a charge to her credit card, she found family history on Everett Goodings. As it downloaded, they heard a soft knock on the door. Thinking their breakfast had arrived, Lucille walked to the door and started unlocking the door. Kathleen yelled at her to look out the peephole. When she did, she quickly flipped the lock back in place.

"Katie, it's those guys. Call the front desk and tell them to get these guys away from our door."

"Little girls, little girls, let me come in," he said in a singsong voice.

"Get away from our door, you perverts, you murderers, you wolves in sheep's clothing!"

"Lucille, let's put this chair under the doorknob. Come into the bathroom. The front desk is sending their security guard to check out these guys." Just as she peeked out the peephole again, she saw the guys leave hurriedly.

They heard a voice say, "What are you men doing there? Come back here." She saw the security guy stop in front of their door, call the front desk, and tell them the men ran out the door at the end of the hall, so they should report them to the police. "Ladies, are you all right?"

"Yes, so far we are fine," they said in unison.

"Ladies, if you will open the door, your breakfast is here."

Lucille looked out the peephole and saw a young man in a white jacket and black bowtie standing behind a cart covered with food items and metal covers. She unlocked the door and let him push the cart in. "Ladies, feel free to keep the cart in here until I come back later. Don't open the door for anyone else," the security man said. They thanked him for his concern.

They moved the cart close to the small round table in front of the television and set out their breakfast and coffee. They were able to eat some of what they ordered, and then put the leftovers back on the cart. The coffee carafe stayed on the table with their mugs. Kathleen went back to her laptop. She looked at the screen and saw a couple of men named Everett Goodings. She punched the key for the one that she thought fit the description. She waited a short time and started reading the information on the family history of Everett Goodings.

Everett Goodings, born March 1, 1948, in Miami, Florida, to Mabel Goodings and father unknown. He had an identical twin brother, Ebert, last known address in Fort Lauderdale and an older brother, Edgar, last known address in New Orleans. Everett and Ebert both had several arrests and incarcerations since they were eighteen years of age. Edgar had been in prison until four years ago for kidnapping. He had served his time and been released. They saw a picture of Mabel with her three sons. The twins were identical at age six and Edgar at age ten did not look much taller. That would explain the difference in appearance last night in the lobby. The taller guy did the talking, but lied when he said they were twins.

"Lucille, I have the answer. It was not Everett Goodings in the lobby last night, but his two brothers. One is his identical twin and the other an older brother. I am calling Walt, if I can reach him. Can you call the local police and tell them who they need to find?" Both friends were on the phone, and Lucille seemed very proud of Kathleen for her good detective work yet again. If she were not so scared, Kathleen would be proud of herself. Now she just felt discomfort and fear.

Walt did not answer his cell phone, but when Miriam answered the home phone, she said that Mr. Alexander just left in the helicopter to go to the Grand Canyon. She let out a big sigh of relief.

She told Miriam if her husband called back to the house to tell him to call his wife immediately. The friends went back to the card games because anything seemed better than sitting, waiting, and thinking. When lunchtime came, they ordered room service again. Half an hour later, they heard another knock on the door.

Lucille walked to the door, peeked out, and saw a man walking quickly away from the door and the security man arrived then with the lunch cart. Lucille pushed the breakfast cart over by the door as Kathleen let the two men and the cart into the room. She handed the young man a tip and he pushed the breakfast cart out the door. The security guard told them he had seen one of the men sneaking out the end door again. "The police are on their way over and we hope to catch the guys soon. When they do, we will let you know."

"We really want to go to the hospital and check on our friend Bernice. We would appreciate hearing that good news," Lucille said.

The security guard introduced himself as Bart and offered to drive the ladies to the hospital when his shift ended at two o'clock. Lucille grinned at him and said, "Oh, that would be wonderful. Would you really do that for us?"

"Of course, ma'am. It would be my pleasure to escort two such lovely ladies in distress," he grinned back with a red face. "I'll call your room when I get off my shift and see if you still need a ride." He backed out of the room and told them to lock the door, which they did.

"Isn't he sweet?" cooed Lucille. "There are just so many nice men in this world who have helped me from time to time."

Kathleen put their lunches on the round table and rolled her eyes at her blonde friend who had the charming personality. "Lucille, you just have a knack for endearing yourself to men who want to rescue damsels in distress. You are something, for sure." They sat down, ate their lunch, and found they had a better appetite than they had for breakfast. After clearing the table, they decided to lie down and rest while they could. They left the curtains closed since they were on the first floor and turned out the lights.

Kathleen's cell phone rang with Walt's special tone and she rolled over and grabbed it from the nightstand. "Hello, dear. Where are you?"

"I am in the lobby of the inn. I did not want to scare you by knocking on the door. What is your room number and I'll be right there," Walt asked. She told him the room number, shook Lucille's shoulder, and told her Walt had arrived. They quickly got up and Kathleen went to brush her teeth and her hair. She heard a knock on the door and rushed to look out the peephole and saw her hero standing there in his cowboy hat, leather jacket, and boots. She unlatched the locks, threw open the door, and grabbed him by the shirt to pull him into the room. He held her for a few moments and then kissed her passionately. He put his hand on her head and held it to his chest. Lucille walked out of the bathroom and said, "Welcome, welcome. We sure are glad to see you." He let go of Kathleen's head, and she turned to look at Lucille who had put on a pair of sandals with heels and freshened up her lipstick.

Walt said, "I stopped at the hospital first to check on Bernice. I wanted to be sure that they were actually keeping a close eye on her. They had moved her to a room across the hall from the nurse's station and were keeping her door closed. She is eager to see you both and to get out of her prison cell as she called it." Both women were relieved that the hospital had taken them seriously about protecting Bernice and that she felt better. They sat down on the beds facing each other while Walt continued to hold Kathleen's hand as they retold the story from the beginning where the two men tried to pick them up in the lobby.

"Everett Goodings has a twin brother, Ebert, and an older brother Edgar. What are the chances of just running into them here?" Kathleen said.

"Our Katie did it again. She solved the mystery of how Everett could still be in prison yet be at the Grand Canyon. Isn't she amazing?"

"Yes, my girl is amazing." Walt had just finished his sentence when they heard another knock on the door. The women froze in fright and Walt stood up. They waited a moment for another knock.

They heard that slimy voice again, "Little girls, little girls, let me come in." Walt motioned for the women to go into the bathroom. He whispered in Kathleen's ear to call security. He pulled back his jacket and took a gun out of his holster. Kathleen's eyes got as big as saucers, but he pushed them both toward the bathroom. He got to the door in about six steps and looked out the peephole.

"Little girls, I know you are in there," said the creepy wolf-in-sheep's clothing. Abruptly, Walt unlocked the door, slowly disengaged the chain, and stood behind the door as he opened it. Two men pushed it open as Walt stepped aside pointing his gun at both of them.

"Hands up now, you low-life creeps." Both men had such frightened expressions on their faces that Kathleen started to giggle from the bathroom door. They looked at her and one of them shouted, "When did Wild Bill Hickok get here? You tricked us."

At that moment, the security guard and a uniformed police officer showed up. After some discussion, they put the two men in handcuffs and took them to jail. Walt hugged his wife and her best friend as he returned his gun to its holster.

"Well, Wild Bill, what next?" Lucille said with a grin.

"How about if I send the plane back to Dallas and I drive you girls home as soon as we can get Bernice broken out of her prison cell? I do not want to stick my nose into your road trip, but I feel the need to protect you. You could just consider me your chauffeur."

Both women agreed that they would like the protection, but he would not be just their chauffeur. "You will be an honorary musketeer, just for this trip, my dear." He grinned and agreed.

"I will sleep with the chauffeur and you get Bernice's snoring all to yourself, my friend," Kathleen said and hugged her husband. They decided they could go visit Bernice.

When they arrived in her room, there were hugs abounding. The doctor had just been in and said she could go home any time now, but did not think a two-day trip in an SUV would be a good idea. Lucille had the solution. "I think that if you sent Bernice and me back to your house in the plane, I can take care of her, and then you two can drive the car back and enjoy a little second honeymoon. We will be waiting for you when you return. What do you think?"

"That sounds like a great idea. Do you girls mind being at the house alone for a couple of days before we get there? Actually, maybe Bernice ought to rest at the inn one more day before traveling," said Kathleen as she looked up at Walt. Bernice agreed to the plan, so Lucille went to the nurse's station to start the paperwork to release her and returned with the good news that they were breaking her out of this joint.

"I think I need one of my skirts because I don't think my pants will fit comfortably over the cast. I hate to ask, but could you go back to our room and bring me a clean outfit?"

Lucille told her not to worry, as they had thought about that. A clean outfit waited for her in the SUV. "I'll go get it and we'll get you ready to leave. How are you doing on the crutches?" Bernice said they were a pain in the neck, but they would do until she could walk on both feet. When she signed the paperwork, Bernice was free to leave the hospital. Walt and Kathleen went to the waiting area and Lucille stayed to help Bernice get into her clothes. When they walked out and saw Kathleen waiting, Bernice smiled widely and held out one of the crutches.

"I knew you could do it, dear. Walt has gone to bring the car up to the door for you." A nurse's aide came up behind her with a wheelchair and told her she had to ride out the door. Bernice gave in and was happy to let Walt push her wheelchair. Lucille carried the plastic bag holding the clothes she had worn into the hospital a couple of days before, while Kathleen carried the crutches. Walt held the back door open for Bernice and carefully helped her get in. They rode back to the inn quietly. As the foursome walked into the lobby, there were half a dozen staff members standing in a semicircle applauding the lady on crutches. One desk clerk handed her a bouquet of wild flowers from the area, while another one took her picture with her friends. The security guard, who had offered to drive the ladies to the hospital earlier, shook hands with Walt and the ladies. Lucille hugged him and thanked him for offering to take care of them.

"I am so sorry I didn't get to know you better. You are such a nice guy and you took such good care of us."

"My pleasure, ma'am. I am just doing my job. I wish you all a safe trip home and hope you can come back again."

Bernice said, "My first trip here with my husband had been a wonderful time. This time not so wonderful. In fact, this trip has been a bust. It has been scarier and painful, although I caused the pain myself. It may be awhile before I want to come back again." They all agreed with her. She turned and headed for their room and sat down in the only comfortable chair in the room and placed her crutches on the floor. "I think I feel well enough to travel whenever we can get away."

"I think if you want to go today, we can get you to the plane and have you on the way to Dallas this evening. The van is taking you to Las Vegas and our jet will be there waiting to take you home. You can lie on the bed on the trip back, sleep, or relax on the way."

"Oh, Walt, you are such a thoughtful man. That sounds wonderful," Bernice said.

Lucille started packing her bags and Kathleen worked on Bernice's bags. Walt made a couple of phone calls and felt he had the plans made to his satisfaction. The girls made one last trip to the bathroom before they headed out the door. Bernice had difficulty getting into the van, so the young driver got out, carefully picked her up, and placed her in a seat. "Thank you, young man," she said and fastened her seat belt.

"What muscles you have, Mac," said Lucille after reading his name on the nameplate on his jacket. He gave her a crooked smile and blushed.

"Come on, Lucille. Quit flirting and get in. We have a plane to catch," shouted Bernice as Mac waited to shut her door. They all waved good-bye, and Walt and Kathleen backed away from the van provided by the inn. As they headed back inside, he took her hand and squeezed it. He thought, *Alone at last*, and she thought, *I hope housekeeping has changed the sheets and brought in clean towels.*

They went into the restaurant for dinner before going back to their room. They shared the activities of their last few days. Walt said that the police told him the Goodings brothers were in jail on other warrants as well as their threats to Kathleen and her friends. She admitted she would sleep better tonight knowing that and knowing she shared a bed with her husband. They took time to sit outside and admire the Canyon and to watch the expressions on the faces of those seeing it for the first time. As they crawled into their freshly made bed, Walt turned out the light and Kathleen pulled up the covers over them. They turned to one another and snuggled together and whispered words of love. Kathleen began to giggle and pulled his face down to hers.

Chapter 21

After breakfast, Walt helped her carry her luggage and laptop to their SUV. He checked them out and they were ready to start their own road trip back home. He got behind the wheel, looked over at her, and winked. "Let's go home, sweet thing." She nodded and smiled at him. He made her feel so safe. As she thought about life since meeting him in Sarasota, she knew she had lived through some of the best and worst moments of her life. Not since losing Tyler had she had such low moments. When Lucille disappeared with Shorty, they were beside themselves until rescuing her. Now she had been threatened by criminals yet again. They thought Bernice might be dead at the bottom of the Grand Canyon and then on the operating table. She thought, *I am ready for some boring days.*

"How about if we go home and have a few quiet years?" she asked.

"That sounds good to me, but not very exciting. You have brought some real thrills into my life. It has been a while since I have had to rescue anyone, other than Shorty, of course. Yes, let's go home and ride around the homestead, paint some pictures, or paint the barn." He laughed and she joined in. They drove for miles in silence and enjoyed it. After hours on the road, they stopped for the night. He found a place with an indoor pool and hot tub so they could relax.

The next day when Walt drove the SUV down their driveway, Lucille and Bernice were on the front porch waiting. Taffy lay on the porch next to Bernice as if she were the protector. She got up to greet her master and mistress. Lucille quickly handed a few flowers that she had cut for Kathleen to Miriam. Kathleen got out of the car, stretched her back, and walked toward her best friends. They hugged and walked together into the house. Walt followed them with her bags and his gym bag and carried everything into their bedroom. Miriam came out of the kitchen to welcome them home. "Dinner will be ready at six, Mrs. Alexander."

"Thank you, Miriam. It is good to see you and so good to be home."

"It is good to have you back. I am sorry your trip didn't turn out as you planned."

"Well, girls, I am going to take a shower and change my clothes before dinner. I'll see you in a few." They waved him off and went out to sit by the pool. Kathleen went in and found Walt lying on their bed with Maggie lying on her pillow. "Dear, are you all right? Maggie, are you taking care of our dear man?" Maggie purred, stretched out, and curled up next to Walt's side.

"Yes, I just want to rest a bit before dinner. I enjoyed our little road trip together. Are you taking a shower? Well, don't use up all the hot water," he said and chuckled. She waved at him and went in. When she came back, Walt snored softly, so she waited until close to six o'clock to nudge him for dinner. He got up, washed his face, and said he was ready for a good meal. Miriam served a great dinner prepared by her husband. Kathleen noticed that Walt only ate about half of the chicken and rice on his plate. He skipped dessert and decided to turn in early. He excused himself, kissed her on the cheek, told the others good night, and left the room He had driven all day and was exhausted. "Ladies, I am feeling my age tonight."

The three friends sat in the living room with a glass of wine until nine o'clock and Kathleen said she also needed to turn in. However, she did not move.

"Kathleen, something is bothering you, right? Spill it, Katie," Bernice said.

"This is such a lovely home, isn't it? Nevertheless, I feel strange at times living in Delia's home. Will this ever feel like my home? Am I being ridiculous? Delia had excellent taste in decorating … and in husbands. This house is so perfect, but it does not feel like my own yet. Maybe it will come with time," Kathleen mused.

Bernice answered, "Kiddo, I wondered when that issue would begin to bother you. It would bother me. Have you mentioned this to Walt? He is a sensitive guy, and I know he would listen. What are your alternatives?" Lucille nodded in agreement.

"No, I haven't said anything to Walt. This is his home and he helped design it, it is located on his property, and I didn't want to sound selfish or hard to please."

Lucille added, "Kathleen, I haven't experienced anything like this, but I also wondered how comfortable you would feel stepping into another woman's house. It is beautiful and one of a kind, but it is Delia and Walt's house. There is enough land here to build another house where you would not even have to see this one every day. You need to talk to Walt about it. He wants you to be happy. See what he says. He is sensitive and sensible."

"What would he do with this house? He may have memories here that he wouldn't want to lose."

Bernice suggested that maybe one of his kids, Nicholas or Nancy and a spouse might be interested in the house. "I wouldn't want Tiff as your neighbor…I wouldn't want Tiff as my neighbor. Sorry, but I do not want you to have a daily dose of that girl. Nancy might love to live in her mom's house and make it her own. You need to talk to Walt about this."

"I hadn't thought about one of the kids, but that might work. Nancy has been so darn nice to me. Walt said Nancy and her mother had a special relationship and it has taken her some time to adjust to the loss. This might be a nice solution for all of us. I will address it with Walt. Thanks, girls. We are a great trio, aren't we? Guess I will go to bed now. Do not stay up too late. Good night."

Lucille and Bernice decided to play rummy for a while before turning in. When Kathleen got to the bedroom and went into the bathroom to get ready for bed, she could hear Walt's quiet snore. When Maggie saw her coming, she moved down to Walt's feet to make room for her favorite lady of the house. She snuggled up to Walt. When he reached out for her, she laid her head down on his outstretched arm. She lay there and prayed for her loved ones and especially for her husband. She ruminated about how to talk to Walt about the house issue. Would he understand? Would he want to give up his perfect home? Time would tell. She closed her eyes and willed herself to fall asleep.

The next day, all four of them had a late breakfast. Walt suggested they go riding, which they all agreed sounded great. Kathleen said, "Oh, Bernice, you can't go. What are we thinking? I will stay and keep you company." Lucille suggested instead that she stay at the house and Kathleen could go with her husband. She felt good to be back in the saddle again. They rode down by the river where they sat on their favorite log for a while.

"It is so good to be home, Walt. I enjoyed my time with Lucille and Bernice, well most of my time, but I am glad to be home. This hasn't been my home for long, but since you are here, it is the only place I want to be." She almost broached the idea of moving, but lost her nerve.

He hugged her. "Honey, this is your home…our home. I am so glad we found one another. For all the irritation that Shorty caused me his entire life, when he found Lucille and her friends, he gave me a gift I would not have found on my own. God bless him."

After some quiet time, they got back on their horses and headed back home the long way around. When they got back to the stable, Walt took Sara's reins and told Kathleen to go back to the house and entertain her guests. "I enjoyed our ride together, but I have some help here who will take care of your horse this time." Kathleen turned and patted Walt on the behind and said, "Thank you, sweetie. You're the best."

Walt said, "Whoa, there, little lady. We are not alone. The horses are watching." They both laughed and she walked quickly out of the stable. She thought, *I never thought I could be this happy. Thank you, Lord.*

Her friends were sitting by the pool. Lucille dried in the sun, while Bernice sat close by in the shade. With her leg in a cast, she had to avoid sweating. She longed to swim across the pool, but that would not be happening for a while. When Kathleen arrived, she asked Lucille if she did not have a date for dinner.

"Oh, I haven't forgotten. Now that you are here to watch Bernice, I am hitting the shower."

"What do you mean...watch Bernice? I do not need a babysitter. I broke my ankle. I didn't lose my mind," she said with a giggle. All three friends headed into the living room and Miriam came in with a pitcher of sweet tea and some little muffins that were just out of the oven. Bernice dropped down into a chair and gently flipped up the leg rest. After Miriam poured their tea, she reminded them that lunch would be in about half an hour. "Would Mr. Walt be back in by then?"

"Oh, I don't think he has ever missed a meal. He will be here. It is Lucille we will probably have to prod a little to get her down here with her wet hair," answered Kathleen. "I hope she and Dave have a nice dinner out this evening. He is such a nice man. If she cannot tease his shyness out of him, no one can. I wonder how shy he was with his wife. Walt said she was very outgoing and bubbly, so she shielded him somewhat. She and Delia were good friends."

"Better friends than Delia and Paige?" said Bernice and she threw back her head and laughed. "I know that Delia and Paige were not friends."

"That's what I heard, little Miss Troublemaker," teased Kathleen.

"Who's the troublemaker?" said Walt as he came into the room.

"Who else? Bernice. It certainly would not be me. I don't cause trouble," said Kathleen trying to keep a straight face. She got up to refill Bernice's glass.

Walt walked by her, patted her behind in her fitted jeans, and said, "That's not what I saw in the stable, Mrs. Alexander." He winked at her and walked down the hall to their bedroom.

"What did you do in the stable, Katie? Should I be shocked or embarrassed? Did you go for a little roll in the hay?"

Kathleen's face turned red and she told Bernice to mind her own business, and she said, "A roll in the hay? Are you nuts? What kind of talk is that? It is nothing. I just patted his derriere and thanked him for taking care of my horse. I am getting audacious, aren't I?" Both of them laughed as Lucille came in with large curlers in her hair and no makeup.

"What's so funny?" she asked.

"Well, for one thing, finding out our Kathleen is audacious and then seeing you in the alien antennae and no makeup," said Bernice. All three of them laughed. Lucille did a little pirouette in the middle of the room.

"Will Walt be scared to see me looking like this across the lunch table?"

"Of course not. I am going to go get Walt and we will go in for lunch. Relax, dear. It is nice to see you *au naturel*." She walked out of the room and came back a few minutes later with her husband. He ushered them into the dining room, helped Bernice get her chair up to the table, and propped her crutches against the wall behind her. Miriam and Maxim carried out their salad plates and a basket of rolls. Walt prayed and they passed the rolls and butter. Lucille apologized to Walt for her hair rollers and no makeup.

"Oh, those are hair rollers? I thought you were communicating with Mars, and then I remembered, 'Men are from Mars and women are from Venus.' Did you reach Dave?" he said drolly. Kathleen patted his hand and apologized for him.

"Lucille, he is teasing you. He knows what hair curlers are and he is not shocked, are you, Walt?"

"Of course not, girls. Lucille, I am glad you are getting ready for dinner with Dave. He is a great guy. Will you be wearing the curlers when you go out?"

"Walt, stop that or I am leaving the table and I won't come back," said Lucille, trying to act as if her feelings were hurt.

"Eat your lunch, Lucy. I will stop teasing you if you promise to finish your meal." When he called her Lucy, they noticed her eyes started to tear up. He realized that had been Shorty's pet name for her. She smiled at him and said, "Thanks, Buddy."

Bernice changed the subject and said that her daughter had called while they were horseback riding and wanted to know when she would be home. "I told her I was feeling quite well and getting around fairly well. The only thing holding us back is Lucille's dinner date with a handsome man. Beth said that if we were having fun, not to rush back on her account. She trusted my friends to take good care of me. Lucille, she said to tell you to have a great time and try not to charm your date too much."

"That girl should talk. Before she got married, she charmed the entire neighborhood. I taught her all I knew," said Lucille and laughed with all of them. Following lunch, Walt went back to the stable to help muck out the stalls. The girls went into the library to play a card game until Lucille had to get ready for her dinner date. About five o'clock, both friends walked to Lucille's room to see what outfit she had chosen. They approved of the purple slacks with tan silk tank top and a long flowing jacket in purple, tan, and a touch of red. Those were her favorite colors that made her feel so self-confident. They left Lucille to get ready.

Chapter 22

At five minutes before six o'clock, the doorbell rang. Walt got up and headed for the door. "Honey, you'd better go get Cinderella." Kathleen started up the stairs and Lucille came out of her room.

"Oh, Lucille, those new sandals are beautiful. He has arrived, so come on down." Lucille looked a little more nervous than Kathleen expected. As she reached the last few steps, Dave and Walt came in from the entryway.

Walt whistled and said, "Ms. Shuman, what did you do with those antennae? You look very pretty." Kathleen smacked Walt's arm to quiet him down. Dave walked over to her, took her hand, and told her she looked beautiful. He looked at Walt as if to ask what he meant by antennae, but he was not about to ask. Walt asked if they wanted a glass of wine before going, but Dave said he had reservations so they needed to leave right away. Kathleen felt as if Dave knew Lucille wanted to escape from Walt's teasing. They told Lucille and Dave to have a good time and to drive carefully.

When they were out the door, Kathleen chastised Walt for all the teasing, but Bernice said Lucille did not mind because she liked the attention. Walt said he thought she liked the teasing, but he would back off because he really did not mean to embarrass her. Kathleen and Bernice knew she did not embarrass easily, but they had fun making Walt feel ashamed of himself. It worked for a short time until he said, "I feel badly that I teased her, but I think she liked it. If I don't tease her, she will think I don't like her and I do." The friends laughed at him and he joined in.

"Okay, dear. Maybe we were being too hard on you. I don't think she minded at all, but you had Dave confused."

"Dave is confused because this is his first date since his wife passed away. It is not easy to start dating in your sixties. You had me charmed the first time I followed you to the dance floor. Dave asked me if his tie looked okay. He is nervous, but Lucille is going to have him relaxed and enjoying her company in no time at all. Should we wait up for them?" Walt laughed. "This is more fun than when Nancy started dating. I gave her dates the third degree and did not give them much slack. It embarrassed her, but a few years ago, she told me it also made her feel very precious to her daddy and mama. She figured out my plan that scared the curl out of that first date's long hair. It worked because he believed me."

Miriam called them out to the patio at poolside for dinner. The house smelled like Texas barbeque, and they all commented how good it smelled and how it whetted their appetites. The Texas sky was lovely, which added to their relaxed evening with spicy barbeque ribs and all the fixings to go with them. After they had eaten more than they should have, they decided to take a little ride in the Jeep. Walt's first suggestion of a walk immediately changed when he looked at Bernice and remembered her cast. Walt drove them down to the river and they saw the wildlife coming out for their evening antics. Walt pointed out the log where Kathleen sat when he tried to get her to say yes to his proposal. Bernice said it looked like a romantic spot. Walt headed the Jeep back toward the barn. When he got near the house, he pulled up by the back door. Kathleen got out and helped Bernice hop out on her good leg as Walt handed her the crutches. The women headed into the house and Walt jumped back into the muddy Jeep and drove off to park it in the barn.

Bernice went to her room to rest and prop her leg up. She took a copy of *One for the Money*, by Janet Evanovich, which Lucille had recommended as a fun read. If she read fast enough, she could finish it before they went back to Indiana in a couple of days. Kathleen checked in with her after a while and brought her a cup of tea. "Kathleen, have you read this book yet? It will put a smile on your face, but don't tell your former parishioners that you read Stephanie Plum books," she said and giggled.

"No, I haven't read any of those books yet, and when I do, I won't hide it. Pastors need to read some of the books their church members read and see some of the movies they enjoy—within reason, of course. I noticed that Delia had the first several in that series. When it gets quiet around here, I will try that one. Walt and I are waiting up for Lucille and Dave. They must be having an enjoyable evening because it is going on ten o'clock and they are not back from dinner yet. Good night, dear. Don't stay up too late."

"Good night, Katie." Kathleen walked out the door and closed it quietly. She stopped by her room and picked up a book she had been reading. When she walked back into the living room, she saw that Walt sat in his favorite chair reading some material that Nancy had sent him from the office. She knew he liked to know some of the details in their business. Kathleen leaned over, kissed him, went to the couch, settled in, and began reading. They were so comfortable just sitting together in silence. *What a wonderful feeling*, Kathleen thought. Shortly, they heard the front door open. Walt got up and went to the front entry and invited Dave and Lucille to come on in for a cup of tea, which Miriam had just brought out to them before she and Maxim retired for the night. Dave and Lucille came in and sat side by side on the couch. Kathleen had moved to the chair next to Walt's so she could reach the tray with teapot and cups and saucers. She served tea all around and asked how dinner had been?

"We had a wonderful time. Dave took me to this classy restaurant with the most beautiful view. I loved the dinner and the service. They treated me like a queen."

Walt said, "I think what my wife wants to know is how you and Dave got along." Kathleen looked at Walt with daggers in her eyes. She thought, *What is wrong with him? I have never seen him so forward.*

"Sorry, dear. I was just teasing. Dave, how was your dinner?" asked Walt, trying not to grin.

"We had a wonderful time. The meal was indeed tasty and done to perfection, but the best part was having Lucille sitting across the table from me."

Lucille blushed and patted his arm, "Dave, my pleasure. I had a wonderful time. Walt, did you know that Dave is also from Indiana? That was a surprise. I noticed that he didn't have the Texan drawl, but didn't recognize the Hoosier twang there." They all laughed.

"I guess I had forgotten that you were from Indianapolis, right? A lot of good things and people come from the Hoosier state. Look at my luck," bragged Walt and pointed to Kathleen. "What did you find out about Lucille that we might not know?"

Dave seemed embarrassed and said, "I found out that she writes poetry. Did you know that? She even shared her favorite with me. She is a smart woman." Lucille beamed but did not seem embarrassed. She took another drink of her tea and excused herself to go to the restroom.

As soon as Lucille walked out of the room, Dave leaned forward with his elbows on his knees, looked at Kathleen, and asked, "How has this lovely, smart lady stayed single her entire life? She is so much fun, so smart, and so thoughtful."

Kathleen smiled and told him, "She loved her students and still keeps in touch with some of them. Actually, she was engaged three times. The first two times, the men saw how entrenched she had become in her teaching career and did not want to compete. One man showed insecurity and the other demanded she give up teaching, stay home, and be a housewife. Neither one of those men really fit our Lucille. You know that she accepted Shorty's proposal just before he died. I think she loved each of them, but Shorty had a special place in her heart. She is a happy woman, secure and self-assured." She saw Lucille coming back down the stairs and changed the subject. Dave leaned back in his seat and tried to look casual. "Walt, have we eaten at the restaurant where they had dinner tonight?"

"No, dear, I don't think we have, but I will take you soon. It is a wonderful place."

Lucille said, "Dave said he likes to play euchre. Do we have time to play a few games tonight?"

Dave stood up when Lucille got near the couch, and they all moved into the library and sat down as couples to play. Dave relaxed and Kathleen noticed that Dave was a competitive man, which would be good for their games tonight. Midway in their playing, Walt got up and offered everyone a glass of wine to finish out the evening.

"Mr. Alexander, don't think you can get me intoxicated to the point that I will get sloppy and let you win. Dave and I have you three games to two now, so none of your tricks." They all laughed and Walt sat back down. The next game, Lucille and Dave won, and he said he needed to be on his way. He told them he had really enjoyed the evening more than he had enjoyed himself in a long time. He shook Walt's hand, kissed Kathleen on the cheek, and allowed Lucille to walk him to the front door. He again told her how much he enjoyed her company.

"Dave, you made this a special evening. Thank you," said Lucille as she reached up to kiss him on the cheek. He turned his head, caught her lips with his, and kissed her. He surprised her, but she did not mind.

"Good night, Lucille. Thank you for the wonderful evening. May I call you again?"

"Of course, but we are going home later this week. Kathleen has my number and e-mail address, if you are interested."

"You bet I am interested. I will talk to you tomorrow. Good night," he said as he opened the door, looked back at her with a broad smile on his face, and left as she held the door open. She waved one last time as he climbed into his white Lexus. She returned to the living room to say good night to Kathleen and Walt.

"I am going to bed now. Winning all those euchre games has worn me out," she said and grinned at Walt who smiled back at her. When she got to her room and flipped on the light switch, she jumped back because Bernice sat in the chair by the window. "Good grief, Bernice, you scared me? What are you doing sitting in the dark? Are you all right?"

"Oh, I am fine. I heard you come in and wanted to hear how the big date went. I had no idea you invited him to stay half the night," she teased.

"We played a few games of euchre and beat the pants off Kathleen and Walt. Dinner was wonderful and the conversation flowed. He really is a nice man. He is rather straight-laced until he gets to know someone, and then he relaxes and is fun." She sat down on the end of the bed and removed her shoes. Going to the closet, she put away the shoes and her jacket. "How would you feel about waiting a few more days before going home? Have we worn out our welcome yet?" She sat down on the bed facing Bernice.

"You know Kathleen would be happy to have us live with her. I am content to wait a few days longer. Is there a reason you are not ready to go home? Gee, I wonder what it is."

"Well, Dave asked if I would be around a few more days. I think he and Walt have something planned for all of us in a couple of days."

"We can talk with Kathleen tomorrow. I am sure this will work out. Bethany is taking care of the horses, since they are really her horses anyway. I am ready for bed now. Have a good night," she said as she got up and hobbled out heading for her own room next door.

The next day, Dave and Walt made plans for a picnic by the river for the three women. Bernice assured them that she could manage to get around with her crutches. The men had folding camp chairs and a folding table packed in the back of the Jeep. Maxim had packed a tasty picnic lunch for them. The women came out to the Jeep wearing jeans, boots, and lightweight jackets. The men and Kathleen were riding horses so Lucille could drive the Jeep with Bernice by her side. They planned to go to a spot farther down the river than where Walt and Kathleen usually sat on their favorite log. Walt had given Lucille very specific directions to the picnic spot and she said, "No sweat, I got it." Walt shook his head in apprehension—had she really listened to the directions? Bernice had the hand-drawn map in her hand. They would be taking the river lane that the family had worn down over the years. The riders would take the short cut across country and be there about the same time. They waved as they headed in different directions.

An hour later, the horseback riders arrived at the spot Walt had chosen. Kathleen was admiring the surroundings and the picnic spot. The birds were singing, and the water was slowly flowing downstream. They dismounted and Walt and Dave walked the horses down to the water's edge and they drank. The men tied the horses to a tree close by. Kathleen looked around for a place to sit. She did not see a log at this spot. Walt took a blanket from the back of his saddle and spread it on the ground.

"If I get down there, will I get up?" she joked.

"I'll pull you up, dear," answered her loving husband.

"But who will pull you up first?" and they both laughed. "I sure hope the girls don't have any trouble finding us. There aren't too many other side roads they could take, are there?"

"There are two spots with Y's where they have to choose the correct direction. I drew them a map."

"Bernice has no sense of direction, poor dear. Lucille will find us, even though you did not think she listened. Dave, have you been to this spot before?"

"No. Walt has kept this place a secret from his friends apparently."

Walt said, "Not intentionally. This is where we brought the kids to swim and picnic when they were in their early teens. As they got older, they preferred the old log area where the river is deeper. I sure hope the girls didn't take the wrong road or have a flat tire or something."

"Don't borrow trouble, dear. Here they come now," said Kathleen as she got on her knees and putting her hand on Walt's shoulder for support, stood up, and waved at the Jeep. Lucille drove very fast, and when she saw Kathleen step out by the rutted lane, she hit the brakes and the Jeep slid sideways, throwing dirt into the air.

"We are here. Let's start the party," shouted Lucille. Bernice held onto her seat and the door with a look of sheer terror.

"Lucille, are you trying to kill us? What is wrong with you?" Bernice shouted, "Walt, get me out of here. She is a crazy woman. I am not riding back with her."

"Oh, for goodness' sake, Bernice. Where is your spirit of adventure? Okay. I am sorry, dear. I guess I forgot this is not the Indy 500, but I have never driven a Jeep before. It was awesome," Lucille trilled.

Dave walked over to Lucille and gave her a hug. "Cille, you scare me. Walt didn't tell me you were sixteen, but you sure drove like sixteen." Lucille hugged him and giggled.

Kathleen came over to Lucille and took her by the arm, "And look at poor Bernice. She is scared stiff. Her hair is standing on end, well almost. Walt, help her out of the Jeep, honey." He moved over to help Bernice get out of the Jeep and handed her the crutches. Dave hurried to the back, pulled out a couple of the chairs, and set them up so Bernice could sit down and prop up her foot.

"Thanks, Dave. Lucille, I am mad at you right now. You drove like a madwoman and risked our lives. I already have one cast and I do not need another. I am telling you right now, Kathleen, I am not driving back with old Lucille Danica Patrick there. Forget it.

I will hobble back or ride a horse, but she is not going to be at the wheel with me."

Dave came over to Bernice and plopped open another chair and sat down beside her. "Bernice, I will drive you back to the house and let Lucille ride Houston back. He is easy to ride, but may give her a run for her money if she spurs him on. Would that work?"

"That sounds great to me, Dave. I appreciate it. You are very thoughtful. I knew you were a gentleman when we danced together at the wedding. I am hungry. When do we eat?" Bernice perked up, smiled at Dave, and patted his hand. Dave's face turned red and he jumped up to help Walt set up the table and the rest of the chairs. They made sure to set the table in front of Bernice so she did not have to move. Dave started waiting on her, fixing her plate, pouring her iced tea, and making her more comfortable.

Kathleen began to worry that Dave might be changing dance partners from Lucille to Bernice; how was Lucille feeling now that Bernice was angry with her? Would she be angry that Dave favored one of her best friends? Bernice seemed oblivious; Lucille did not seem to care. Walt raised an eyebrow at Kathleen and she shrugged her shoulders. The afternoon had not turned into the carefree, fun afternoon the guys had planned. As the meal progressed, they mentioned how good the chicken tasted, the excellence of the potato salad, and the yummy baked beans. Lucille was trying to fix the situation with Bernice, but Bernice did not seem to want to help. Finally, before the chocolate cupcakes were uncovered, Lucille got up from her chair, walked around the table, and asked Dave to give her his chair for a minute. He got up and held the chair for her.

Lucille leaned over to Bernice and said, "Bernice, you are one of my best friends, and of all the people in the world, I do not want you angry with me. In my stupidity, I took chances I should not have. I promise not to do that again. I am sorry. Please forgive me." She put her hand on Bernice's arm and said, "Lucy, 'Cille, girlfriend, I can't stand you being mad at me. Look at me. I am sorry." Bernice finally looked up at Lucille and felt sorry for her. They had been best friends for so many years.

"Okay, I forgive you…but don't you ever do anything that dangerous again. Do you hear me?" She reached for Lucille and gave her a hug. All the women were wiping tears, and the guys got busy clearing the table for dessert wanting to stay away from the angst they felt coming from the other side of the table.

"Is anyone ready for dessert? I am starving now," said Kathleen. "I can't believe I am going to eat this huge cupcake. Just a few months ago, I went to Weight Watchers to get healthier, and now Maxim is tempting me with chocolate cupcakes. What am I doing?"

"My dear, you are splurging just once in a while. I have been watching you. You are swimming every day and riding Sara. Looks like your pants are getting baggy. I like you just the way you are. Enjoy that cupcake," said Walt and gave her a kiss on the cheek.

The rest of the afternoon became more relaxed. Walt pulled out the fishing poles and tackle boxes and the guys found a spot under a tree and settled down. Kathleen finished the cleanup at the table, stored the leftovers back in the coolers, and watched as Bernice and Lucille chatted more calmly. Everything seemed back to normal, whatever normal is for the musketeers. Dave pulled a bass out of the river and the girls applauded. "Ladies, I think you are having fish for dinner," he said.

Kathleen called back, "Dave, if you provide the meat you have to stay and eat…or the fish." Walt looked more determined, and after a short time, he pulled out a slightly larger bass than Dave's. The girls gave him equal time with the applause. "Any of you girls want to fish? There's another pole here."

Lucille went over, picked up the pole, and put on her bait. Each of the guys caught another four fish between them; Lucille had not caught a thing. Kathleen suggested they needed to pack up because the sun was getting close to the horizon. The guys were happy with their catch of the day, but Lucille gave up. "This has been one stinking day for me," she said with regret. "Dave, I will ride Houston back for you. I deserve the punishment on my derrière."

"Are you kidding? The Jeep wasn't exactly a smooth ride, Ms. Lucille," Bernice mumbled. "Dave, help me to the chariot please."

"Yes, ma'am," Dave said as he jumped up and went to her side and extended his arm so she could pull herself up on her good foot. He handed her the crutches and walked beside her until she got to the Jeep. He opened the door, lifted her up, and carefully set her on the passenger seat. He left her door open while he stored his fishing pole and helped put the chairs and table into the Jeep. He came around and shut her door; everyone said his or her farewells. Dave slowly turned the Jeep around and drove off. The other three mounted the horses and started trotting back home down across the country trail.

Later, when Walt and Miguel were grooming the horses in the stable, the women went back to the house. On the way, they looked in the barn and noticed the Jeep had not arrived yet. Each one decided to take a shower and get ready for dinner. "It is a good thing that Walt brought the fish back, or we might be eating dinner at midnight. Dave certainly is giving Bernice a slow ride home," said Kathleen.

"I think he is sweet on Bernice since I took her on a joyride that scared the pudding out of her. I think they make a cute couple, don't you?" said Lucille.

"Are you kidding me? Lucille, he wanted to go out with you first. Does it bother you that your boyfriend switched to one of your best friends? Maybe he is just being kind to Bernice because she seemed so upset."

"I only had one date with Dave. He is very nice, but he is not very exciting. Compare him to Shorty. Albie gave me lots of laughs and fun, fun, fun. Dave is too serious for me. My feelings are not hurt if he rejects me for Bernice. Anyway, she says she does not want a man hanging around her. Let's see where this goes," said Lucille with a wink. They parted at the bottom of the stairs and each went to relax, shower, and get ready for the evening.

When the guys came in, Walt headed for the shower. When he came out in clean clothes, the Jeep still had not returned home. He went to the kitchen to ask Maxim to wait until Dave and Bernice arrived to start the fish. "No problem, Mr. Walt."

Walt found Kathleen and Lucille sitting poolside playing rummy and sat down to watch. "Where do you think they are? Should I go look for them?"

"No, let's give them some time. Dave is a good driver," said Kathleen. They dealt Walt into the game on the next round. Maxim came in at seven o'clock and said, "Madam, should I start dinner yet?" Walt and Kathleen both looked at their watches and were amazed at how late it had become.

"Walt, I think he needs to start the fish, don't you think?" Walt agreed. Later, Miriam came in and called them to the dining room. Miriam set the table for five, but only three sat down to the meal. When they had almost finished the meal, the back door slammed shut. Walt got up to see if it might be Dave and Bernice. When they all heard Dave swearing, they scurried to the back hallway. Dave and Bernice stood there side by side, looking very frustrated. Dave proceeded to tell Walt that he needed two spare tires. "I can't believe that two tires went flat on the way back here. Two tires, Walt. If Miguel had not been out riding, we would still be at your old log by the river. Bernice, I apologize for my language and my ineptness at fixing flat tires."

Bernice leaned against the wall, shaking with laughter. "Oh, Dave, you were so much fun. I really think Lucille ruined the tires when she ran off the road on the way out and hit that piece of steel thig-a-ma-jig. However, we made it home safely. What a day. Is there any dinner left?"

Kathleen helped Bernice to the hall bathroom and went to get her a change of clothes and invited Dave to use Bernice's bathroom to clean up before dinner. Later, as Dave and Bernice sat down for dinner, Maxim brought out hot, freshly fried fish for the two of them.

"Maxim, how kind of you to hold back some of Dave's catch for us. I am sure this is the fish you caught, Dave," said Bernice. Maxim nodded and smiled at her. He looked satisfied that he had made the right decision. He did not like to serve warmed-over food to anyone.

Lucille excused herself and went to her room. She could not remember a day when she had made so many mistakes and felt so ashamed of herself. She wanted to go back home to Indiana and lick her wounds. As she sat in her chair looking out the windows, she heard a knock on the door before it opened. Bernice stuck her head in the door and said, "May I come in?" Lucille nodded and Bernice hobbled over to the bed and sat down, facing her despondent friend. "Lucille, I know you must be feeling down, but I don't want that. I am sorry I behaved so badly about your driving this morning. I made a mountain out of a molehill. I became over the top and silly. In addition, when Dave started taking care of me, I enjoyed it. I wondered how you were feeling about being moved aside by your date."

Lucille interrupted her, "Dear, this has been the worst day of my life since you girls rescued me from the killer, when Shorty died, or when we almost lost you on the operating table. Those were the worst, but this day has been my own disaster. I cannot remember the last time I acted this bad and stupid. Is there any hope for me? Am I losing my mind?"

The door opened again, Kathleen walked in, and sat down on the end of the bed. "Girlfriends, life was crappy today, but tomorrow is another day. What can I do to help, Lucille?"

Lucille just shook her head, "Nothing. I acted bad, dangerously, and I feel like an idiot and a fourteen-year-old high school student. I have helped them work through bad days, but now, I truly know how deep in the well they must have been feeling. It is bad." She chuckled and took a deep breath. "How do I face Walt and Dave now? Oh, heck, I am a big girl. I am an old girl and I feel like such a disaster. I do not want Dave as a boyfriend, but I do not want him to think I am mixed-up broad either. Can you smuggle me out to the airport and get me out of Dallas unseen?"

Kathleen and Bernice both laughed and Kathleen said, "We aren't smuggling you anywhere. You simply showed your wild side, which is still alive."

"My dear, we are not angry or embarrassed or disappointed in you. This just gives us another story to tell," said Bernice as she pinched Lucille's ankle. "Come on back downstairs for a card game. In addition, for your information, I do not want Dave either. He never said he thought you were a fruitcake or goofy or mixed-up. Relax. You are an enigma to most men. You keep them guessing and they like that. Let's go downstairs."

The three of them headed out the door and Kathleen winked at Bernice because she knew the men would not say a word about Lucille's disastrous day. She had threatened them before she went upstairs to bring Lucille down. When they got to the library, Walt had set the table for five people to play a new game Dave planned to teach. The rest of the evening became lighthearted and not a word slipped from their lips about the calamitous day. When Dave needed to leave, he kissed each of the three women on the cheek, shook hands with Walt, and walked out the door still wondering what had happened to him that day. He could not be sure that he had a chance at another date with either Lucille or Bernice, but he certainly had a rocking fun day.

They all decided to turn in after such a strange day. Lucille helped Kathleen carry the mugs and plates back to the kitchen while Walt put away the cards. When Kathleen slipped into bed with Walt, she lay back and let out a big breath. "What a day. I hope not every secret event you plan has this outcome. What happened?" She turned and gave him a kiss. He took her in his arms and whispered in her ear, "I have no idea, except I need two new tires on the Jeep, Dave went home without a future date, and Lucille went wacko."

Kathleen smacked his arm and said, "Lucille is not wacko. She just went a little wild as she used to when we were in our twenties. But you are right, she seemed a little out of character for her age." She laughed. "Good night, dear." She turned her back and snuggled up.

Two days later, Bernice and Lucille were packing to go home. Miguel helped Walt carry their bags to the limo. Miriam and Maxim were at the door waving good-bye as the four of them headed to the airport. When they got to the plane, Walt and Kathleen hugged the two Hoosier friends and wished them a good trip home. "Call us when you get there, girls. We were so glad to have you here. We look forward to your next visit."

The happy couple got off the plane and walked back to the limo. They turned and waved when they saw the faces of Lucille and Bernice pressed to the windows. They looked happy and Kathleen relaxed. Her two best friends were on their way back home, and they would soon be planning their next visit in a few months. It had been a most eventful trip, and she reveled in the fact that she was again alone with her new best friend, her handsome husband.

Walt hugged her and said, "Darling, I love your friends, but I am sure glad to have you all to myself again…safe and sound. Whoever said that the retirement years could be boring have never met the three musketeers. They have never met my lovely Kathleen. Let's go home, sunshine." Kathleen turned, and keeping her arm in his, they walked together back to the car.

Thank you, Lord for this gift of a second chance at love. Maybe when they got home, she would take him out to the patio and they could talk about getting a "Kathleen/Walt" house.